Beast

BRIE SPANGLER

ALFRED A. KNOPF
New York

THIS IS A BORZOI BOOK PUBLISHED BY ALFRED A. KNOPF

Visit us on the Web! randomhouseteens.com

Educators and librarians, for a variety of teaching tools, visit us at RHTeachersLibrarians.com

Library of Congress Cataloging-in-Publication Data
Names: Spangler, Brie, author.
Title: Beast / Brie Spangler.
Description: First edition. | New York: Alfred A. Knopf, 2016. |
Summary: After falling off the roof, fifteen-year-old misfit Dylan must attend a therapy group for self-harmers, where he meets Jamie, a beautiful and amazing person he does not know is transgender.
Identifiers: LCCN 2015048797 (print) | LCCN 2016023777 (ebook) |
ISBN 978-1-101-93716-7 (trade) | ISBN 978-1-101-93718-1 (lib. bdg.) |
ISBN 978-1-101-93717-4 (ebook)
Subjects: | CYAC: Self-help groups—Fiction. | Interpersonal relations—Fiction. | Transgender people—Fiction. | Dating (Social customs)—Fiction.
| BISAC: JUVENILE FICTION / Social Issues / Dating & Sex. | JUVENILE FICTION / Humorous Stories.
Classification: LCC PZ7.S7365 Be 2016 (print) | LCC PZ7.S7365 (ebook) |
DDC [Fic]—dc23

The text of this book is set in 12-point Mrs Eaves.

Printed in the United States of America
October 2016
10 9 8 7 6 5 4 3 2 1

First Edition

To Matt
Because I wanted to quit more times
than there are words in this book and
you always said, "Keep writing."

ONE

I don't know what fell first, me or the football.

In theory, it was the football because good old me, all meat and muscle, can't be trusted to walk and chew gum at the same time, let alone rescue a misthrown ball. Glad no one saw me climbing out onto the roof, because I'd never hear the end of it. Same stupid stuff, like Don't do that, You're too big, You're too tall, You're too furry. Everyone loves to remind me about what I look like. As if I don't own a mirror. But it was quiet up there. Nothing moved, not even the wind. I edged toward the corner where the gutters met and stood on a row of shaky tiles. My shadow cast itself on the grass below, long and lean.

I shouldn't have looked.

It's bad enough I'm closing in on six foot four and have enough body hair to insulate a small town. No, I need to shop in the Minotaur department too. Regular standard-sized uniforms don't fit. Before the new school year kicked off, my mom had to sew the stupid school patches onto maroon jackets and white polo shirts the size of baby grand pianos. I look like an ogre who drifted in from under the Fremont Bridge and decided a reasonably priced Catholic education was the way to go.

Today didn't start off as the worst day ever. When I ate a small breakfast of six pancakes, four pieces of toast, and a quick fistful of bacon, I thought maybe Mom was onto something when she said, "This is your year, Dylan, I can feel it!" Because, I don't know, perhaps after this epic crap-storm of foot-long growth spurts and shaving since the sixth grade, sophomore year *would* be my year. It'd be a nice change. I even saw a good-luck penny lying heads up on the sidewalk on my way to the bus stop. A sign from my dad that he was thinking about me. But that false hope of One Good Year shattered when St. Lawrence had to go and ban hats and long hair on guys. The whole entire school turned around and gawked at me.

Every day my hair is the same. Part it down the middle, comb it down so it covers as much of my face as possible, put the hat on. Mom hates my hair. It hangs in my face, she says. Hides my eyes. My hair is my thing.

Correction: was my thing.

Madison blurted out, "Oh my god, now we're going to have to see the Beast's face every day." She really did say that. Right in the middle of the school assembly. I sat one row behind her. Of course JP laughed. When Fern Chapman rolled her eyes at Madison and told her to shut up, my chest bounced off the floor like a rubber ball.

Thank you, Fern Chapman. This is why I'm so stupid in love with you.

She's so pretty, it's hard to be in the same room as her. The air tightens.

"Take Madison back to your cave first, Beast." JP elbowed me from his chair and waited for me to laugh. I gave in because, screw it, that's what you do when the principal is standing on the stage announcing to the world that St. Lawrence Prep is hell-bent on exposing you for the genetic wasteland you are.

Sitting next to my best friend, JP, only proved my theorem. Not in some crazy quadratic reciprocity way. No, more like: one of JP's freckles > my entire physical everything. Squared. If we're going on looks, JP is the gleaming hero in shining armor mounted on an all-white horse, who unleashes his broadsword from its gilded hilt and slays me dead while the townsfolk cheer. Which is pretty much the truth. His motto is *"Simul adoratur,"* which if you plugged that into Google Translate, it'd humble-brag: "He is worshiped." Watching how he gathers up girls like a butterfly collector kills me every time he pins one through the heart.

But in a weird way I love JP because he's not afraid of me. Making friends was never easy. Mom was always like, "Talk to the other children. Show them your beautiful smile!" (Mom . . .) But when I tried, they ran the other way. Or even worse, pretended I wasn't there. When I had thirty pounds on every other first grader in town, JP was the only kid who asked, "Wanna play?" Of course my answer was yes. And if he asked me to rough up the occasional somebody here and there, I did it because he wanted me to be his friend. It wasn't too bad. Usually standing over the kid and staring down did the trick. Besides, hanging out with JP is a badge of honor at St. Lawrence. I'm not about to sacrifice my seat by his side at the lunch table.

He's the best, except sometimes I hate him. Like right now. If it weren't for JP, maybe I wouldn't have gone onto the roof and maybe I'd still have hair. It was JP's idea to go to the barbershop after school. He said he'd pay and I was like, awesome, because he's stinking rich and I'm poor as hell. JP must know I'm really down, I thought as I sat in the chair. Nice thing for him to do. So I told the guy I wanted it cut like JP's, just like JP's. He tosses it to the side and it always looks perfect. Girls run their fingers through it whenever they get the chance. I want that. I'm telling the barber this and the dude goes and buzzes a strip right down the center of my head. What the hell? I jumped out of the chair, stupid plastic cape and all, and towered over the guy. He cowered, like they always do, and pointed at JP. Told me JP slipped him an extra twenty bucks to buzz it. And right on cue, JP starts laughing. I laughed too, but that's different. I had to.

So now I have a buzzed skull. I don't like it. Reminds me too much of chemo. I wonder what my dad thinks about my new haircut. He'd be the expert on this particular hairstyle. If he still does think, that is.

I tried to block out hating my new chemo head, but that only lasted until I got home, took my hat off, and saw my reflection in the hallway mirror. If anyone asks, yeah, the busted glass and dribbled bloody trail leading up to the roof was me. Big deal. I needed some fresh air. I picked up the long-lost football, took a deep breath, slipped, and we both came tumbling down. Perfect end to a perfect day.

And then it just got better! My neighbors the Swanpoles heard me dent the earth and my hollering that went with it and called an ambulance. Now I'm in the hospital, waking up from surgery with two spiral fractures in my right leg, and all the beeping from the monitors is driving me crazy. Does it have to do this with every heartbeat? I wish someone would turn it off. The beeping, I mean. Every time it repeats, I hear Madison's voice on a loop. *"Oh my god, now we're going to have to see the Beast's face every day. Oh my god, now we're going to have to see the Beast's face every day. . . ."*

My eyes close to block out all the white-white-white of my hospital room, and I'm feeling vaguely disappointed. Didn't think I'd end up here. Not what I had in mind. My right leg is attached to the metal skeleton of the bed, with spikes and pins and wires all jutting out of it, and in my morphine-drip haze, it's like my very own trippy puppet show. I settle into my hospital bed and inhale the room's chemical sterility as though it's Fern Chapman's perfume. Or deodorant; whatever it is that always makes her smell unbelievable. I can't lie: I've had dreams where I'm invisible and all I do is walk behind her and inhale.

I guess in my dreams I'll have to hobble now. Crutches are perfect. Now I will be known as the Guy on Crutches. "Hey, look at that guy on crutches," I'll hear people say as I go by. I like the thought of that. It feels so amazingly ordinary.

The silence is short-lived.

Mom comes flying into the room. "Dylan!" There's

no chai-tea-for-the-ride-home in her hand. She must've raced all the way here from Beaverton, where she works long hours and gets us shoes at the employee store. A wave of guilt crashes over me. There's not enough chai tea to wash away her kid being rushed to the hospital in an ambulance and having emergency surgery while she got the call at work. She might need to switch to kombucha.

"Sweetheart!" she cries out, and zooms across the room, smothering me in a massive hug. "I got here as soon as I could. Your doctor brought me up to speed while you were knocked out—he says you'll be okay. Are you okay?"

I could use some more morphine. Not because I'm in pain but because it's morphine. "Never been better."

"Can I get you anything?"

A genetic do-over. "No."

Mom pulls away and takes in the hospital tomb. I mean room. A shudder slips down her back. "You look so much like your father," she murmurs. No doubt. Looking at me attached to tubes, bald, and more pasty than glue must be like being thrown back in time to when my enormous father sprawled across a hospital bed.

A fresh smile blooms on her cheeks, the one that crinkles up too high when she's trying not to be too gushy. Mom lets go of the metal bar on the side of the bed. "But I like your new haircut—I get to see your face again. Looks so much better than hiding behind all that hanging scruff." She lightly cups my cheek like she did when I was small. "You're just like him in every way."

I say nothing because okay, I've seen the pictures and it's true. You can swap out a photo of my dad and think it's me.

Same massive picture-clogging bodies and camera-breaking faces. But lucky me, I'm the hairier one.

"Oh, Dylan." My mother sighs as she fluffs my pillow. "The doctor told me you were trying to get a football? We could've found a better way to get it down, you know."

"Mmmm . . ."

"I thought you hated football."

Ignoring that, I reach for the pain pump instead. Pump-pump-pump.

"Stop," she says, taking it out of my hand. "The last thing I need is to drop you off at the methadone clinic before school every morning. We are not getting addicted to morphine today, thank you very much."

"S'good schtuff."

"I bet," she says. "Well, while we were waiting for you to wake up, I called the school and let them know you're going to kick off the school year with only one leg."

I roll my eyes underneath my lids, getting a rush from the painkillers as I do. "Whatever. Who else did you tell?" Fern Chapman?

I swear if Fern comes gliding in through that door, I will die.

"The school, the family," she says.

"My friends?" I'm afraid to ask. "Please tell me I'll be the first to tell JP."

"Don't be mad, honey. . . ." She bites her lip.

"But you already texted him," I finish for her.

"No, no—he texted me! He heard something happened and wanted to make sure you were okay. Isn't that what friends do?"

"I guess so."

"Don't shoot the messenger. You two were the ones who decided you were brothers when you were little kids, not me. He was watching out for you." Mom tries to chuckle. "Well, JP might not have seen you in full flight, but I bet Dad enjoyed his front-row seat."

We laugh together but it feels rehearsed. I mean, what can we do? Nothing. The man I look more and more like every day, from the height to the fur to the never-ending bodily expansion, has been gone for twelve years. He died a long, hard death from cancer, so I hope if anything, he's up there laughing his ass off.

My head feels cold. I touch it slowly and feel all stubble, no weathered cotton and a stiff, frayed bill. It's gone. "Where's my baseball hat?" I immediately say.

Mom glances about. "Not sure."

I sit up and jerk left and right, looking for it. "No really, my hat—where is it?"

"Lie down," she stresses. "Dylan, your leg, the traction."

"I'm fine." Things begin beeping and nurses run in, yelping for me to quit moving. "All I want is my hat," I try to say as slowly and calmly as I can. Doesn't work. A billion panicked hands and arms press my body down. Guess I am as big as they say. "It's not my leg," I try to assure them. You'd think they were holding down a thrashing water buffalo. It's just me, people! "I just like my hat, that's all."

"A hat?" one of the nurses says.

"I can get you a hat," the first nurse volunteers. "Be right back."

Mom comes over and rubs my shoulder. "It's okay, sweetie," she says. "You're a handsome guy, you know. You don't need to hide behind a hat. You are a beautiful person, inside and out, and someday—"

"Mom, don't."

Mom. Jeezus, where do I begin? The bleeding sincerity? If a total and complete stranger stubs their toe next to her, she will be the first one offering a ride home and half her life's savings just to make sure they're okay. In my case, it means a constant maternal bludgeoning so I am painfully aware of my epic wonderfulness.

The fact that she has to try so hard annoys me more than any of the words.

"Here we go." The first nurse returns, holding up a white cotton skullcap.

I take one look at it and drop it on the side of the bed. "Thanks," I tell him all the same. Don't feel like wearing any hat that's not my baseball hat. My hat's been through a ton of crap with me; it's my helmet for battle. This hospital hat couldn't protect me from shit. I look at the metal frame. The system of pulleys and wires keeps my leg still and high. My leg. Emptiness vibrates through me as I stare at it. Like it's lifeless. A marlin that fought the good fight, only to be strung up and measured at the dock.

"Dylan, honey, are you okay?" Mom asks.

"Hurts." I fake some physical agony. She doesn't budge, so I squirm some more. She was so excited to see my face again, I crush it up into little pieces with sheer anguish, just for her, and she lets me push the pump. (Yay.) "I need to talk to the doctor."

The first nurse tests the nerve response from my toes as the second nurse leaves the room. "I'll find him," she tells me.

I chew my upper lip. Should I really do it? Ask him a question I've only asked Google? I'm kind of thinking yes. Some twenty minutes later, my orthopedic surgeon, Dr. Jensen, enters and surveys the scene. "What's the problem, Mr. Ingvarsson?"

His bedside manner is nothing if not direct. "Never mind," I mutter, embarrassment circling back in full force. "I'm fine now."

Everyone stares at me. The doctor looks to my mother. "Might I have some time with my patient?"

"Sure thing," she says. Mom stands firm, blinking innocently.

The doctor raises his eyebrows at her until she can no longer ignore the hint.

"I will, uh . . . go get a snack. I'll be back in a bit." Mom pauses. The nurses stop mid-step, just as they're about to leave with her. "Can I get you anything?"

"No," I say.

"Are you sure? Can I run out and get you a burger or something? An apple pie? You love apple pies."

"Mom!"

"Okay, all right, fine." She disappears.

Dr. Jensen regards me once we're alone. "Okay, now what's the real problem?"

His eyes are lasers. "It's, uh . . . Well, ah, can you . . ." I shake my head, my pathetic head.

"Can I what?" Dr. Jensen checks his watch.

I sigh and try again. This might be my only shot. "Can you refer me to anyone who can change . . . me?"

TWO

I'm not complaining; it's just unfair.

And the worst is that if I ever bring it up with anyone, all I get is: suck it up. Unless it's my mom, and then I get a "you're so wonderful and amazing and I love you, hooray forever and ever" pile of Mom pom-poms (Mom-Poms™). Which is why I never talk to her about the stuff that really bothers me anymore. Besides, it's not like she can stop me from getting hairier.

The first time I wore a T-shirt to school in the seventh grade, Madison said it looked like I dipped myself in glue and rolled around on a dog groomer's floor. After that, I didn't wear short sleeves until the ninth grade, when we had a heat wave in late September and it got so hot I couldn't stand it anymore.

It's no fluke that my nickname is the Beast. Or Furball or Sasquatch or Wolfman. It changes by the day. I laugh, but I hate them all. I'd rather not be a hairy slab of meat, or have a five o'clock shadow by noon. I'd rather not have knuckles so furry you can't even tell if I'm wearing my dad's ring or not. Rather not have chest hair squirt up the neck of my T-shirt. Front and back.

I've heard girls whisper that it's gross, that I'm nasty. I am aware.

One of the worst days in my life was when I went to get my back waxed. The fact that Mom was willing to take me to her salon was mortifying enough, but I was desperate. Last summer my friends and I were going to Splish-Splash and I wanted everyone to see I was capable of de-cavemanning. Sue me, but I thought if certain young ladies could see that I'm loaded with enough solid muscle to throw a cow over each hairless, smooth shoulder, their perceptions might change. Unfortunately, I found out manscaping one's back is impossible if you have the dexterity of a T. rex. I couldn't reach it all myself and needed the help of trained professionals, so Mom brought me to her nail salon. Cue the laugh track.

The lady brought me behind a curtain and I stood there, glued to the floor.

She looked all the way up at me and took a step back. "What do you want?"

"What do you mean?"

"You." She flicked her hands like she was shooing a big fly. "Where do you want wax?"

If she only knew how hard it was for me to walk behind this shabby white curtain, maybe she might not look so disgusted. I swallowed and thought of Splish-Splash. Of being a normal fifteen-year-old. “My back?” I said in a small voice. “My shoulders?”

“Take your shirt off.”

I did as I was told.

She clicked her teeth and sighed. “Lie down.”

I did that too. It took four hours. Four of the most painful hours ever, but when I was done, everything was smooth. The lady sat slumped in the chair and my mom gave her a big tip.

We both knew it was gross if Mom said anything, so she didn’t, but when I got home, I hung my hair in my face and turned around and around in the mirror. It was all gone. I didn’t look like a throw rug. I looked like a person. It was amazing. I was ready for Splish-Splash. I was ready for Fern Chapman to jump up and sit on my shoulders so we’d win at chicken in the pool.

Fern. What can I say about Fern? She’s gorgeous and smells like a flower. She’s the type of girl I want next to me so JP can nod, like I did good. She has big blue eyes and she’s small enough that I can definitely save her from a burning building or a car wreck or something. Pocket-sized, as JP would say. She’s perfect.

Splish-Splash was not. I couldn’t go down the slides. Against the rules to go down with a hat. So I sat by the deck chairs because I didn’t want anyone to look at my face. I straight out lied. Said I didn’t want to go down the slides and then ha-ha-ha, everyone laughed and said, “Good—you might break them.” And to top it off, turns out waxing my entire body was worth a pile of shit tacos. No one said anything. Said anything nice, I mean. JP was like, “Where’s the floor-to-ceiling carpeting?" More laughter. Slaps on my sore, bare back because it's so incredibly funny.

And if I was the butt of everyone's joke, why did they stay even farther away? Girls skirted around me, like they were afraid of me. At the snack hut, I offered to buy this girl from my Spanish class her french fries because she was fifteen cents short. Nothing weird or crazy about that. I was freaking gallant. I was the full-on "pull out the wallet, extract three dollars, and say, 'Here, let me get that for you' " kind of guy. I stood over her and looked down nicely, smiling the whole time. The friendliest way I know how. And what did she do? She mumbled something I couldn't hear, made the *ohmygod* face to her friend, and bolted. Left her fries on the counter. It's like no matter what I do, I'm disgusting.

So I put a shirt on and sat down on a plastic lounge chair under an umbrella and pretended to read really important texts. All that did was get me a front-row seat to JP giving Fern Chapman his towel when they came out of the pool together. She took it and smiled at him.

Dr. Jensen clears his throat.

A poke to my arm and the day at Splish-Splash fades. My leg. The white walls. Dr. Jensen checks his wristwatch. "You here?"

"Yeah," I mutter. "I'm here." Still here in the hospital.

"What do you mean by finding a doctor to change you? Can you elaborate on that?"

"Elaborate?"

"It means give further expla—"

"I know what it means," I snap. In probably not the best way, but I'm not stupid. Never have been, never will be. I just don't want to elaborate beyond saying thank you for the referral.

Dr. Jensen flips some papers on his clipboard and makes some notes. Bores a hole through my head with his precision dagger stare.

My thumbs molest each other. "Like maybe plastic surgery or something," I mumble. They work miracles. Surely they can snip away the ogre and tweak me into looking like a normal human person. I've seen the Discovery Channel.

"So what does a plastic-surgery referral have to do with your broken leg?" he asks.

"No, not like that. . . . Like saying 'plastic surgery' sounds bad. But it's just, you know, it's something that I would, um . . ." Something I would get the nanosecond we won the lottery?

"I need more words."

Heat rises up. My cheeks burn. "It's just, this isn't what fifteen is supposed to look like."

"Trust me, fifteen looks like many things, and there are far worse fates than being almost six foot four, two hundred and sixty pounds. Sounds like a football scholarship if you ask me," he says, taking his pen from his pocket. I roll my eyes. See, this is why I hate football. It's the only thing people think I am capable of doing. Big + Ugly = Football. Dr. Jensen flips a page up, scribbles something. "When did you first place a value on your looks?"

"A value?"

"When did the way you look become important?"

"I guess the sixth grade."

"And when did you begin puberty?"

"Ten or eleven," I say. "Like, fourth grade."

"That must've been fun." He jots it down.

"Hmph." No, it was not.

"How's your self-esteem?"

If I'm honest, it's in the toilet. If I'm doubly honest, I've been depressed for four years and counting. "Not the best."

"On a scale of one to ten, ten being the highest, how significant does the way you look factor into your daily life?" Dr. Jensen asks. "In regards to mood, extracurricular activities, social life, and so on."

Eleven. I'd give anything to be a hundred pounds lighter and a foot shorter. To be normal. That's all I want, to be normal. "I don't know, maybe a seven," I lie.

"Uh-huh," the doctor says with a sniff. "Ever had a girlfriend?"

"No."

"Would you like to?"

"Yes."

"And why do you think you've not had one yet?" he asks.

Twist the knife already. "You know a face only a mother could love?" I point at my mug shot.

"It's not so bad," he says. "If anything, you look rugged."

More like Cro-Magnon, but whatever.

Dr. Jensen's pen scratches across a new sheet of paper. "What's school like?"

"Fine."

"How's home life?"

"Fine."

"Mom? Dad? Siblings?"

"Mom's great. A bit pushy. No siblings. Dad died when I was three."

He rests the pen a moment. "Sorry to hear that."

"It's okay," I say. I know it should bother me more, but it doesn't. He died when I was so young, all I knew of my father was that he was a very sick man. As far back as I can remember, everyone enforced the idea that for him to die was a good thing. I never knew it any other way.

The pen goes back to work and more notes are made. "Would you say your new haircut was a contributing factor to your broken leg?" he asks with technical precision.

"Um . . ."

"Why the pause?"

"How did you know I got a new haircut?"

He smiles to himself. "Summer's over, brand-new back-to-school haircut. Looks like you wore a hat too."

"Oh. Well, ah . . ." I try to laugh. "See, they made this new dress code at school and now we can't have long hair and we can't wear hats. They banned hats."

"When did they ban hats?"

"Today." Now the pen scribbles furiously. "But, I mean, it's a coincidence."

"And today you fell off the roof and broke your leg at"—he flips the pages—"around three-thirty in the afternoon."

"I'm fine."

"You have two spiral fractures and titanium rods and pins holding your leg together. That's not exactly fine," he says. "Do you have a history of self-harm?"

"What? No! I don't 'self-harm.' Are you serious?"

"Dylan, you fell off the roof the day they banned hats." He raises an eyebrow.

"Because I'd rather be known as Guy on Crutches than a freak show!"

"There it is." Dr. Jensen's eyes flick back to the clipboard and he almost writes a book on the last piece of paper. "I think there's someone you should talk to. I'll get in touch with her. Her name is Dr. Burns. She's the codirector of psychology and she runs a wonderful outpatient group therapy program for troubled adolescents here at the hospital."

"Wait, I'm not—Dr. Jensen, I'm not *troubled,*" I say from my hospital bed.

Patting my arm as he strolls out of the room, he smiles. "I'll have a word with your mother."

"No, don't—" He disappears and I'm alone in the room. "Shitshitshitshitshit."

I spend a minute looking for an escape route before Mom shoots through the door like a bullet. Dr. Jensen trails behind. "Oh, Dylan!" she cries, rushing over.

"No, Mom, no. It's not what you think! I'm fine."

"You did this on purpose?" Her hands flutter over me, smoothing and brushing all the loose bits.

"Sort of," I confess. "But not in the bad, crazy way. It was an accident."

"I knew you weren't up there looking for a football!" She looms over me. I never felt dumber. "Well, whatever that therapist recommends we'll do, because you're not running up to the roof every time life gets tough. You could have landed on your neck and died!"

She says it like that's a bad thing. "I only meant to sprain my ankle."

"Is it your father?" Mom says, laying a hand three times smaller than mine on her chest. She's the polar opposite of me. If I'm a Minotaur lurking in a labyrinth, my brown eyes burning red in the shadows, then Mom is a doe lightly munching dandelion greens in a field, blinking her big brown eyes so frigging much, the hunters become vegetarians. I don't get it. I almost want a maternity test. "Do you miss him that much? Do you want to be with him in heaven?" She jumps straight to blaming my dead dad because that's her go-to when things go wrong with me. "Is that what this is?"

"Mom, no, it's really not that big a deal."

"It kind of is," Dr. Jensen chimes in. Smug bastard. "But Dr. Burns is great; she'll help you learn some usable coping skills so the roof is less tempting in the future."

"Actually—"

"He'll be there," Mom butts in. "With bells on."

"Good." Dr. Jensen gives my mom a white card. "I'll have her call you later today with the information." He goes off to harass his next patient.

Once we're alone, Mom whirls around to face me and taps the card stiff in her palm.

"Hey—" I try to cut her off.

"Don't even try to talk your way out of it, buddy," she says. "You're going to therapy."

THREE

"The Beast is mobile!" JP hollers when he sees me wheel down the hall on my first day back. My right leg clears the way. "Everyone make a path—there's a tank coming."

Fair comparison since I feel like a bulldozer. I can barely walk on two legs without knocking over anywhere from one to a dozen things, but a wheelchair? Forget it. Wheels are definitely not my friend. Too round. Since my mom dropped me off at the front door, I've managed to bang into the trophy case, one fire extinguisher, and a bucket of dirty water left behind by the art kids painting a mural over the principal's office. At the end of the day, this poor wheelchair is going to cry itself to sleep.

But I'm slowly discovering I love being in it. In the chair, I'm normal-sized. The Beast is contained. I don't have to duck under doorways and I can make eye contact with the girls instead of towering over them.

"Hey, hey, make way," JP says, and the group of guys loitering in a semicircle around him step aside for me. "How are you? Does it hurt? Did you get the pizza I sent? I wasn't sure if the hospital accepted pizza."

"They did! It was awesome, one large pepperoni and—"

"Mushrooms," he finishes for me, and we both nod because that's our favorite. "Cool, because I was like, shoot, I can't go visit but I know what's good."

JP can't just get rides on a whim. His parents aren't good with that sort of thing. We might not be able to drive yet, but pizza makes everything better. "Nailed it," I tell him.

This kid Whatshisface hangs on the outside of our gathering group, angling his way in because him and JP were on the same baseball team last summer. JP doesn't acknowledge Whatshisface so I don't either. This kid sends out ping after ping to JP's radar. Like, *What gives, JP? We were teammates—we talked about girls and shared a laugh. Why are you ignoring me now?* Just want to tell him, Sorry, man. If JP says you're not in, you're not in.

"You're finally the shortest one," JP says.

"Yeah." For the first time, I don't have to stoop over and hunch down to hear what they're saying.

"What's up, man? How do you feel?" Bryce asks.

"Beats rotting in the hospital. Can't believe I was there for a whole frigging week." I peer up at my friends and blink.

"How long are you in the chair?" Bryce asks.

"For the next few weeks, until I can get the side pins out," I say, looking him in the eye as I answer his question. This is so bizarre. "Then I move on to crutches." Truth be told, I don't want to get rid of the chair anytime soon. So many times, people just throw words up at me. I wonder if since I'm smaller, maybe they'll actually listen to what I have to say.

"You guys, Dylan is a total badass," JP says, thumping my shoulder. Everyone in a twelve-block radius nods in agreement with him, and I eat it up. Can't help it. I'm filled with toasty warm kittens right now.

"Yeah, well, it was me against the roof, and the roof won."

"Liking the dome," JP says, cupping his hand over my shorn skull. I hate this stupid buzz cut, but it feels like he's anointing me in front of the whole school, and it feels good. Here is my first mate, my best man. Here is the one I choose to stand beside me. Or in this case, sit.

The bell rings and I wheel off to my locker.

JP walks with me. With me in the chair, I can't bump his heels like I used to and he can't back-kick me in the ass. But we'll figure something out. "Don't forget to use that thing for all it's worth. It's a pity magnet," he says.

A scenario and device that spark sympathy from the female population? Golly, what desperate loser would stoop that low? Answer: Me. And how. "I'll see what I can do."

"Lucky bastard. Your house good after school?"

Ordinarily, yes. We play video games almost every day at my house until our eyes bleed, but today I can't. Stupid therapy awaits. "Can't," I say. "Doctor's appointment."

His shoulders slump. "Cold shit on toast, Beast, because I just got this new controller. Maybe you heard about it? Like, only the most amazing one ever?"

"No way, nuh-uh, the Wormhole? You got a Wormhole?"

"Oh yes. Oh so very yes."

"Are you serious?" That thing costs four hundred dollars and has a five-month wait because it has to get shipped over from Korea on a bed of angel-driven clouds. It is insane. It's pulse sensitive and auto-responds in time with your heartbeat, so if you get all amped up and your heart beats fast, it will adjust precision time. I would fall off another roof to have one.

"And . . . I might've gotten you one too."

"You're shitting me."

"It's yours. But hey, you know Adam Michaels?"

"The senior? Yeah."

"Next time you see him, remind him he owes me that thing, will you? He'll know what you're talking about."

And I know exactly what JP is talking about. I bob my head, delirious with Wormhole dreams. "Yeah, yeah, sure. You got it."

"Anyway, later." JP claps me on the back and runs off toward his homeroom, bobbing away into the scrum.

Holy crap, the Wormhole. If I didn't want to go to therapy before, I absolutely do not want to go now.

Mom, Mom, do it for Mom. One and done. Deal with epic bullshit today, play with new Wormhole until my corneas dissolve tomorrow.

I open my locker, only to have it clang into my cast. "Ow, ow, ow, ow . . . ," I mutter. That freaking hurts. I swivel the chair in another direction so I can actually spread the door wide; but then once it's ajar, I can't reach my books. They're too high.

There is something humbling about being unable to do

things for yourself because your body simply can't. I briefly consider asking someone for help but immediately squash it down.

So I hitch myself up on my good leg and ignore the rush of pain as I stretch my arm high to get my books and cram them into my backpack. Hey, look at me *coping* and using *skills* to go on! I don't need therapy this afternoon. Pretty pointless: I can do this by myself, but whatever. I'm only going for one day to make Mom happy, and that's it.

I have all the time in the world to get wherever the hell I want. While everyone else races to beat the clock, I get an extra ten minutes to wheel my furry ass down the halls.

Perhaps sophomore year is going to rule after all.

Trundling all around in a wheelchair kinda makes me feel bionic, and in homeroom everyone makes a huge to-do over my leg. I get tons of signatures on my cast. Except most of them are like: *Get better, Fuzzball! Feel better, Beast! Hey, Sasquatch—Next time stick to the woods!*

JP was right: it is a pity magnet. All the girls in homeroom go, "Aww . . . !!" in that cute, high-pitched way. They touch me. Pat my shoulder and give me quick little side hugs and stuff. Nina gives me a piece of gum. I save the wrapper in my pocket.

The bell rings for first period and I take a breath.

Even though we have this stupid rotating schedule that I can't remember for shit, I know someone else's schedule better than my own. If I stall a little before going to my class, there will be someone coming in with her books and sitting down in the seat in front of mine.

I waste some time and lo and behold, Fern Chapman.

She comes into the room and it's like time stands still. St. Lawrence gives girls an option between navy blue pants or a skirt and today she chose the skirt. I'm almost positive she did it for me, to make me and my broken leg feel better. She comes closer and I can feel my pulse in my fingertips. My rib cage might be the size of a small bathtub, but that doesn't stop everything inside from bubbling and quaking like jelly.

I will pretend body hair directly correlates to confidence.

"Hey, Fern," I say, mushing my books and papers in a pile.

"Hey," she says. And then she sends me the tiniest of smiles. I think I might pass out.

When it comes to girls, I want to be a gentleman because if you break it down, you're a gentle man. That's what I want to be. A gentle man. Figure if I'm polite and nice and not manbearpigboy, everything will go well. So here goes nothing. "H-how are you?" Wonderful. A stutter. I clear my throat and cough. She frowns. Great, now I can't speak or breathe right. Course correction and proceed to do-over. "What's up? How's things?"

Fern sits down and swings an elbow around the back of her chair. "Going better than for you." She laughs.

I laugh.

We share a laugh! Time to buy prom tickets. "Yeah, I . . . I fell off . . . ah . . . the roof."

"I heard," she says.

Fern turns to her homework from the night before and underlines a few answers. No tea and sympathy? I fall off the frigging roof and that's all I get from my future wife?

Cold, Fern. So cold. I check the clock. I should go, except I don't want to. But she's not even looking at me anymore. "Um," I say.

She looks up, in a "What the hell does this troglodyte want now?" way.

"You want to sign my cast?"

"M'kay," she says.

"I have a Sharpie," I say, and hold it out.

She hesitates before she takes it. "Why do you have a Sharpie?"

"Um . . ." Because I've been waiting for you to sign my cast since I woke up from surgery. "It was JP's idea. The marker. He said pen works like crap on casts. He's always looking out for me."

"JP's so smart," she says.

No, he's not. He's always "checking" his homework with me from the night before because he's a lazy dumbass. Let's leave my far more appealing best friend who's already hooked up with half the class, okay? Bending over to make her mark on my ankle, she finishes and I read: *Poor Beast. —Fern*

Time to get a refund on those prom tickets. I take the Sharpie and put my books on my lap. Wheeling backward, I knock into the desk behind me. Her eyes snap up at the loud bang. My chin stiffens. I'm down but not out. Prom's two years away, I still got time. "See you in study hall," I say.

"Huh?"

"'Cause I don't have gym anymore. I have study hall in the library instead," I say. Same time as Fern, and I prefer the term "observer" over "stalker." Just because I memorized Fern's schedule doesn't mean I'm going to be hiding in her closet with a rag full of chloroform. "So I'll see you."

"Okay," she says.

I sit in the chair. Is she going to say anything else?

"Dylan . . ." My homeroom teacher, Mrs. Dobrov, butts in. She swings her thumb toward the door. "Class is starting soon. Don't abuse your privileges."

"Right." I roll my eyes at Fern. "Because having a broken leg is such a privilege."

Fern laughs again and I almost throw up. I got her to laugh twice. Suck it, JP.

"Dylan, homeroom is over!" Mrs. Dobrov snaps.

"Right, fine, I'm going already," I say, and rumble my wheelchair into a whole row of chairs. They catch on my stuck-out foot and their metal legs shriek against the floor, but I don't care. Only three periods until study hall!

After that, I seriously don't care about the rest of the morning. Trig: blah-blah-blah. English: blah-blah-blah. Physics: blah-blah-blah. Aw yeah, study hall. In which I hope to not study at all.

Just my luck, physics is on the other side of the moon compared to the library, but no worries. I got wheels and it takes almost seven minutes to get there.

I get inside the library and listen. If I happen upon Fern "by accident," it'll be less weird than if I plow over to her table and am all, HI. IT IS I. I AM HERE.

Way over by the biographies, I hear girls talking. I ease forward. Definitely Fern. And probably Madison too.

Methinks now would be the perfect time to check out a super biographical book.

I push myself through the aisles so carefully, concentrating on stealth mode. Mom would be proud. I never pull this off on two feet, let alone on four wheels. She'd be stoked I'm not clearing swaths of books from their shelves and leaving a path of destruction in my wake.

"Oh my god, that's so creepy," I hear Madison say. I'm this close to coming around the corner. Deep breath, keep it casual.

"I know, right?" Fern says back. "He was all, 'Dur . . . Me fell off roof!' and I was like, what kind of dumbass falls off a roof? I mean, seriously!"

My breath freezes in my throat. I'm a dumbass? What the hell? I take trig with juniors, Fern takes algebra with freshmen, and I'm the dumb one?

"No kidding," Madison says. "I see him and I'm like, go back to your cave."

Fern laughs. "I feel so bad, but it's so true! He weirds me out, no joke," she says. "Does he even understand English? I'm just like, ew, don't talk to me."

"Maybe if you paint pictures on the wall, he'll get the point," Madison says.

They giggle and I sit back in the chair.

"And his hair? Why did he shave it all off? He looks ridiculous."

"Ugh, I know. His head's all bumpy at the top," Fern says.

I touch the top of my skull. That's why I never wanted to shave off my hair before. Even my bones are ugly.

"I just can't with him, you know?" Fern goes on, but I want her to stop. Please stop. "I only talk to him because he's best friends with JP."

"Ohmygod, I know," Madison drones. "Why someone as hot as JP hangs out with the Beast all the frigging time, I have no idea."

I reverse my wheels and roll away. In the corner behind the computers, I drive into an open bay of one of those forty-year-old study cubbies that smell like pee and bury my face in my hands. My head. I touch it. Run the palm of my hand across the skin from front to back, feeling the new stubble.

"Whatever," I mutter. Suck it up.

I feel an ache to study. Doesn't matter what, I have an urge to open a book and read things that dare me to figure them out. I'm dying for a problem to solve. One that doesn't involve people, unless they're there to be impressed. Like in trig. I love murdering those problems, stepping back, and having the whole class admire my handiwork. That I can do.

My phone buzzes in my pocket. I leave it there. Keep my head in my hands, feeling the rasp of my scalp with my fingertips. Like sandpaper.

My phone buzzes again. And again. I pull it out.

The first one blares: *DON'T FORGET! This afternoon, you've got therapy.—Mom*

And worse: *You've got therapy, fyi.*

Then even more worse: *Dr. Burns said u need to try one session. Reminding u it's today.*

And finally: *Wanted to touch base—therapy/this afternoon, k?*

Got it, I text back.

Another buzz and I look down. *btw, ilu.* Jeezus, Mom, enough.

I'll be there. Stop texting me, I send back before she can pop off one more.

What I really want to say is this: leave me alone.

FOUR

"I'm so sorry I took so long," Mom says from the front seat.

"What are you talking about? You picked me up from school right on time," I say, yanking my baseball cap down hard. School's out; hat's on.

She stares from the rearview mirror at me in the backseat, where I'm stuck just like some little kid because of my leg. Her brows furrow with worry. "I had a meeting that ran long. I didn't want you to think I forgot you."

It's easier to let my mom fret about nothing than try to help her not worry, because *spoiler alert* she will worry.

We pull up to the hospital. Mom parks in a handicapped spot and puts on the hazard lights. "No one will mind; we'll hurry-hurry," she says, opening my side door.

She lugs my wheelchair from the trunk and pops it open on the sidewalk in front of the outpatient wing of the hospital. People trudge in and out of the sliding mechanical doors. Pregnant women, kids hugging teddy bears tight, old people with humped backs and walkers, and me. We're all here to dip in and out for our scheduled hour.

I unbuckle the seat belt and lurch out into the sun and into my chair.

"You all right?" she calls out.

"Fine."

She stuffs some money into my hand. "For some snacks," she says. "Try to get something healthy. Like an apple."

"Okay."

"Maybe a banana."

"Okay."

"Or even an orange, if they have one."

"I know what fruit looks like, Mom."

She gives me a kiss on the cheek and squeezes my shoulders. "Want me to go with you to the room?"

"Nope."

"Are you sure? I could help get you set up, find a good spot, carry your bag. . . ."

"I'll be okay, Mom."

"All right then." She sighs and then smiles. "Have to get back to work. I'll pick you up as soon as you're done. I'll be waiting in the parking lot. Unless you want me to be here in the bay?"

"Mom, seriously, it's fine. I'll see you in ninety minutes."

"I'm proud of you, you know," she says, eyes filling with enough sap to fuel a greeting-card factory.

"Bye." I leave her in the parking lot and push myself into the giant box of glass and shiny surfaces. I find Room 12, no problem, but all I want to know as I wheel through the door is how to seem *untroubled* enough to never have to come here again.

The room where we're expected to hold hands and sing "Kumbaya" is plain. Bleached linoleum floors in a gray-on-gray checkerboard pattern with beige walls to box us in. Opaque shower-curtain-type blinds on the reliably rectangular windows. Fire-retardant furniture in a sloppy circle. It's the kind of room where you take one look and don't bother breathing because what's the point? Even the plants listing in their wicker baskets look like they're begging to be composted.

A girl is already sitting pouty-style on one of the couches. She glares at me before going back to tearing fresh holes in her shredded fishnets. Black hair, black makeup, black clothes, black combat boots, black nails, and radiating a sullen aura as strong as the stench of her old cigarette smoke. I could chew the ennui.

Of course this girl is at Therapy for Self-Harmers 101. If I'm being honest, I'm guessing her parents only send her here because they got tired of their credit cards getting maxed out at the local hardware store for all those chains around her neck.

The girl in all black says nothing. I pull my baseball hat down, park in an empty space, and drum my fingers on the armrest.

"You're in Dr. Burns's spot," the girl says.

"Oh." I shuffle my wheelchair far over to the left and nudge aside a plywood armchair exploding with foam cushions. I check to see if this is a more appropriate spot, but she never stops picking at her nails, so I drop my bag on the floor and claim it.

In time more girls file in. Based on Little Miss Sunshine over there on the couch, I worry this is going to be a bottomless pit where they all [fill in the blank] just to see if they can feel. But they seem more normal than my welcome wagon. With any luck, these girls are like me and were sent here by doctors and mothers who mean well. We're all fine and we can all go home and forget about the whole thing. Except their tugging at and fidgeting with their long sleeves is too obvious.

It doesn't make any sense why they would hurt themselves, they're all so pretty. And everyone—except for the Child of the Night—is friendly, nodding hello and saying hi. You'd never guess why they were here. They could be any girls from any school anywhere. T-shirts and jeans. Normal girls. The circle grows with lots of meandering small talk from everyone but me. I am the only guy here. This is not my scene. But whatever. I'm only here for a day, no point in butting in.

Instead I observe, bio-lab style.

This one girl, oh my god, when she enters the room I have to look down because there's a part of me I keep locked up. Not the amiable furball joking in the halls at school, not that guy. The real beast. One look at this girl and the key is turned. The cage is open. I want to grab her hips and hold on for a long ride. Wavy blond hair rippling with every step she takes. What's the word . . . "diaphanous"? Yeah, she's like that too. She flows. Like a goddess on a throne, and I'd kill all the lions in the Colosseum if it meant she'd be underneath me.

I want to get her on my lap and roll with her right on out the door, and we'd catch the bus to my house because my mom is still at work, and we'd . . . oh yeah. In my version, she'd be excited to go with me. I'd finally have my first kiss. A real one, not that stupid one with Tara Jardin. This girl, this goddess, she'd want me—and oh, the things I would do to her.

Except once the goddess sits in her chair, her body screams she's off-limits. She is not here. A part doesn't fit right, and it shudders to the surface as she holds her knees and lightly rocks and rocks to try and knock it back into place.

I want to pull my skeleton out through my nostrils so I can punch myself in the face.

There is no hope. I need to learn how to slowly turn to coal from the inside out so I stop falling ass over teakettle for anyone who claims the pronouns "she" and "her."

I can't fall for another girl again. I can't. I look at the Raven Queen and that does the trick. She's like a living cold shower. The real beast goes back to his cage and I lock him in. I remind myself of what I'd rather be. A gentle man.

I notice a poster on the wall mocking a dangling kitten with HANG IN THERE in all big, white letters. My eyes slide off that and they fall on a bust of Nefertiti. Except she sniffles and wipes her nose. Holy shit, she's real.

Directly across from me a very tall girl sits on an

aluminum folding chair. I'm instantly into everything about her. Even if I don't want to be because girls, boo. Girls despise me; why wouldn't this new one be any different? But she's striking. In a way that's like a neon-yellow bubble in a level not quite lining up, so instead she tilted the world and said, "There. That's where it should be." Everything about her is good and crisp: the skirt, the scarf, the boots; nothing has that super-relaxed, worn-in look. No scuffs, no soft folds. It's all new. But then again, what do I know? I wear a uniform every day. She gets to wear whatever she wants to school.

She's reading a book I read over the summer, and I can see she's almost at the best part. I want to start a book club with her where we sit over cookies and talk about the strange ending where everything was just bathed in sun and then it was over.

As she reads, something about her catches all the light and holds it in her skin, divvying it about the room like cards for poker. Her legs, her willowy long legs. (Stop . . . keep it clinical.) She has two of them. She crosses them all ladylike despite, or because of, her short-short skirt and sky-high boots. Her dimpled knobby knees smile like they're happy to be there. She plays with her long, curly brown hair and wears a loose purple scarf streaked with glittery bits. Our eyes hook as she lightly drapes it around her neck.

"Hi," she says in a voice that reminds me of cinnamon being grated into a mug of hot apple cider.

"Hello."

"You're new."

I nod once.

"I'm Jamie."

"Dylan."

"Hi," she repeats, and goes back to the book. Long hands hold the spine. Long fingers flick the pages one after another.

"Sorry I'm late. Hi, guys!"

A woman comes busting through the door, holding a fat trapezoid pillow and dragging an office chair behind her. She can't possibly be the doctor. "I'm late, I'm late, so horrible, forgive me," she says. I can tell when she was a little kid, she must've been cute. Like, overalls and lisping, "Mithter, would you like to buy a glath of lemonade?" cute. The ringlets and freckles give it away.

She angles the trapezoid pillow behind her and settles into it. As she sits, her pants hitch up, exposing mismatched socks. Now I'm all irritated. She's a doctor. She should wear a white coat, be on time, and wear matching clothes. "Ahh . . . ," she breathes. "Never deadlift televisions in your youth, guys. It may not hurt now, but I swear your back will remember forever." The girls laugh but I smirk at the thought of anyone in this circle deadlifting anything heavier than a tissue.

"So we have a new person. Welcome!" she announces. "I'm Dr. Burns and this is group. We meet once a week, but I consider it more like hanging out in a really ugly room." More laughter from the girls. Dr. Burns reaches into her bag and brings out a crusty notebook splitting at the seams with papers and stickies. "I think what you guys have to say is very important, so please don't mind if I take notes. Does anyone want to go over some rules? Jamie?"

Jamie keeps her legs crossed and leans forward on the lip of her chair. Lucky lip. "Everything is confidential; we're here to share, not to give advice. No interrupting. Anyone can ask whatever they want but no one has to answer," she says like a trained monkey.

She's been at this way too long.

"Good," Dr. Burns says. "And most of all, I believe in laughter, so feel free to give in and laugh if you feel like it."

I check on Mistress Raven, and I'll be damned if she's not smiling.

"Because we have a new member"—she refers to her notes—"Dylan, please raise your hand, thank you—we finally have an even number!" Dr. Burns high-fives the sky. Oh my god. "So let's start off with an icebreaker by pairing up with the person directly across from you. I want you to tell each other five good things about yourself and then your partner will share your good things with the group, so pay close attention to one another. It can be anything. Okay? Go for it."

The room rumbles as the girls shift about, and I watch as Jamie gets up and drags her folding chair across the room. She dunks it in front of me with authority and sits, instantly crossing one knee over the other. They line up like a lock and a key. I enjoy wondering which one is which. "I figured it would be easier to come to you," she says, rearranging her scarf. "What happened to your leg?"

"Broke it."

"Oh," she says. "How old are you?"

"Fifteen."

"Me too," she says. "I thought you were older."

"I'm sure you did."

"You're so big—how tall are you?"

"Is this what you really want to talk about?"

"I just . . . I'm tall too." She looks away.

"You want to go first?" I ask. She's probably done this a billion times already; she might as well.

"Sure," she says, and takes a breath. "Five good things about me are . . . um . . . Okay, one: I helped my mom make breakfast and when I could've said something that would've set her off, I held my tongue. That was hard, but I did it. Two: I'm transferring schools—finally! Three: my dad said I looked nice today. That was amazing. Um. Four, hmmm . . . Okay, four: I saw a shooting star last night and I made a wish—"

"Did you wish for fascinating things to say?" I interrupt her with a joke.

Her face falls. "Excuse me?"

I wince. Too far. "I was only, um. I don't know."

"You're lucky I'm forced to talk to you right now. Why would you make fun of someone's wish? Do you know how many shooting stars I've seen in my life? One. And you just shat all over it."

I hang my head and smooth my furry knuckles with my thumb. "What was your wish?"

"Like I'll ever tell you."

"I'll tell you one of mine?"

She peeks over at me, waiting for my confession or something. I don't know what to say; I never tell anyone this type of stuff. Like JP would give a shit about what I wish for? He'd just try to buy it for me, but what I want can't be bought. I think of a safe one. A wish I'm pretty sure everyone's had at least once. Or for me, a minimum of fifty thousand times. "I wish that I could wake up and not be me. Just for a day."

Jamie perks up. "Like in what way?"

Um, the fucking obvious ogre way? "My exterior."

She sits tall and nods. "Right. Sure, yeah. The packaging, I get it."

Of course she does. She has two working eyes and they are looking at me.

Jamie reaches into her bag and fidgets around, pulling out a camera. "The fifth thing I was going to say was I'm really good at photography. Maybe if I took some pictures of you so you could see how the light—"

"I hate cameras."

"Oh." She sinks her camera back into her bag.

"I mean, if you like it, that's cool. I don't."

"Do you know anything about photography?"

"Pictures are cool."

"Pictures are cool," she echoes. Jamie sits back in her seat and tucks her long fingers underneath her thighs. I imagine it's quite warm under there. She narrows her eyes and smiles. "How can pictures be cool if you hate cameras?"

She's pushing me and I'm starting to sweat. I need to nip this in the bud because I get pungent. "Can I just say my five good things now?"

Jamie frowns. She's disappointed. Fine, I'm used to it. "Go ahead. Your turn," she says.

"Okay." Since this is my only session, there's no point going beyond the basics. "Five good things about me. One: my mom and I are cool. She can be annoying, but I love her to death. Two: I'm in all Level I and AP classes at school and I have the highest GPA in my class. Three: I've got a great seat at lunch because it's next to JP, and he and I hang out all the time. Four: I'm a nice guy. Five: I have nothing to complain about—I'm fine."

She bobs her head. "Well, all right then. How about that."

"How about that."

"You have nothing to complain about."

"Nope."

"Even though you made that wish."

"Yup."

"Lucky you," she says.

"They don't call me Dylan Luckiest Guy Ever for nothing."

"Except you don't seem like a Dylan."

"What did you think my name was, Throg the Rock Crusher?"

She giggles. After Fern in the library, I don't want to hear another girl laugh ever again, but she has the best laugh. "I admire you for making a joke. I'm not there yet."

Now I squint at her. "What could you possibly need to joke about?"

"Um, maybe everything!" Her laughter comes from a way-deep place and erupts. "It wasn't the wish I made on the star last night, but I've had your wish too. Maybe that's why it didn't come true for either of us. We're overloading the system."

"Maybe the wish factory needs a new call center."

"You're funny," she says. "Even if you are a liar."

"What? Why would you call me a liar?"

Jamie bends near enough for me to see her pores. Except there are none. She has the most perfect skin I've ever seen. It's like cream. Her face reminds me of almonds. Her chin, her forehead, her cheekbones, all smooth, but just enough subtle edges and sharp points to leave a mark if you push too hard.

"If your life is so flipping fantastic," she whispers, "then why are you here?"

FIVE

Why am I here? Because I fell off a roof, duh, but I'll never tell her that.

I look right into Jamie's eyes. "I don't know why I'm here."

"Hmm." She drops her line of sight to her knees, and it feels like someone hit the dimmer switch. Everything goes dull. She switches legs, unbraiding them and recrossing them on the opposite side. Maybe she'll look at me again and bring the light back, but no. Those eyes of hers, their corners lifting high despite the purple bags underneath, they land on everything else in the room but me. The fake plants, the dull linoleum floor. They sit for a spell on the hospital's interpretation of what decorative knickknacks should be. Like that poster of a kitten dangling from a branch. HANG IN THERE. Because a kitten with shitty manual dexterity will solve all our problems? Done. Can I go home now?

Jamie's attention eventually strays to my cast. After she reads the doodles and messages, she looks up at me. The light comes flooding back (don't look, don't do it, don't fall) and I shut my eyes.

"The Beast?" she says. I open them and there she is. A face that launched a thousand somethings. Cars. No, tugboats. Ships. One of those.

"Is that your nickname?" she asks. "They call you the Beast?"

"Guess so."

"Why?"

I lift my forearm and show her. My bare palm facing me and the hairy full-length sweater facing her. Fur everywhere, all the way up, even coating my knuckles.

"Can I touch it?" she asks.

"Uh . . . okay."

She gently smooths her fingers across the back of my hand, like she's touching the head of a newborn. "It's soft."

I sneak my hand back. Am I like a dog now? Did she just pet me?

"Shall we come together?" Dr. Burns asks. "Anyone have a topic they'd like to discuss?"

A girl in the corner raises her hand, and if I saw her coming down the street, I'd step aside so I wouldn't accidentally breathe on her and mess her up. Everything about her is precision perfect. Like she parts her hair with a laser and resews every button so each row of little holes lines up north to south. While my bag lies dumped on the ground with all the crap spilling out, her bag stands at attention by her foot like a guard dog. "Dr. Burns," she says, not asks.

"Yes, Gabrielle?"

"I still find it difficult to illustrate to my family that what I'm undergoing is a legitimate concern. They thought I was crazy when I used to cut," Gabrielle says. "They said black girls don't do this; it's a white-girl problem."

"How did that make you feel?" Dr. Burns asks. I inch my wheels closer to the door. If that's the default follow-up question to everything, no wonder these girls are robots.

"Like they didn't care," Gabrielle says. "Like no one cares."

I want to laugh. Oh, Gabrielle, take it from me. No one gives a flying shit how you really feel. Not your friends, not anyone.

"Thank you, Gabrielle." Dr. Burns nods and looks at me. "Dylan? Would you like to add anything?"

"I don't hack myself up with razor blades," I say. "So I don't think I should be here."

A way-too-skinny girl, Hannah, jumps out of her seat. I'm surprised she has the energy. "If he doesn't think he should be here, then he should go," she says. "Because what he said is insulting."

"I agree," Jamie says.

Jamie lists to the side like she was punctured with a pin. I suddenly feel bad.

Our Lady Black of the good ship Weltschmerz raises her hand. Dr. Burns points at her. "Yes, Wretched?"

"*Wretched?!* Your name is *Wretched*?" I burst out.

"We're respectful toward others," Dr. Burns says to me.

"I'm sorry, I'm sorry, I shouldn't have. But that's perfect."

"Fuck off, Caveman Jim," Wretched snaps at me.

"Name-calling," Dr. Burns says, playing referee.

"I can call myself whatever name I want," Wretched spits. "I don't need some misogynist acting like he has a say." She looks like she's about to throw a chair at my head. "You know nothing about me."

"Likewise," I say.

"Oh, but it's okay for you to get all up on your high horse because of someone's name or what they look like?" Wretched sneers.

"At least you chose—" I stop. I pull the brim of my hat down and dunk my hands in my lap. Shut up, shut up, shut up, I chant in my head as I squeeze my hands into fists.

"At least what, Dylan?" Dr. Burns asks.

"Nothing." I glare at my fingernails. My hands relax and I look up. I grin at the room so they'll see I meant no harm. I'm a nice guy. Besides, I know when I'm outnumbered. I don't want them to rise up and drown me in lip gloss. "Nothing. Sorry I said anything."

Wretched sighs and rolls her eyes toward the ceiling. "I would like to know what you were going to say."

"Me too," Gabrielle says.

"Me three," Jamie says.

She sends me a smile, a small peace offering.

Gripping my jaw, I drag my fingers across my chin. The raspy five o'clock shadow that sprouted after lunch scritches louder than sandpaper. I take a breath. "I was going to say"—I debate how to put it—"at least Wretched chose to look that way and call herself that name. That's all."

"Um . . . ," a tiny voice says.

"Yes, Emily," Dr. Burns says to the blond goddess. Except she's not a goddess and I'm not a gladiator about to bang her in the backseat of my gilded chariot. We're just two people sitting in a circle.

"I can relate," her soft voice whispers. "Because I'm twelve and sometimes I feel trapped. Like I didn't choose to look like this, like there's nowhere to go. It's a cage. Or jail, or something. I'm afraid to raise my hand in class. I don't want to give anyone a reason to look."

"Thank you, Emily," Dr. Burns says. "That's very heartfelt."

Her little mouth full of purple braces grins at Dr. Burns and I'm sick. She's *twelve*? My throat seals shut and I almost choke. Oh god, I'm a pedophile.

No wonder every girl on the planet avoids me like the plague.

I turn off the volume and tune out.

The session lasts forever, and outside of telling everyone the five good things about Jamie, I don't say another word. For the rest of the time, I'm gone. This isn't for me and I'm fine with that, so okay. I went to therapy to make my mom happy. I gave it a shot and now I'm done. The end.

Emily elbows me. "What?" I ask her.

She points at the group. They're all staring at me. Jamie fidgets, a nervous smile stabbing her hot red cheeks. "Are you still with us, Dylan?" Dr. Burns asks.

"Uh . . . yeah?"

"Great! Would you like to add to the conversation? Any thoughts regarding what Jamie just said?" Dr. Burns says.

About what Jamie said? The five good things? "I . . . um . . ." Shit.

The girls don't blink. They wait for an answer.

This must be what being on trial feels like. "I think what she said is fine."

"You do?" Jamie asks.

I shrug. "Uh, yeah. Why wouldn't I? It's cool."

She smiles. A real smile, not a fake one like before.

Time's up and I get my things together to go home. Dr. Burns puts her hand on my shoulder as I'm halfway out the door. "I look forward to seeing you next week."

I shake my head. "I only had to go once, and I think once is enough."

"Well then, it was nice meeting you," she says. Dr. Burns steps back and lets me leave.

Freedom! Even the air smells better outside that room. So claustrophobic. And I don't turn around to see the girls leave, no way. I push my wheels into the hall and keep on going. I don't want to see Emily scurry back to the sixth grade. Don't want to see Hannah's death stares from her skin-hugging-skull face. Don't want to hear Gabrielle's polished shoes storm off to conquer the world. And I definitely don't want to see Wretched. Like, pretty much for anything, ever. I'll pass on that one.

They won't miss me. Jamie won't either. She probably already has a boyfriend. Or nine. *Right, Dad? Did you watch this whole pile of ridiculousness? What'd you think of me getting shot down by a roomful of girls? Par for the course, right?* I glance around, looking for any sign my dad agrees with me from above. A crooked stripe in a pattern, a loose shoelace on someone walking by. Something.

I'm always looking for that one something extra to tell me he hears me. If I'm locked in my head thinking about something that's bugging me, that one blip—a text that won't load, milk that's got one day left before it expires, anything—is my dad telling me, *I got you. I'm with you. I'm still here.*

Instead, I get nothing. Silent as always, so I push his non-answer into a little box inside my gut and shut it tight. As soon as it's all locked away, my phone buzzes. Digging it out of my pocket, I turn it on and see I have one text from JP. It's a quick one that says: *Did you talk to Adam Michaels yet?* And shoot, the answer is no. Not looking forward to that—he's a senior on the basketball team. Could be a challenge to collect, for once.

The other eighteen missed texts are from Mom, all in pigeon talk because she's the COOL MOM. This is what COOL MOMS do.

So sorry! Running late, big mtg!

Sorry Sweet <3! Work . . . u know how it is.

Pls don't b mad!

FYI ILU!

I'll make it up 2 u w/McD!

(Even tho McD is evil corp)

I know u <3 chicken nuggets!

I'll get u a 20 piece meal

(although chickens r ground up into goo)

(And tortured in sm. cages)

K?

Or do u want Big Mac?

2 Big Macs? (Even tho cows suffer to make beef & cheese)

Lemme know asap . . .

After that it was her emoji fetish. Emoji purple heart, emoji smiley, emoji pink heart, emoji panda bear (why a panda bear? Is McDonald's selling a McPanda now?), emoji burger and fries . . . *I got your messages,* I text back to her. *I will study while I wait for you. Stop worrying.*

What abt chix nuggets? she immediately texts back.

Fine, I text, and find the money she gave me so I can get a candy bar and a bag of pretzels. Debate getting a soda too, but decide to pass. Screw fruit.

ilu!!! she texts.

I sigh. It's not like I haven't encouraged her to use actual English; I have, but she's stuck in 2003.

Love you too, I text back. I have to. If I don't shut that down, an avalanche of emojis will destroy my data plan, and I need that to talk to my actual friends. Like when JP wants to humble-brag about how he didn't tap whatever ass fell on him from the sky because "she deserves a guy who cares." How magnanimous of him.

Snacks in my lap, I make my way to the front of the hospital. I sit under the wide awning and wait. There's not a great deal to look at. To my left, there's an off-ramp from a highway. To my right, there's a bus stop. Nothing special, just a boring clear and metal box with some posters and a bench and a schedule on a pole. One of the posters tugs at my eye. It looks like an advertisement for my favorite podcast about stuff you missed in history class. It's literally called Stuff You Missed in History Class. I listen while I do homework because I like it when my brain bounces around, the colliding information zinging between hemispheres. Graphing the derivative of *f* while learning about an eighteenth-century vampire panic in New England must be what smoking a whole bong feels like.

I wheel over to the bus stop. The poster turns out to be a regular old band poster. An upcoming show. One band is called Stuff (original) and the other is called Missed History. I clench my fist and shake at it, old-man style. Curse you, poster. Making me wheel over here under false pretenses—get off my lawn. I'm about to wheel back when I slam on the brakes.

In the far corner under the giant plexiglass dome, huddled in a tiny little ball of boots and legs and skirt, kneels Jamie.

SIX

"Jamie?" I say, and she snaps up to her feet.

"What are you doing here?"

My gaze darts to the left before landing back on her. "I was looking at a poster. What are you doing here?"

She looks at the camera cradled in her hands. "I was taking pictures."

"Of what?"

Jamie shrugs lightning fast, a tightly coiled spring. "There's some, um, rust, you know, in the corner over there," she says. "It's red. The pole is blue. Looks cool."

"Rust." I back up my wheels, and her shoulders instantly soften and relax. My back teeth press together. We were just talking like twenty minutes ago. What happened to our five questions? She's acting like I'm about to murder her or something. "Okay. I'll let you get back to it."

I reverse in a three-point turn out of the bus stop when

the back wheel skips off the sidewalk and into a small ditch of dirt next to some newly planted seasonal mums. My right leg stupidly sticks out, awash in signatures of mediocre intent, and I glare at it while trying to push off. Mom will be here any minute, and I'm not ready for her slaughter of questions. I pivot and push but go nowhere.

Swiveling around in my seat, I look below. That one lump blocks me from going forward. I'm stuck. "Come on." I give my wheels a shove forward, throwing my chest out for momentum.

"I'll help you." Jamie comes up behind.

"Don't. I can do it."

She steps away from me, hands up, as I grunt my way back onto the sidewalk. "All good?" she asks.

I don't say anything. Maybe this is one of the rules of therapy; how should I know? Gripping the wheels, I turn them toward the hospital. Mom will freak if I'm not there.

"Hey," Jamie calls out.

I pause.

"Can I take a picture of you in your wheelchair?"

"No."

She dashes in front of me. "No?"

"No," I say again, head down and staring at my lap. Those happy knees of hers are standing in front of my chair. I can't go off-roading, that's been proven. My only option is the sidewalk, and she's starting to look like a very attractive speed bump.

"I can't take one shot? Just one?" she asks.

"No way," I say. "I don't even let my mom take pictures of me."

"Really? Why?"

I look up at her. "What the hell do you care?"

Her mouth drops open. "You don't have to be rude."

"Hold on. You're the one acting like I was going to slit your throat in the bus stop, and now you're all, sit still and pose for a picture?"

"You caught me off guard."

"It's a public space."

"Well, maybe I get nervous in public spaces."

"Well, maybe you're crazy."

She smooths her skirt. "Maybe you don't know what it's like to be a girl."

A giant red stop sign shoots up inside my head. Cease and desist. JP always says when girls start whining about how hard it is to be a girl, smile and nod and move on as soon as possible. "You make a fair point."

"Thank you. So can I take your picture?"

"No!"

"Dylan . . ."

"What?"

"Look." Jamie comes near, stoops down, and shows me the screen of her camera. "I really am a photographer. See?" She flips from one frame to the next. Shadows behind a door, a pencil with a broken tip, an empty syringe surrounded by needles, someone's bare back, a twist of yarn, uneaten food, empty prescription bottles, a half-pulled-back curtain, a close-up of her eye, and then finally the rust.

"You have no idea what you're doing," I say.

"What!" she explodes.

"I mean, not like you don't know how to use a camera, but what are you taking pictures of?"

"Life, you asshole," she snaps. "Because we're human beings who should care about being alive, not about the glory of sitting next to some jamoke at a lunch table."

"Wait, hold up. Don't throw one of my 'five good things' back at me. That's not fair," I say. "I had to say something in that stupid room, and yeah, maybe having a prime seat next to the most popular guy in school is a bonus for someone like me."

"Someone like you."

"You know what I mean." I angle my head back down and hide behind the hat.

Jamie slides the lens cap over her camera and slips it into her bag. "Yeah, I know. Stupid me for thinking there was more to it. Now, if you're going to continue to be a cryptic a-hole, my bus is coming."

"I'm not being cryptic," I say, wheeling after her. She doesn't slow down. It only makes me louder. "I'm not!"

Jamie steps onto the bus and pays her fare. The driver sees me and hits the hydraulics to lower the bus down to the curb with a wheezing hiss. A metal flap unfolds and the driver waits for me to roll on, so I do. If I see a white car drive by, right now, this second, then it's a sign from the afterlife that I'm supposed to get on the bus.

A red car flies by, followed by a silver truck. Then a white car.

Close enough, Dad.

The bus gobbles me up, seals the door tight, and eats my money. My nostrils flare. I'm inside. I'm on the bus. I look with wide eyes at the parking lot. If my mother's there, I don't see her. And then I realize I don't care.

I'm on a bus and I'm going far, far away to another place, and this is amazing. A smile breaks out across my cheeks so hard, it feels like a sunburn. I give my armrests a squeeze and gaze headily at the trees whizzing by. "You okay?" Jamie asks.

"I am so okay right now."

"You look high."

"I am not that kind of high," I mumble. "But I wouldn't know, that's your arena."

Her head bobbles. "I'm sorry, I didn't hear you properly because it sounded like you just called me a drug addict."

"The syringes." I lean in and whisper. "On your camera. I saw them, but don't worry, I won't tell."

The farther Jamie's neck skews backward, the more her eyes stay locked on me. "Did you ever think those needles and syringes might be for medicine that keeps me alive?"

"Like for diabetes?"

"Something like that."

"So . . . ," I drag out. "You're a diabetic?"

Her lips purse like she's sucking a lemon. "Yes," she finally says.

I look at her wrists, but they're covered with long sleeves. "Where's your medical bracelet?"

"My what?"

I point to her right and left hands. "For the EMTs. In case your insulin gets too low and you pass out walking in traffic."

She whips her hands up under her armpits. "I don't wear one. They're ugly, so stop looking."

I scratch my chin. "I'm guessing you've got type I

juvenile-onset diabetes, so I'm not sure what the pill bottles are for. Maybe high doses of—"

"Okay, enough, Dr. McKnowitall. I get it: you're *smart,*" she interrupts me. "But this is not Jamie's Medical History 101, so let's talk about the weather."

"But you're in therapy."

"So are you."

I shake my head. "Not really. I only went to one session to make my mom happy."

"Your mom sent you to therapy?"

There are so, so many ways I could answer that question. "Uh, no. Not quite. My orthopedic surgeon did."

"An orthopedic surgeon sent you to therapy? Holy shit, Dylan, did you break your own leg?"

"What? No!"

Now Jamie is the one who leans in tight. I try not to get heady from the closeness. "We're in therapy for self-harmers." She gestures to my leg. "So if you did this to yourself, you need way more than one session."

I turn toward the window. "Where are we going?"

"We?" she chokes out. "I'm sorry, were you under the impression *we* were going somewhere? Because you got on by yourself. I don't tend to go on bus rides with people who insult my work and assume I shoot up black tar."

She gets up from her seat and sits across the aisle, arms crossed and legs folded.

Suddenly the bus is cold. "I don't know anything about photography," I say.

"That's obvious."

"Why do you like it?"

"Why should I tell you?"

"Because I want to learn."

Jamie's eyes return to mine. She reaches for her bag and takes the camera out, pinching the sides of the lens cap and smuggling it away inside a pocket. Her finger nudges a tab and the shutter twitches to life with a click. She looks through the viewfinder and snaps a picture of the empty rear of the bus. "It sees more than I can. Captures those tiny moments in time. Things you think are soft but they're really solid. Like light," she says, but I can hardly hear her above the engine. "Unexpected things. Vulnerabilities."

The camera lands on me and I hide in my sleeve. "Don't."

It sinks down, revealing her face.

Hers is such an interesting face.

"Take a self-portrait," I say.

"I have," she says. "Thousands."

"Thousands?"

Jamie hugs the camera to her cheek. "You think it's egotistical?"

"No." But I might be a little jealous.

She tugs her skirt down and rests the camera on her leg. I swear it nestles in like a pet cat. "I could take a nice picture of you in your uniform, if you want."

"What uniform?"

"Your football uniform."

"I'm no more a football player than you are a heroin addict."

"You're not?" I hate that she's surprised. "I figured, football season, your leg, you can't play. Benched. Depression, self-destruction, all that jazz."

"Time to change your tune."

I can't bring myself to look at her face after that.

The world will never see me as the smart guy, the guy who likes to sop up equations like crusts of bread dipped in warm soup. Everyone but my mom thinks the rows of A's on my report cards are a quarterly mistake. Why am I killing myself over grades when I could just be running into other meatheads, bringing glory to our town?

If I were a withered, hundred-pound string bean who could barely hoist a backpack, no one would think twice. It'd be, Oh hey! Look at Dylan dominating the honor roll again. Of course he did; isn't that jolly. Indeed. Pip-pip, cheerio, send him off to Oxford on his Rhodes Scholarship, where he can squirrel away in a turret and ruin his eyesight by reading all those tasty history books.

And there it is. My dream.

I've never told a single person alive that I want the Rhodes. That I want to wake up in an eight-hundred-year-old dorm room in England and dash to class in a building that looks like something out of a Harry Potter novel. That I want to drink a tall pint and talk about All the Things at The Bird and Baby, the tavern where J. R. R. Tolkien hashed it out with C. S. Lewis every Tuesday at lunch.

I want to understand cancer, and not just the cellular kind. All cancer, because that shit is everywhere in all forms. There's very little difference to me between a malignant tumor and the Salem witch trials of 1692. Faced with his entire world going to hell, a seventy-year-old farmer named Giles Corey refused to plead guilty to practicing witchcraft, so they pressed him to death. And what did he do? He looked them all in the eye and said, "More weight." That's amazing to me. I like to think my dad was similar in his final days. Dead at twenty-six. I'd like to think he threw up the double birds and said, "More weight," because fuck you, cancer.

I don't know if there's such a thing as a historical oncologist or an oncological historian, but I don't see why I can't be the first. It's a solid step up from some bullshit major like underwater basket weaving. Oxford is the perfect place for a Dr. Dylan Ingvarsson, MD, PhD, to do quite a bit of both.

Only my dad knows my top secret dream. Being dead makes him magic because he's officially become a part of history, however small. But if I told a living, breathing person my biggest wish, of somehow blending obscure history into the cure for cancer, they'd be like, that's nice—here's a football.

Try not to chew it too hard.

My gut falls into its very own tar pit and right now, all I want is to go home and sink into bed. I take my phone out and hit the screen. Twenty-two messages. All from Mom. I should get off this bus and call her. Tell her I thought I'd make it easy on her and take the bus home.

A bus that ended up going in the wrong direction.

"Hey," Jamie says. She stands. "Come with me."

"And do what?"

The bus skids into a blank patch reserved on the pavement. The door opens. She looks over her shoulder. "Now or never."

Her boots tap-tap-tap down the aisle. My phone starts to vibrate. I don't think about how fast I'm shoving it back into my pocket; I'm too busy giving my wheels a giant push. The driver sees me and the bus starts to kneel. Now or never.

SEVEN

Downtown Portland looks like what a five-year-old would doodle up if you gave them a piece of paper and some crayons and said, now draw a city. There are rectangular buildings with glass windows standing tall in various heights on square blocks. Very basic. You'd win at Pictionary. But with any city, it's not always the surroundings that make it worth visiting; it's the people—and this town is the ultimate grab bag. Fixie-bike drag racers, eco-warriors, steampunk foodies, zoobombers, caffeine snobs. You need to fulfill a lifelong search for someone with a fork tattooed on their neck? We got you covered. Couple years here in the rain and everyone wears the same thin coat of moss. It keeps us huddled together and loving weird things like bewitched donuts and refusing to use umbrellas when it's pouring out.

It's the people that make a city great, and today that's us. Jamie and I, we are great.

In the middle of this block-tower paradise, there's a splat of bricks called Pioneer Courthouse Square, and that's where we sit near the steps, me in my wheels and her in a folding chair, holding hot cups of coffee. My first. Jamie bought one for me. "You think it'll work?" I ask.

"It's why I started drinking it. Five foot nine is tall enough—I have no desire to be a giraffe. So please, coffee"—she cradles it lovingly in her hands—"stunt my growth."

Jamie smirks as she sips.

"I don't blame you. I think girls should be short too," I say, and take a sip myself.

"Hold up—don't put words in my mouth," she says. "I'm talking about me. My dad's a former Trail Blazer, my mom's Swedish, and I'm trying to stay under six feet tall so I can comfortably fit my knees in an airline seat, thank you very much."

"Your dad's a Blazer?"

She stares at me like I have nine heads. "Did you hear anything I said?"

"Well . . . yeah, but you have to admit, that's an interesting factoid."

"A factoid. Sure. He played two seasons before he tore both his ACLs and retired. Rip City, do or die. Now he sells boating equipment." Jamie checks her phone for the time.

"I can sympathize," I say quickly. I don't want her to leave. "About the airplane. Those seats are so small, it's unbearable."

"What exactly did you mean, though, that girls should be short?"

I shrug. "It's what I've heard."

"From who?"

"My best friend, JP. He's got standards. Girls should be short, not talk while you're playing video games, and have long hair."

"He sounds like a real prince."

I scowl and look down at my coffee. It's too hot. So far it tastes terrible. "I'm just saying."

She motions to a lady walking across the plaza. "Her. That woman in the glasses—what do you think about her?"

"Like, in general?" I give her a once-over. "She's got to be almost forty, too old to be wearing a hoodie and jeans. And they have holes in them. She looks like a hobo."

Jamie nods curtly and points to another lady. "And her?"

"She needs to stand up straight; she's too hunched over. It's like she'd be pretty if she tried, but you can tell she's not going to."

"What a shame."

"Well, kinda," I say. "She looks like she'd be a nice girl if she smiled."

Jamie gets out her camera and takes pictures of the two passersby before they disappear from the plaza to parts unknown. "You know what I think? They're phenomenal as is. Maybe you'll figure that out someday." She stands up, gathering her things. "I don't think I want to know what you think about me. Later." Jamie throws her empty cup in the trash and walks away.

"Wait," I call out after her.

She spins around. "Of all the people the universe has ever barfed up, who are you to judge, Dylan?"

I drop my coffee, brown liquid drenching the bricks as I

roll after her. "Because I'm living it, okay? Every day. I am the one everyone sees and thinks, thank god, at least I don't look like that."

The wind kicks up her scarf and she smooths it back down.

She's standing there with all her bones lining up in the most aesthetically pleasing way possible, and now I'm the one to roll my eyes. What a joke. She's pretty and she knows it. Constantly seeking approval. Always looking around to see who's staring back at her, and once they make eye contact, Jamie tosses her hair and gives a little smile to herself. Like it's a check in the yes column.

Jamie can be all, wow, you're such a dick, look at you judging others—but she's perfect. There's nowhere she can go where she won't be welcomed, because she is a very attractive person, and humans like looking at attractive people. It's science.

I twist it in. "Someone like you wouldn't know anything about it."

Jamie takes her camera with two hands and looks into the viewfinder for a good long while before she looks up at me. "I'm happy with who I am."

"No doubt. You're gorgeous."

She launches into a nervous waterfall of laughter. "Oh my god." Jamie turns away, hiding her bright pink cheeks.

"But who cares, right?" I say. "Because what we look like doesn't matter, right? We're all smiling beams of sunshine in the sky, on the ground, under the trees, and we're all equal and extra-special flower petals, or whatever." The words bubble up, pumping a deep spring in my gut. "If you believe that garbage, that we're all beautiful little snowflakes, that's great. I don't. I haven't believed it since the sixth grade, and I'm not going to start now."

Pity coats her face and I hate that it's for me.

I back my wheels up.

My leg is killing me. Dr. Jensen gave me a prescription for Demerol, and I begged my mom to fill it, but she refused. Apparently all it takes is one Demerol and I'm going to end up in some abandoned warehouse giving head for meth. Instead, Mom loaded up a little plastic baggie with ibuprofen and stuck it in the zippered pocket of my book bag. I pull out the baggie now and dry-swallow. "I should call my mom."

"No, don't do that," she says with a softness that wasn't there before. "Mothers should be avoided at all costs."

"Yeah, well, my mother's probably filed a missing-person report by now."

"So what?" Jamie says. She takes her camera and snaps a few shots. "Don't we deserve some time to ourselves?"

"Oh, are we doing a 'we' now? Because I thought you were leaving."

"Maybe I changed my mind."

She eyeballs my chair and walks around the chrome frame and rubber treads in a slow circle, her finger itching to push the button. I concede. "You can take pictures of the wheels," I tell her.

"Thank you!" She bends to one knee and fires the camera to life. "Your leg too?" she asks, never letting the SLR leave her eye.

"Okay, but that's it."

She feasts. What she's probably been hoping for ever since we met in group. The button clicks a million times. When Jamie comes up for air, she licks her lips. Sated.

"You know, we're not so different." She fiddles with the lens cap but doesn't put it on. The thing is still alive. "I have a confession to make, or maybe it's more of a warning." Jamie tucks a loose curl behind her ear. "Those thoughts you think? About how people look? I have them too and they don't shut up. My last school was full of catty girls and I was one of them. You couldn't walk two feet without one of us making a snarky comment like, oh my god, she is such a blubber nugget—those jeans are a million sizes too small. I made a lot of girls cry in my old life and I don't want to do that anymore. I'm trying to be better. At least, I want to be better." She beams. A frigging Girl Scout.

"Would you have talked to me in your old school?"

Her grin wilts. "Probably not."

"Ouch."

"It's the truth," she says. "I have . . . issues. When you surprised me at the bus stop, it brought me back to a bad place. I'm trying to get past it."

"So, what, hanging out with me is like karmic clean slate for you? Because you used to be mean to ugly people, you get soul credits for a cup of coffee?"

"When you put it that way, it sounds pretty bad, doesn't it?"

It's a blow.

I sit back in my wheelchair and stare at the sky. No clouds. No birds. Just glaring gray haze. When I come back down to earth, Jamie sits in her chair next to mine like nothing ever happened. If I had two functioning legs, I'd take a big step away from her. But then . . . why? Because she's a reformed mean girl? In a stupid way, I still am one. "Long story short, I guess we're both horrible people," I say.

She laughs her great laugh. "If that means trying to be a little less shitty each day, then yeah, I hope we are very horrible people."

"Let's go kick a pile of sleeping kittens."

"Pfft!" she scoffs. "You and what leg? Let's go punch babies in the face."

"Topper."

"And how." We smile at each other, but she breaks. "I would never punch a baby."

"So there's still hope for kicking kittens?"

"You're terrible."

"You mean horrible."

Jamie holds up an invisible goblet. "To us, the most horrible people in the world."

"Cheers," I say, as we clink our lost coffee cups together. We drink air.

"But thank you," she says. "For being cool. With me. That's pretty awesome."

"Uh . . . why wouldn't I be?"

Her hands raise another toast before she scatters whatever remained of the faux cup to the winds of the square. "And that's why you're so cool." She smiles.

I die. I try not to, but I do anyway. I'd ask her to pinch me, but that's technically touching and I might die some more. The best I can do is reach up and scrape the scruff on my cheek instead of smiling. "You're welcome."

"Dylan!" My head whips around at my name.

Oh my god. Mom.

Beige coat flying, she tears toward me. "There you are! Sweetheart, you scared me half to death! What happened? Where were you? Who was that girl?"

I go to make a flustered introduction, but Jamie's off and sprinting down the steps. "Jamie!" I call after her. She doesn't look back, speed walking across the bricks like she's late for another bus. "She's gone," I say.

"Why weren't you at the hospital?"

"She didn't say goodbye."

"Dylan." Mom claps a hand on my shoulder.

"Sorry," I say in a daze.

"That's all you have to say? Sorry?" Mom grabs the handles of my wheelchair and gives me a big shove. Our car is double-parked and blocking traffic. I'm maneuvered toward the backseat; my bag is removed and tossed in through the open door. Her hands grip under my armpits, as if she could lift me, and I come to.

"I can do it," I tell her, and get into the car by myself.

"Wonderful," she says, lightly dripping with sarcasm. "I wasn't sure. I thought you might have brain damage or something terrible."

"You mean horrible."

"Fine, horrible. Why weren't you waiting for me at the hospital?"

The city whizzes by. Somewhere behind me, Jamie's taking pictures. I want to be there with her as she listens for the cracks and dents to call her camera near.

"Dylan!"

"Sorry." The inside of my head feels like whipped butter. I scoop out my story. "I thought I'd make it easier on you and take the bus home. It was the wrong bus. We ended up downtown."

"Who was the girl?"

"Jamie. We met in group."

"If you two are in group together, then that's where you two should be. Not flying all over the city together."

The car feels very small. More than usual, given that the shotgun seat is all the way down for my broken leg, and my toes can almost touch the glove box.

"You should've called, Dylan. Or texted. I searched the hospital. I asked security; I asked every doctor and nurse in the hall. No one knew where you were. It was very upsetting. I'm very upset."

"You mentioned that."

"And you don't seem to care!"

"I care," I mutter. Jamie didn't say goodbye.

"You need to call me before you pull a stunt like that," she grumbles before launching a giant sigh. "Okay. Compromise. You can ride the bus with your friend, but you have to call me first."

"I can't have some time to myself?"

"I am not having this argument with you right now, Dylan."

"It's not an argument!"

"Don't raise your voice at me."

I glare at her in the rearview mirror. Fighting with my mom is a lose-lose situation, so I drop it. Her version of brass knuckles is guilt. No matter what I do, Mom snuffs it out with her trump cards: Widow, Single Mother, and We Don't Have a Lot of Money. Whatever I'm going through, it pales in comparison to her struggles. Because I *have no idea how hard life is. . . .* I usually run to my room with my books, but I'm stuck in the car with her this time, and I don't even think studying would make me feel better right now. "How did you find me?"

She looks to heaven. "I asked your father for a sign. He told me where I needed to go."

My eyes bug.

Mom pats her heart and drives on. We aim for home. I say nothing and look at the sky with jealousy. Over the years, I've asked my dad a million times to help me with a million different things. I'm still waiting for an answer.

EIGHT

One day later and it's like my escape to the city never happened. Mom and I are tucked snug into our tiny two-bedroom bungalow with one extra plate at the table tonight. But we don't mind. JP has a stacked, infinity-bedroom, infinity-bathroom palace far away in Irvington, and yet he lives in a tree house his dad had built for him instead. It's a nice tree house, don't get me wrong, all hooked up with electricity and stuff, but it's a little cold and crappy in the wintertime, so Mom and I just say hi when he comes here. A place to be, a house on the ground, where he can sit and eat and feel normal. When we were kids, I always wanted to go to his house—his toys were way better—until I realized there's a stark difference in parenting techniques between his mom and mine.

We never talk about it. Ever. But it's there, like shadows attached to the bottom of your shoes, following you in silence. Because I mean, shit, if I were JP, I'd never go home either. And I'd be sitting on my best friend's living-room floor and playing video games too, which is exactly what we're doing.

"Get the fuck out of here, you piece of shit." JP's fingers fly with his new controller.

I run over his corpse as it evaporates and switch guns. "Kiss my ass," I say.

"You mean, kiss my Sasquatch ass." JP wastes a life and respawns at the start of the level way the hell over by the crumpled-up Empire State Building. "In which case, that'll never happen," he says, and runs to catch up. "I don't want furballs."

"Whatever," I say. "Come over here again. I'll still kill you." Angling my guy to jump off a pile of crushed taxis, I stall. I hate this part. I always screw up here. Something about jumping doesn't sit well with me anymore.

Crap. I die and regenerate over by the Empire State Building.

"And the Beast chokes again," JP says.

Sometimes I want to choke *him.* He's always just . . . I don't know. Lucky. He's lucky. I have no idea how he does it, but whatever tricks he has up his sleeves, girls practically wait for their turn with him. If only they knew his skater bro shit was a farce. He might look like one of the original Z-Boys of Dogtown, but in reality he gets off the bus two stops early to fake like he skated the whole way to school.

JP curses me out after I kill him: "Blow me, you hairy asshole."

"Blow yourself."

"Nah, I'll get Katie to do it later."

I grumble to myself because here's the thing: I have no idea if that's true or not. JP is north on the compass, no doubt about that, but there's no way of knowing if anything he says is the truth or just him exaggerating. He's been caught doing both, so I let it go.

JP claims he's done it, but he says it was with a girl he met while he was at baseball camp. Wait, there's girls at baseball camp? Oh, no worries, she was at the softball camp. Same fields, different buildings. Sure. Why not? And she was from California, where they have no email or phones, so there's no need to keep in touch. Sounds good.

Oddly enough, now I've got the same problem. I want to tell him about Jamie, but there's no proof. No number, no email address, no glass slipper, no nothing. Jamie's real, but she sounds too good to be true. A girl—no, wait—an interesting girl, who even JP would think is hot, bought me (yes, me) a cup of coffee and we talked. For a couple of hours on a perfect fall day, we were a We. I never knew what that was like before (it was awesome) and I might never know what it's like again, which is depressing.

"Hey, uh, Adam Michaels? Talk to him yet?"

"Shit." I totally forgot. And/or slightly hoped Adam Michaels had paid up by now. He's kinda older and not as big as me but big enough to leave a mark. I like it better when they can't fight back. "Will do."

"Thanks, man." JP jerks to launch another round of flame bullets at the little baddies protecting the big baddie in the corner. "How's the Wormhole?"

"Amazing," I say, because it is. Then I chuff to myself

because it's funny, the stupid things we do for each other, JP and I. But fine, I'll go talk to Adam Michaels.

Mom leans in from the kitchen, bringing the smell of simmering spaghetti sauce with her. "You guys ready for dinner?"

"Yeah," JP answers for both of us.

JP puts the game on pause, hops up and out of the beanbag chair, and trots into the kitchen like a dungaree-wearing farm boy whose mama done rung the dinner bell. Left for dead, I lug my corpse up from the deepest depths, mentally scream in agony because my leg freaking hurts like hell whenever I move, and hop stupidly to my place at the table. Even if I'm not supposed to be up and about just yet, I have no choice. My wheels are folded up and left by the door like an umbrella because our house is too small for me to actually use it indoors. I have to use a cane to hobble around the house instead. I try to gently bumble, but when was that possible back when I had two working legs?

The wooden chair groans under my weight. I lift my cast for elevation and wait for the pain to stop. It doesn't and I wish I could rub the bones straight. Mom ladles organic, grass-fed meatballs onto the plates heaped with pasta and sauce. Two for her, five for JP, and twelve for me. Fair is fair. "Ready?" Mom asks.

Both her and JP bow their heads. Mom thanks the Universe. JP thanks God because unlike me, he's an actual Catholic and not going to St. Lawrence because it's the best education in town. While they say their own version of grace, I pretend to. Although I never know where to send prayers, so I just think: *Hi, Dad.*

Their heads pop up and we begin to eat. "Go easy on the cheese," Mom says to me.

I lift the Parmesan from the grater. "Why?"

"Because that's the last of it for the month."

Money. As in, as soon as I finish dinner, I'm off to go study so I can get a full ride to Stanford or Yale or Harvard or MIT with all the bells and whistles. One day this mutt will have a pedigree.

But as I shovel food in my mouth (from the ever-rising food bill we never ask JP to help pay because apparently lost boys eat for free), I wonder . . . would I change places with my best friend? The answer is yes. In a heartbeat.

I imagine waking up in his body. One smile from my perfect teeth that align one perfect row on top of the other, and I'm wrapping up girls in my new lean arms. My brains in his body with all his money? Unstoppable. The world won't know what hit it. I'd never give his body back. He'd be stuck inside my old one and man, would he be miserable. But I bet, dollars to donuts, he'd take my body and do something real stupid with it. He wouldn't turn to a book to keep it in check. He'd go whole hog and end up in prison. No doubt.

My hand squeezes into a fist underneath the table. Sometimes I wonder what would happen if my fuse really lit. I haven't punched anyone since last year. Some junior. JP had asked me to do it, like he'd done a thousand times, but this time I enjoyed it. Way too much. It's not my size that scares me. It's what I'm carrying inside. My secret Hulk is always crouching under the surface, needling me. But I know the tricks to keep it locked up.

JP doesn't have control. He's all id: I want, I want, I want.

He'd want to beat the shit out of someone and he wouldn't know when to stop.

I drop the fantasy. He'll always be him, and I'll always be me. He'll have his face, his genes. All he has to do is hold on a few more years and he's gone. His dad will pay for college without breaking a sweat. JP can dick around for four years and earn some bullshit degree, smile with his pretty teeth, and he'll get by forever. Not me.

But whatever. It's science. It's fine.

Mom reaches out and lays a hand on my shoulder. "You okay, sweetie?"

"Huh?" I snap to.

"You look a little down."

"I'm okay," I say. My plate is empty, food eaten on autopilot.

JP guides half a meatball through thick red sauce, his eyes tracing its trajectory. "It's been one of those weeks."

"Right?" I side with him.

"You're not kidding," Mom agrees. "Can't believe it's only Wednesday."

"Hump Day is the worst. It's like all I can do to make it to Friday," JP says. "And even then, I don't want to deal with Saturday and Sunday."

"You know you're always welcome here," Mom says.

JP nods. "Thanks. It's just, I don't know, like my mom's like even worse these days and it's like no matter how—"

My chair shrieks to the side as I get up. "I have a test on Friday. I should go study." Throb goes the leg as soon as I stand.

They both stare at me. Mom frowns.

JP puts on the same face I catch him in all the time at school when he's talking to the guys at our lunch table. The slightly glazed half smirk. His mask. "Kill that test with fire, Beast," he says, one pump of his chin to finish off the sentence.

The two of them pick up where they left off, JP starting to elaborate on the most recent rage his mom was in. She's a mean drunk. It kicks me out a little faster. I just can't hear about it, I don't know why. It's like I want to be there for him, but I prefer to leave it at that. I got you, we're friends, moving on. Hearing about JP's mom issues gives me a mild temptation to go down to the basement and see the trains.

When my dad first got his diagnosis, he started building a train set. I was a baby at the time, so Mom told me all this later, but it's still down here. Dusty and lost. As the years went by, my father expanded the table and added tiny mountains and villages. It takes up an entire corner of the basement next to full-length mirrors. Maybe he wanted the fake little trees and tracks to reflect into infinity. A miniature father and son wait at a faded red train station for a locomotive that will never come.

The whole thing works. All the lights and switches and town houses with doors and windows that open up. He even left behind Christmas bunting for the entire town to get gussied up for the holidays. Mom tried to get me into the trains when I was eight and then again at ten. I never wanted to flick that switch and make them run. They made me deeply sad, but I didn't know what kind of sad to call it.

I still don't.

I wander into the living room to get my school bag, but my leg hurts so much I have to rest. Mom would've filled that frigging prescription if she knew what it felt like to have your bones try to grow inside a cast.

I'm growing again. I know it. No book or quiz or podcast can save me.

I think of Jamie. She understands.

Another cup of coffee sounds so good right now—let's stunt these legs right up!—but group is so far away. One more week. All I have to do is hold on, and we can be horrible again.

I sink into the oldest, softest chair we have and disappear into the cushions. No wood to creak, just worn-out springs that gave up years ago. Mom hates this chair. When she sits in it, she can't climb out because it's an abyss of threadbare plaid and compressed foam. Once it was my dad's, but I've made it my own.

Pulling some books from my bag, I open one and shake my head sharp and fast. Focus. Study. Chemistry. Let's get pulled into Coulomb's law, pun intended, because opposite charges will produce an attractive force while similar charges will produce a repulsive force. I'm ugly as fuck, so let's get some lovely equations to give me a lap dance.

"How are things at home?" my mom says loud enough so that I know she's making sure I hear too. I should've gone upstairs.

JP sighs. "She tripped and knocked herself out on the coffee table. Again."

"Did you pad the corners, like we talked about?"

"Yeah, but then that pissed her off even more and she

threw them away. She's like, 'I'm not a baby!' and all that, but she's real bad right now."

"And you sent that email to your dad?"

"He doesn't care," JP says. "I could get a plane to write it in the sky over his office and he wouldn't give a crap. He's like, no one can make her go back to rehab, so it's not his problem anymore."

There's rustling. I don't have to see them to know they're hugging.

My mom hugs and I punch. Go figure.

When JP started doing this loan-business stuff back in the eighth grade, I didn't give it much thought. Why would I? I was there for the first transaction. Chase Cooper wanted a pack of gum and was short a dollar. JP spotted him and a week later, with my help, got two dollars back. It was even a little fun shoving Chase into the wall; I'm not going to lie. It's a rush. Now we're in high school and his side project has gone school-wide, which is weird. Especially since he doesn't need any cash, ever, but it's his thing and we all have a thing. Something to distract from real life. He gets off turning guys who need a favor into clients who owe him. So if I can make him happy in some dumb way, then that's what I do to help. Better than sitting in the kitchen.

When Mom gets up and fills their glasses with more ice, I sneak my things into my bag and whisper away off the couch. The cane is wood with a worn-down rubber tip that normally tack-tacks against the floor, but I work to be as light as a cotton ball.

It takes forever. I breathe once I'm in my room and the door is closed. I hop over to my window and stare at the roof. That football still taunts me. I close the curtains and sit at my desk to ignore the pull to go get it. I search for a podcast I haven't already heard, but I've heard them all, so I randomly pick the one about dazzle camouflage. The spine of the chemistry book cracks as I lay it flush against the flat wood. I'm reading, but my eyes slide down the page. My mom and my best friend are downstairs talking about wine-bottle-dodging strategies while my leg screams in pain.

I mean, jeezus. His own mother throws empty bottles at him. I've seen the welts. He's shown me. And afterward JP's head would shake, and his perfect hair and perfect body and perfect face would follow as he slumped against the wall, looking like a young Greek god on a bad day. It dawns on me I would still trade places with JP. Any day. So WTF does that say about me?

NINE

"Strip down and climb up onto the bed," the nurse says. "We have to measure you."

This is what all kids want to do at 8:30 on a Tuesday morning. Get half-naked in a hospital and wheeled into surgery. Yesterday I had an emergency appointment with Dr. Jensen and he looked at the X-rays and was like, yeah, that cast needs to come off ASAP.

"You should've told me as soon as your leg started hurting," Mom says.

"Your mom's right," the nurse says. He logs into the computer and types some stuff. "Growth plates could get messed up, if they haven't already."

Mom inhales sharply, like she's the one in pain.

"You need to strip," he says to me, and then gives my mom a look.

"I'll step out." She slips out of the exam room and shuts the door behind her so the metal knob clicks.

The nurse's head turns toward me. "Anything you want to ask while your mom's gone?"

I shake my head.

"Now's the chance," he coaxes.

What does he think I need to ask him, where's the nearest whorehouse? I tilt my baseball hat and look up at him from my wheelchair. "I'm good."

"All right. Skivvies and a gown." He tosses a threadbare green number in my lap.

He's joking, right? That thing is as small as a Kleenex. "Thanks."

"No problem. I'll be in the hall with your mom," he says, taking the clipboard with him.

A full-length mirror beckons on the back of the closed door, and I pivot my wheels away from it. Being anywhere near naked is one of my least favorite hobbies. Especially when I always hope to see someone else looking back at me.

But not today. I have to go into surgery, get these stupid pins removed and replaced, and get a new cast. Hooray. This is why I'm here when I'd rather be in trig.

Everyone's in a tizzy about my leg healing in a confined space. The bone will bunch up and I'll be all lopsided. To which I say, I don't care. It'll give me an excuse to slouch.

A knock at the door and the nurse is inside before I'm finished. "I'm not done yet," I say as I struggle with my jeans. They're stuck.

"Here, let me help," he says, reaching for my jeans before I get a chance to say whether or not I am cool with that. But I sit there like a mute as he wrestles off my pants over the cast. When he's done, he re-hands me the gown and the obvious dawns on him. "Whoa, dude, this isn't gonna fit." Nurse Ryan, as per his name tag, digs under the counter and pulls out one that's more my size.

He stands above me. "You sure you're only fifteen?" He makes something that could be confused for a laugh.

I push off the wheelchair and now I'm the one to stand over him. He's a good half foot shorter than me. I put on the gown, but why I don't know. Modesty? Pride? I doubt there's much left. "Yeah, I'm fifteen."

"All right, show-off." He points to the scale. "We should weigh you first. Hop up."

Easy for him to say.

He fiddles with the sliders. His eyes bug. "Two hundred and seventy-two pounds."

"Is that bad?"

"No. It's solid muscle," he says, squeezing my bicep as a prop. The nurse steers me toward the clean white sheet of paper covering the flat hospital bed. "Get on there and lie down."

Two knocks on the door and Mom pops her head through the crack. "Can I come in now?"

Hail, hail, the gang's all here. The nurse motions for her to take the empty chair next to my clothes. I swing my bad leg up and it hits the paper with a crunch.

"You're wincing." Mom wrings her hands. "Be careful—go slow."

"He's fine." Ryan slaps his hand on my back so hard it feels like a million hornets. "He can take it; don't worry about him."

You're right, I only notice pain when a mastodon's goring me.

"Let's get the tape measure. Lie flat and still." He takes a yellow roll from his pocket and hands the end to my mother. "Pin this down by his heel." The nurse walks toward my head, the tape unwinding. He presses it by the side of my head. "Six foot five and a half. No wonder your leg hurts: you've grown almost two inches," the nurse says. He takes the measuring tape and wraps it around my upper arm. "Flex."

"Huh?"

"Make a muscle."

I squeeze it tight.

"What does this have to do with his leg?" Mom asks.

"Nothing. I was just curious." He takes the tape back and clamps it between two fingers, running the length with a stupid grin on his face. "Jesus . . . twenty and three-quarter inches! What do you bench?"

I put my hat back on. "Nothing."

"Not buying it. Schwarzenegger's arms were twenty-two and a half inches when he was competing. There's no way you're at twenty and three-quarter inches by doing nothing."

"We're here for my leg," I say, dropping the bass in my throat as low as it goes. So low, my chest rumbles as I speak. "Get to it."

Ryan backs away. "Hey, man, no problem." He raises his hands up, soft palms facing me.

Mom and I lock eyes and she turns to him. "We'd appreciate it if this could be wrapped up as quickly as possible," she says. "Dylan wants to get back to school. He loves school—he's very smart."

The nurse smiles but I can almost smell the drops of piss I alphaed out of him trickling down his leg. "It's just guy talk," he mumbles. He clicks the mouse and snaps the computer to life, bringing up my X-rays, and whips his little pointer all around the screen. "All right, so here we are. It's the pins that are causing the problem because they're screwed into your bones, and as you've grown, they're pulling against the body of the cast. Hence, the pain. So Dr. Jensen wants to move up the schedule, install some new plates, and redo a cast so it's smooth. No pins."

Fine. We already went over this yesterday during the freak-out. When we found out my bone might be permanently effed.

"You should feel proud of yourself," the nurse says. "They usually pull the pins out while you're awake, but your break was so bad and you grew so much, you need surgery."

"Defenestrate" is one of my favorite words. Not the version where you shitcan someone, although I'd really like to fire this nurse-guy, but the original meaning where you throw them out the window. King James II of Scotland defenestrated a dude, and if it worked for him, I imagine it'd work for me. Why not? I would like to pick up Nurse Ryan with my mighty twenty-and-three-quarter-inch arms and defenestrate him.

Splat.

I bet Mom would hold the window open.

She sits there, her leg jimmying up and down like a piston

and her mouth mashed into a razor-thin line, so pissed she can barely speak. "How much longer?"

"He's prepped for 9:15 AM," the nurse says. He slams a hand on my back one more time, and my eyelid twitches. "All right, man, I'm off to talk to the doc. No food. No liquids. See you soon."

Mom grunts as soon as the door closes.

"This is supposed to be the best orthopedic practice in Portland," I attempt to justify.

"I almost don't care anymore." Mom rises and comes over to where I'm plopped on the bed. She lays her hand on top of mine. "You must be sick of it," she says.

"Happens every day," I say.

She nods.

"When will I stop growing?"

"I don't know."

"How are you so small and I'm so big?" I ask.

"Genetics are funny." She squeezes my hand and I squeeze back. "You take after Dad. He was a big guy. You're just like him, in every way," she says.

Then I have only eleven years left until I die too.

Mom brushes off invisible pieces of lint from my stylin' gown. "I just wanted you to know you're not alone." She touches her nose to my shoulder. A little nudge. "If you ever feel too big, it's just because the world can be a little small sometimes."

My stupid head lands on her shoulder. Her cheek presses on top of my scruffy buzz cut, and her arm wraps up as much of my shoulder as it can reach.

A new knock at the door and we both tense. It's time. "Yeah?" I ask.

An orderly comes in with a standard-sized wheelchair. "I'm here to take you to surgery," she says, sucking her lip when she sees me. "Oh . . . I don't think . . . Hold on, let me get another chair."

I hop down and get into my old one. Super deluxe and supersized. "No problem, use mine," I say. The orderly pushes me and I wave goodbye to my mom. "See you in a couple hours when I'm back in the big, wide world."

TEN

Waking up from this surgery isn't as much fun as the last time. No pain pump with a super-cool button to push. No doubt Mom put the kibosh on that. Ah well.

She sits in the far corner of my dark hospital room, reading a book. On the cover a woman in a torn red dress with crazy hair and bare shoulders is getting mauled in the neck by some pirate dude. The spine's cracked. Must be one of her favorites. Another of the hundred and ninety thigh-slapper novels that she hides under her bed and I accidentally find when I'm looking for ski poles, I bet. "What time is it?" I cough out.

"You're awake," she says, ramming the book into her bag. By my side in no time, she scoots a stool close and sits down near my head. "How do you feel?"

"Fine. Groggy." I rub my eyes and flatten a palm against my head, the hair starting to stubbornly grow back. Feels like I'm rubbing a hedgehog.

"That's normal," she says. "Dr. Jensen said it went well and you can go home tomorrow. New cast, want to see?"

I roll over and check. All the names are gone. No more Fern Chapman. I smile. Good. She's not allowed to sign this one. "Cool."

"You had a visitor."

"I did?"

A sneaky little smile takes over. She points. I follow the line and on my bedside table, there's two daisies in an old iced-tea bottle by my bedside. "Where did these come from?"

"A girl dropped them off. I'm guessing she's the same girl from that day when I caught you at Pioneer Courthouse Square," she says. "Jamie? Is that her name?"

I almost explode off the bed. "Jamie was here?"

How did she know I had surgery? And she came into my room? With daisies? Do I smell them for clues or something? I pick up the bottle. The two daisies droop against the side of the open mouth. These aren't store-bought daisies. Their petals are all gamey and chomped on by bugs. The two ragged stems swim in cloudy tap water.

"So what happened?" I ask, as nonchalantly as I can. "She came in?"

"It was the strangest thing. I'm sitting here, reading my book, when she barges in, all bags and boots and then I could see the girl underneath it all. She's pretty."

She says that like it's a surprise—maybe it is because she was here for me. "Did she say anything?"

"Not at first, no. I was like, can I help you? And she almost ran for the door, but I talked her into staying."

I bet. Patron Saint of Small Talk right here. "What did you say?"

"What do you mean?"

"What embarrassing story did you tell her?"

"Give me some credit." She sniffs. "I found out you two met in group. Jamie was here for a doctor's appointment of her own, and I learned her favorite food is crab cakes. So there."

Crab cakes. I will remember that.

Mom sidles over. "So that's the girl from the square."

"Mystery solved."

"I wish she hadn't run away that day; she's a sweetheart. And poor thing too. She's got such a hard road ahead." Her head tilts to the side, heavy with sympathy.

Now I'm confused. It's not like diabetes is an instant death sentence. The discovery of insulin put an end to that. "She didn't choose to be that way; it's how she was born. I don't think there's anything wrong with her."

Mom nods. "You know what? Good for you, Dylan. That's the right attitude. As long as you know."

Mom the drama queen. I turn my attention to the flowers. "But she brought these?"

"Yeah, about that," Mom says in a way that makes me go uh-oh. "Jamie told me to tell you in big bold letters that those are daisies, and daisies are for friends."

"Seriously? She seriously said that? You're not making that up?"

"She seriously did."

"Hokey."

"Hey, you got flowers from a girl, didn't you?" she retorts. Touché. "I have to say I agree with her. I think you two will make great friends. It's good to have friends."

"I agree."

"So that's where your relationship stands?"

"Mom, there is no relationship." Yet. I'm hoping. Although these daisies are sending that hope straight up into the sky like a balloon.

"For the best," Mom says, and smiles. "Jamie did take some pictures before she left."

I grab on to the metal triangle dangling above and yank myself upright. "She took pictures of what?"

Mom bites her lip. "You."

"What!"

"I asked her to."

"How could you do that to me?"

"Dylan . . ."

"I was unconscious!"

She sits and pins her hands in her lap.

"I want to go home," I say.

"No way! You need rest."

"You know I hate when people take pictures of me."

"Hear me out," she interrupts. "Jamie said it was the first time she's seen you without a big puss on."

"A big puss on." I fold my arms. "Again . . . Seriously?"

Mom's eyes shoot to the ceiling. "Okay, that was my way of putting it, but fine. *Jamie* said it was the first time you didn't look like a sulking axe murderer. Then she asked if she could take some pictures. Said she forgot her camera but her phone would do in a pinch."

So she Instagrammed me. I've been filtered.

"She showed me, and I asked her to send some to me because I am your mother and you are my son and I have no pictures of you. None. You haven't let me take your picture since you were in the fifth grade." Mom turns her head away, dabbing the corner of her eye with her knuckle.

"You don't have the right."

"Well, maybe you don't have the right to pretend you don't exist. Did you ever think of that? Because for your information, you do exist. And you have people who love you." She stares down at the phone resting in her clasped hands. Sticking it in my face, she clicks open a picture with her thunb. "Look."

It's a shot of me. A close-up. Very still, very quiet. My eyes are closed, and the shadows hovering around the rambling bedrock of bones that make up my face are soft.

"Look how handsome you are," Mom says.

"It looks like I'm waiting for a plaster death mask to be poured."

Mom pulls her phone away and tucks it inside her palm. "Oh, for crying out loud, it does not." She runs her finger down the side of her phone. "I think she captured you."

"Delete it."

"No."

"How did you get that picture anyway?"

"Jamie texted it to me."

I wedge myself up onto my elbow. "You have her number?"

Mom looks up at me with a glint in her eyes. "I have her number."

"Give me her number."

She grins. "Well, look how it's suddenly not so *annoying* for your dear old mom to be friendly with your friends, huh?"

"Mom . . ."

"Suddenly that picture I have on *my* phone is looking pretty good, isn't it?"

"Don't make me beg."

"All right." She twirls the phone in a loop. "I have a proposition for you."

"What?"

"If I give you her number, I get to keep this picture."

"Fine." Gimme, gimme, gimme. I have daisies to discuss.

"And," she adds, "any other future pictures she takes of you."

"There won't be any."

She smirks.

Commence eye rolling. "Deal. Text it to me."

Her little firefly fingers go to work, and my phone buzzes. I snatch it off my bedside table. Mom gets her coat on. "You must be hungry. I'm off to get a pizza," she says.

I wave goodbye. At least, I think I do. I'm busy working on what I hope is the perfect first message. *Hey, Jamie. It's Dylan. . . .*

ELEVEN

Thursday. It's the last class of the day, and all I can think is Jamie, Jamie, Jamie. . . .

"Dylan?"

Except I'm still in English. I look up from doodling *Dr. and Mrs. Ingvarsson* in the margins of my notebook and scribble it out so hard it rips the paper. "Yeah?"

Mrs. Steig waits patiently, but annoyed. "Your thoughts on *The Scarlet Letter*?"

"Which part? The slut-shaming part? The Victorian era masquerading as the Puritans? The familial guilt from Nathaniel Hawthorne for his ancestors being jerks in Salem?"

Mrs. Steig's so sick of me doing this, but she's smiling because she loves me, so I just wait for her to sigh and throw her hands up, and she does. Right on cue. "Have you read the book, or is this tangent time?"

"Yeah, I read it." In like the eighth grade because I was bored once, but whatever.

"I take it you're not interested in *The Scarlet Letter,*" she says.

I shrug.

Mrs. Steig looks at the clock. Ten minutes before the bell rings. "All right, go ahead."

"So it's not really about *The Scarlet Letter,* right? Because that book's been beaten to death. We get it. It was amazing at the time, revolutionary, a big slap in the face. Everyone is a hypocrite and no one's better than anyone else, so quit judging, but it was a major coincidence for Hawthorne because it was almost foreshadowing the time to come, both his and in the book, you know?"

She folds her arms and smirks. "How so?"

"It lines up perfectly with the holding country, England, as a last gasp before the Restoration, when everything pulled a one-eighty once Charles the Second came back on the throne," I say. "Like, we're all talking about Nathaniel Hawthorne using Hester as a metaphor or a trope or an analogy or whatever, but did you know that one of the most prolific and bestselling authors in Britain during Hester's time period, mostly, was a woman named Aphra Behn?"

Mrs. Steig's arms drop. "I've not heard of her. She was more prolific than Shakespeare?"

"No, he was dead by the time she came up," I say. "But she wrote a lot and made good money for it. She was a legit full-time writer, which is not what you think when you imagine guys in tights and long curly wigs." The Restoration is one of my favorite time periods. You'd think everyone was all prim and chaste, but they were anything but. "Read her poem 'The Disappointment' and tell me if Hester wouldn't have been one of Aphra's contemporaries."

That poem is bold.

A shepherdess is crazy into this shepherd and wants to lose her virginity by banging his brains out. And this poem about a girl wanting to bone sold like hotcakes during the 1600s. It's kind of nuts.

Mrs. Steig gets her phone out and pulls it up. She swizzles her head and shoulders all cheesy-like, fake stage style, and reads in a booming voice:

> *"ONE Day the* Amorous Lisander,
> *By an impatient Passion sway'd,*
> *Surpris'd fair* Cloris, *that lov'd Maid,*
> *Who cou'd defend her self no longer ;*
> *All things did with his Love conspire,*
> *The gilded Planet of the Day,*
> *In his gay Chariot, drawn by Fire,*
> *Was now descending to the Sea,*
> *And left no Light to guide the* World,
> *But what from* Cloris' *brighter Eyes was hurl'd.*
>
> *In a lone* Thicket, *made for Love,*
> *Silent as yielding Maids Consent,*
> *She with a charming Languishment*
> *Permits his force, yet gently strove ?*
> *Her Hands his* Bosom *softly meet. . . ."*

Mrs. Steig stops. She reads far ahead, eyes widening, and puts her phone back in her bag. "Oh my, we can't read this in class." Now everyone's all writing the name of the poem for later. I grin to myself. If there's one charming thing passed down through time, it's that humans are all a bunch of horny nerds who can't wait to talk about *it.*

Wait until they get to the end. The shepherd dude can't seal the deal, and the girl—the girl!—has blue balls. I didn't even know that was possible, but turns out I'm about four hundred years behind the times.

"Well, that's an alley I didn't anticipate getting clubbed in," Mrs. Steig says. "Where did you learn about Aphra Behn?"

"A podcast." And then I found a book of her work at Powell's and read that too.

Everyone in class stares at me, but in a good way. They're floored. This girl Bailey and I have a pissing match over grades, and even she crinkles up her nose with admiration.

"Must've been a heck of a podcast," Mrs. Steig says as the bell rings.

I merge into the flow of traffic in the hall and get carried away to my locker. A note gets dropped in my lap by a cute girl who sprints away so fast, I barely have time to be confused. I think that was JP's newest girlfriend? It's so hard to keep them straight. All the note says is *Adam Michaels?*

Shit. I turn the other direction to find the wing where the seniors have their lockers. Everyone in the whole school can't wait until they have the senior wing's because their lockers are painted glossy black and left in the far back of the school where nobody bothers them. I find Adam Michaels crouching in a ball on the linoleum floor and cramming last-minute this and that into his messenger bag.

He peeks at my wheels. "You owe JP," I say, dropping my voice and giving him a long, hard stare.

"So?" Adam Michaels stands up, and all six feet, two hundred whatever pounds of him looms over me. Well, this has never happened before. How curious. Today of all days, I have to be in this chair?

I stand up and now I'm the one looking down at him. Two can play at this game.

Adam Michaels gathers up the last of his things and zips out of reach on a pair of fleet feet. Frigging Mercury over here. "What's a cripple like you gonna do about it?" he says, leaving me in the hallway like a skid mark on a fresh pair of tighty-whiteys.

"Shit," I mutter to myself. Stupid chair. Stupid JP.

I'm not chasing after him, the hell with that.

I sit back down with a plop and hope no one saw. Then it's like . . . Dammit. Now I feel obligated to beat the ever-loving shit out of him just to keep my edge.

Had a similar incident last year, but it didn't end well for that guy. There was this junior who wanted a sweet set of rims that looked like razor wire for his Toyota Camry, but he didn't want to wait until Christmas (because let's be honest, Jesus, Santa, and the Easter Bunny would laugh their asses off with that one). So JP gave him the money. Unfortunately, the guy thought he could blow off repaying some scrawny freshman with a dewy pout and a fat wallet. I proved that junior wrong.

Haven't punched anyone since that guy, though. Just . . . because. Seeing him down on the ground and rolling around, holding his face. I don't know. Wasn't the first time

I laid someone out, but it was different. I broke his nose and cheekbone with one punch. I really hurt him. It scared me. Sat in my gut like an axe left in a tree.

I asked my dad about it, silently and in my head. *Was it right? Was it okay?* I know whenever Dad went into a bar, he'd scan the room for the drunkest guy because it was only a matter of time before some dumbass wanted to prove his machismo and take it outside. My mom told me that story when she tried to prepare me for what my size could bring. He'd tower over the entire room, sizing up the crowd, and she'd always get up and kneel on a bar stool and ask him, "What are you looking for?"

And he'd say, "The biggest idiot."

My dad did it—he punched other people. So it must be okay because that's what I'm doing, punching idiots.

Except I don't want to get into it with Adam Michaels. But I fear I will, and now I'm wondering, What does it mean? Is this just leveling up? Maybe this is how it's supposed to go.

This is like having the world's strongest magnets inside, pushing against each other. Punch, annihilate, crush bones. No, don't: let it go, make peace. Wipe the floor with his face; you can't let someone disrespect you like that. Laugh it off, who cares, let bygones be bygones. Push, pull. I want both, I want neither.

Maybe if I put Adam Michaels in a coma, I'll never have to do this for JP again. My reputation will speak for me.

It's an appealing thought.

Who knows what Adam wanted: headphones? New Jordans? Like I said, none of my business. I don't care. Besides, who cares about Adam Michaels when Jamie's on my mind? She's always on my mind, it just depends on the corner.

I hear a voice call my name.

"Dylan!" My name comes at me. "Dylan! A word, please! Don't go home yet!"

I am not in the mood for any more delays. "Hey, Coach Fowler."

He jogs down the hall, his silver whistle bobbing all over the place. Dignity, my man, you lost it when you started harassing me to play a sport I want no association with. Panting, he arrives and lays a heavy hand on my shoulder. "I know we've chatted before . . . ," he begins.

"Yeah, and my leg's still broken."

"But it won't be next year!" he says. "We could really use you. It would be a great help to the school if we had you on the team."

"You know the farthest I got was Pop Warner when I was ten."

He throws his hands up. "I don't care! I'll take you under my wing, give you a recommendation to any school you want. Heck, I'll even drive you to tour the colleges!"

"I already said no." Go Team Brain.

"If you're worried about being behind, you've got plenty of time to learn."

It's not hard to learn how to be a brick wall. "Once again, not interested."

"Dylan, please . . ." He leans in and whispers, "Think of the girls!"

I grin. "Already got one," I say, turning my wheels to go. "Later, Coach."

Leaving him hanging in the hall was good, but even better? Going to see Jamie and get more. More bus rides and more five good things about her and just plain *more* of everything. I want more. We've only seen each other once in a room full of nutters—but now I'm the one feeling something crazy. I feel hope.

Mom picks me up and starts lecturing as soon as my seat belt buckles. "No running off today. You say hello to that girl and have a nice visit, but you stay at the hospital, understand?"

"Yeah."

"Yes," she demands.

Jeezus. "Yes."

She rambles on about therapy and how worried she is, blah blah blah. There's no convincing her I am fine and do not need therapy, so I nod my head to the beat. Yes, I'll be there when you pick me up. Yes, I'll listen to the doctor. Yes, I'll participate. But the whole time my heart is thumping Ja-mie, Ja-mie, Ja-mie, Ja-mie. . . .

We slow down in front of the entrance and she helps me unload. Mom hands me my bag and looks me dead in the eye. "You'll be here waiting for me, when?"

"Ninety minutes from now."

She smothers me in a big hug. "I love you, sweetie. Have a good session. Be strong."

Inside the lobby, I roll toward our dismal room and wonder if she'll be there early, like me. "Hey," she says from behind.

I spin around. It's her.

Jamie leans against a metal fire extinguisher cubby. "Want to get out of here and do something horrible?"

"Yes, immediately."

TWELVE

Ten minutes later we're across the street at a little park where tiny kids take turns falling off a slide onto a squishy sponge disguised as grass. Moms pretending not to check their phones while they push their tots on the swings. I wonder if they have actual things to check or if they're just bored. The kids don't care. They swing and jump and play under the drifting leaves among the last rays of afternoon light.

It's not like Jamie and I want to be here with all these moms, but the park is close enough that I can be back at the hospital in ninety minutes. We meander to nowhere in particular and end up under an old dome that's been repurposed into a rotunda. She holds on to a wrought iron pole and lets gravity swing her down to the stone step below with a plop.

"I just didn't want to be there, you know?" she says. "I'm tired of it. The drivel."

"I hear you." It's crisp without the threat of rain, and I lift my face to the sun. My eyes might be closed, but I can see her clearly through the blistering red and yellow leaves. Jamie stands in my mind like a figure cut from different layers of stone. Strong and unexpected. As nervous as I am to be here, and I am beyond nervous, I'm happy.

I hope she is too.

Jamie gets up and takes some scattered pictures of the park. "I decided I don't need therapy anymore," she announces.

"Yeah? Why's that?"

She shrugs. "Because I'm the most normal person I know."

"I don't think I need it either. Big waste of time."

"Hooray for us, we're cured."

"I'd rather be here."

She shuffles lightly with laughter. "Me too."

Jamie's leaning on a pole and watching the kids play. Not taking pictures, but hugging the camera like she's wistful. Pining. "Penny for your thoughts," I say.

"Cheapskate." She grins. "I was just thinking about what it was like when I was little. Like, I knew exactly what I wanted to be, but I didn't know how to get there."

"What did you want to be?"

She looks me right in the eye. "I think I wanted to be a mommy, but I didn't understand it yet. Does that make sense?"

"Uh . . ." I glance at the kids and then back to her. "So have some babies ten years from now when you're ancient, like almost thirty. Not that hard."

"For me it is," she says. "I can't have kids."

The diabetes. I've heard about this. My mom always cries at *Steel Magnolias.* "Adoption. Surrogacy. There's a million ways around it; you can still be a mom."

"I know, I know." Jamie swings her camera to the trees and takes some shots of dappled sunlight and listing leaves. "And I will be. Just adjusting to the idea now." She stops shooting long enough to send me a small smile. "You don't think it's weird I want to be a mom?"

"No." I shake my head. "Why would I? Don't lots of girls want to be moms?"

She sighs, her smile curling like an idle leaf. Carefree. "I like being out with you."

Uh, duh, being at the park on one of the most glorious days of the year with her is amazing. "I like being out with you too."

"This is why you're so cool, Dylan, I'm telling you. Points for humanity right here."

"Can I cash in my points and ask you something?"

Jamie shifts and stands straight. "Okay."

"It's something I've been dying to know."

Her spine stiffens. "Go ahead."

"The daisies," I say. I was too mortified to mention them before. It'd be like I would go to text *so those daisies, huh? coolest flowers ever!* and it felt so stupid, I just deleted it and talked about favorite movies, music, books . . . everything but daisies.

"Oh my god, the daisies! I forgot all about them!"

"Well, I didn't."

"Sorry," she quickly says. "I didn't mean it like that."

"Fine. How did you know I had surgery?"

"I have eyes everywhere."

"Can't you just tell me?" JP says girls play games. This must be one of them.

"I'm at the hospital like a billion times a week. I know people."

"But how did you find me?"

"It's embarrassing." Jamie's fingers sweep the side of her face, but they're jumpy and she ends up tugging on her earring like it's an anchor. "But I might have told a certain person who works at the food court next to the orthopedic suites about a cup of coffee I bought for a guy on the bus. And we might have chatted at length about it. And she might have seen or heard about someone matching your description being wheeled into surgery. And she might have violated all the HIPAA confidentiality laws by telling me this, so don't breathe a word to anyone. I don't want her to get fired."

"You talked to someone about me?"

Jamie aims her camera at her face and grimaces a hideous shape with her mouth, pulling it down at the corners and grinding her teeth so they buck as the button goes click-click-click. She cracks one awful face after another, wincing sneers and scowling underbites. It looks like someone's branding her with a red-hot tire iron. "What are you doing?" I ask.

"Self-portraits," she says.

"Why are you screwing up your face like that?"

"Because it's how I feel right now."

She goes to make another monstrous face and I push the camera down. "Stop."

"Excuse me?" She whisks the camera away.

Her stare makes me feel like I've been dipped in boiling water. Stripped and raw. "I don't want to see you like that."

"What if it's the true me? Can you handle it?"

I blink. Maybe that's Jamie's beast bubbling up. "Yes. I can."

She puts the camera down and scrolls through her recent photos, deleting some and keeping others.

"Why are you at the hospital so much?" I ask.

"I'll tell you if you tell me," she says, not looking up.

"Deal."

"Therapy." Jamie sinks down next to me. "I'm in so much therapy, sometimes I don't know where my mind is," she says. "Family therapy, individual therapy, group therapy, it's endless."

"Why so much?"

"My parents are 'afraid' for me," she says, air quotes and all. "There was an incident at my old school. I took some things out on myself. They panicked. Fast-forward to now: my mom says it's all part of the healing process."

"An incident?"

"I got beat up, okay?"

"One of the mean girls?"

"No. It was a guy."

I'm furious. "A guy beat you up? Are you shitting me? What piece of scum would do that to a girl?"

"Points!" She throws some more my way.

"Who is he?" I growl. I want to know.

"So chivalrous." Jamie shines at the thought. "But yeah, that happened and then I got busted for doing something stupid that I don't want to talk about. Your turn."

"Something stupid?"

"That I don't want to talk about. Your turn."

My turn. "I fell off a roof."

"Fell or jumped?"

There's really not a verb for what happened. I confusa-jumplefell. My mouth wants to clarify with a flurry of words, but it opts for only one. "Fell."

"That's it? That's all it took to get you into group?"

"That's it."

"Well, that's a bit overzealous."

"Right?" I ask.

Whatever I had left of my nerves disappears. Vanishes. I'm with Jamie and Jamie's with me, and it's like the jumping beans in my gut have been drugged.

She springs up and tries to climb the railing of the bandstand.

"What are you doing?"

"I want to get a big shot of the park," she says. "The light's really good."

"How high do you want to get?" I get out of the wheelchair and hop over to her.

"What do you mean?"

Bending down, I hold out my hand for her to step onto. "I'll lift you up."

"I don't want to hurt you," she says.

"You won't."

She lightly steps with the ball of her foot into my open palm. "I hope you realize how much I'm trusting you. With everything."

"I won't let anything bad happen. I promise."

"Ready." Jamie holds her camera in one hand and steadies herself against the pole with the other.

I plant my left foot and raise her up, nice and steady.

"Holy crap! Holy crap!" she yelps. "You're doing it with one hand?"

The sun blankets her hair with a yellow glow and casts her face in shadow. She's so high above me. So slight, I could do this for hours. I feel her weight shift in my hand, like a broom you guide so it stays straight. "Don't worry," I say, not looking up her skirt. Even though I want to. "I'll catch you if you fall. Take your shot."

Her fingers balance against the dome, testing her center. Jamie's stomach tightens and sends vibrations all the way down into mine. I got her. She will not drop. There's a release in her feet after she takes her pictures, and I make sure she's holding on to the rotunda. I hope she got what she needed.

"One last thing," she says.

I look up.

The camera is pointed down at me. "Can I?" she asks. "Is it okay? This is too fantastic to miss."

One flop of my wrist and she could be on the grass, but that snap reaction is gone. I don't feel like hiding. Not with her. "Okay," I tell Jamie, half expecting each click of the shutter to fall like drops of acid, but they don't. It's okay.

I gently lower her to the ground, where she jumps off with a tiny leap. "That was amazing," she says in a rush.

I duck my head. "Aw."

"No, it really was—that was incredible. I don't know anyone in the entire world who can do that. It was like . . . flying!"

"I could really launch you if you wanted."

"No doubt—you're crazy strong. Like, insanely strong. I weigh way over a hundred pounds and you're just like, boop, here, let me put you eight feet straight up in the air, like it's nothing. Mad strong."

My mouth presses shut. "I know," I finally say.

"It's a good thing!"

I realize this is the first time we're standing together. I haven't been in the wheelchair for a while now, and she's looking up at me for once. She's talking and I can actually hear what she's saying. I grin. It's a revelation. Here's to the tall girls. "Today, it's a good thing."

"Be proud."

In a new way, I am. "Thanks."

My chair looks rigid and miserable. Let it stay by the steps; I want to be free. I relax onto the grass. It's damp and clammy. Jamie sits down next to me, unasked. "I set the ringer on my phone."

"To do what?"

"So we get you back to the hospital," she says. "In case we lose all track of time."

I go to kiss her. "Don't." She stops me.

"What's wrong?"

"Do you really want to do this?"

"Jamie, I'm so into you." I'm nervous, telling her that, but her smile is so big I know it's okay.

"Points, points, points." She leans in, lightly pressing her lips to mine.

I'm light-headed. We kiss, but it's stubborn. Each heartbeat grows more scattered and clueless than the last. We try too hard to be every movie we've ever seen, and it's awful. She angles her head, I do the same, but it's the wrong side, and we buck. I'd laugh, but I'm too embarrassed. I've read how many books and seen how many movies, and this is putting study into practice? I feel like a fraud.

There's a wall of gritted teeth keeping me out. It's like she's terrified. I am too, because this is my first real kiss. This one actually counts and I want it to be good. Scratch that: I want it to be amazing. I want this day to never end.

But she's not there. I pull away. "You okay?"

Her eyes are clenched shut. "No. Can we stop?"

My insides collapse. The cliff slides into the ocean.

"I'm scared," she whispers.

It's so unfair—I know what her lip gloss tastes like now. Pineapple.

"Did I do something wrong?"

Jamie opens her eyes. Her hand is soft as it touches my cheek. "No," she says firmly. "You're wonderful."

Warmth creeps up my spine and floods my chest. Another person, who's not my mom or another blood relative, thinks I'm wonderful. "We don't have to do anything, if you don't want to."

Her head plunks against my chest. "Thank you," she murmurs.

We'll just pretend it never happened. I reach for her camera and place it in her lap. "Here. Take some pictures."

She pushes it to the side. "The only subject I want to capture is off limits."

I reach for the camera, take off the lens cap, and turn it on. The SLR chatters itself digitally awake, flinging the lens in and out with a jolt. I hand it to Jamie. "Knock yourself out."

"Really?"

I take a deep breath. "Really."

She aims the camera at me. My face twitches into a smile. It feels worse than getting my back waxed, but I want to do it. For her.

"Be natural," she says, her finger on the button. "Pretend I'm not here."

"Impossible."

"All right, then think of something that makes you happy."

I think of her and turn red. She fires a million shots, and I dunk myself backward on the grass to soak up the sun. Jamie hovers and slinks up alongside me, snapping shots again and again. There's no place I'd rather be. There's nothing I'd rather be doing. In the distance little kids squeal and play, and I feel like one of them.

That magical time when you were really, really small and all that mattered was finding an open swing. Back when you let go and ran however the hell you wanted to. Before other people's opinions mattered. Being with Jamie feels like that. Free and good. I didn't know one person could make you a better version of yourself. And the sun is shining down and saying, *welcome to the world, dummy.* Tale as old as time.

But it's pretty cool when it's your song. I smile and she laughs with me. "I like you," I tell her.

"I like you too," she says. "You are a wonderfully horrible boy."

She brings the camera down and our noses slowly creep closer.

The timer on her phone rings, splitting the air between us like a barb. The day I wished would last forever is done. I hobble and huff back to my chair. Jamie takes the handles and pushes me.

I let her.

THIRTEEN

I'm skeptical about luck.

Nothing dramatic, just real used to the fact that if I go to grab a lucky rabbit's foot, the bunny will whip around and bite me. When I was a kid and things would go south, I'd ask my dad to please help me out. *Please influence that kid to invite me to his birthday party, please give me all the right words before I try talking to that girl. Please let me know you can hear me.*

If anything remotely good happens, it's my dad pulling a few sky strings from above, because luck and I are not on speaking terms.

It doesn't apply to school. As long as I do the work and study hard, my academic achievement is never touched by the chill finger of doom. It's everything else that occasionally goes to shit. Whenever things start to go my way, I sit back and wait for a kick in the teeth.

Oh, I just get an actual shirt that fits, like with buttons

and everything? Just kidding. The armpit rips open as I reach for a jar on the high shelf. Maybe that one happy day when I found twenty bucks on the street? Oh man, I immediately started planning all the food I was going to buy with that thing. I'm talking double cheeseburgers, extra bacon, and several bags of Doritos to wash it down. All the stuff my mom hates me eating. But wait! Some ranting woman charged up and started hollering that I stole it from her. There's no way that was true, since she was at least twenty paces behind me when I found it, but that lady threw such a fit, people actually came out of their coffee shops to gawk, so I just gave it to her. When you look like the opposite of innocence, no wide eyes or cherubic cheek in sight, you end up sighing and shrugging a lot.

So when I asked Jamie if she wanted to meet up at Peninsula Park in the rose garden, I had my doubts things would continue being great. Just because.

I flag a bus and take a long, slow trip there because she said she would come. Doesn't matter how happy she sounded when I called; I'm still worried. Maybe this will be the day when she gives me the friendly pat on the head and says, "Stop dreaming."

But that's it right there. I can't stop dreaming.

In my mind's eye we spend the day leisurely drifting in and out of straight rows exploding with flowers that surround the wide, circular fountain. Drops of water sparkle in the sunlight. Roses burst from their bushes in all colors and sizes. Tiny little white ones woven in between big lusty red ones. Thousands and thousands of roses blooming as one. Her feet treading across the weathered brick path, my wheels pushing along beside her. Perhaps we'll lean in to smell the same rose at the same time, and my lips will brush her cheek. The sun will beam down with golden rays of warmth, surging through our very beings and carrying us forward with the endless time of days.

Oh my god, shut up.

I dent the window of the bus with my head. Everything outside is bleak. Gray with dripping clouds. A small touch of hope thinks the sun will shine over the park, just for us, but an increasingly large feeling of dread rises up—it's the perfect backdrop for Jamie to sign off and go her way.

The bus slows to a stop. I'm right outside the park. There's a sidewalk and a ramp on either side of the rose garden, so that's nice. I'm even on time. Still, the dread grows. I want to cancel. Maybe stay on the bus and keep going.

Because what if Jamie is just humoring me?

The bus kneels and I get off. My stomach straightens out. I'm the one who called her, I remind myself. I want to see Jamie because maybe this is the one day my shirt won't burst apart. My nerves shake with each push to our meeting place by the little bandstand. I don't see her. I raced to get here as soon as the bell rang and I'm still covered in school. All loaded up with my book bag and wearing my uniform. I pause to take off the tie. I don't want it to seem like I'm trying too hard.

When I get to the bandstand, Jamie's not there. I check my phone for the time. I'm early and no messages from her. Maybe she's somewhere else taking pictures. A massive meadow, brown and dusty from last summer's relentless sun, lies surrounded by tall pine trees screaming up into the sky. She's not taking pictures of the grass or the trees, so instead I look for what might be rusty or cracked and check to see if she's crouched before it, working to find beauty in the forgotten and the grotesque.

"Boo!" Jamie's breath hits my ear like a shot.

"You scared the crap out of me!" I jump and land with a big, dumb smile on my face.

She hops in front of me with a little kick of her heel. "I wanted to surprise you." Some of her hair got trapped in her lip gloss and she pulls it free. One tug with her finger and the tendril flies back and blends with the rest of her hair, which is long and smooth today. I think I smell perfume, but it could be the flowers.

"That was the best surprise all week," I say. "Want to see the roses?"

"The roses? Uh . . ." Jamie makes a face. "I'm afraid I have bad news for you."

Here it comes.

"Well, I mean, it was kind of inevitable, wasn't it?" she says.

"I know, I know." Come on, let's rip the Band-Aid off already.

Jamie points toward the rose garden below the bandstand. "They're dead. It happens."

"Wait, what's dead?"

"The roses? As in, there aren't any to see today?" she says in concerned tones. "Are you okay? You look a little off."

I actually look at the rows of empty bushes. They're all

pruned. Some are wrapped in burlap. Dreams dashed. "What happened to the flowers?"

"It's fall. They go dormant. Old ladies in funny hats come in with pruning shears and put them to bed." Jamie takes a picture. "It's still a beautiful day, though."

"Is it?" It's all cloudy and the roses are dead.

"Do you want it to be an awesome day, or would you rather mope all over it? Let me know so I can plan accordingly. Go get a poncho or something," she says, not exactly hiding the sarcasm.

As her disappointment grows with her folded arms, my apprehension fades. Jamie's not telling me the next stop is Friendtopia. She's with me in a boring park on a shitty day with nothing to do but stare at a bunch of dried-up bushes. Meaning she actually wants to be here. With me. I want to give the world a high five.

Bravery surges through me like antidote after a snakebite.

"I'm glad you came," I say.

"Me too. It's good to see you."

Last time we hung out in a park, it ended with a kiss. I think we should begin with one today because I want it to be everything it should've been last week: stunningly perfect.

I stand next to her, using the bandstand for balance, and do what the violins tell me to do. The park melts away into a soundstage. It's our big close-up in a movie. Makeup artists fuss over Jamie, using all the crimson in their paint boxes for her lips. Fangirls are going to break Tumblr with GIFs of us kissing with Jamie swept into my arms like they're the last refuge on earth and me powerfully embracing her against the vicious winds of a ravaged tundra. Or jungle or postapocalyptic landscape or something more exciting than Portland on a cloudy day.

We're on set and as she turns toward me, the wind machines gently pick up, her face softly lit and glowing. The director helps me out and says, Lean in, little bit more . . . slower. Still slower. Now cup her cheek with the palm of your hand. Brush her skin lightly with your thumb, not too much, but just enough. Good, now—

Jamie grabs my hand and pulls it down. "What are you doing?"

I blink. The boom mikes and bounce lighting disappear.

The park sits around us, as dappled with midfall depression as ever.

"I was going to kiss you," I say, deflated she smacked it down.

"I got that. And maybe you're going to think I'm a complete prude, but please don't do that." Jamie edges back a touch and hugs herself. "I got to the park and it was like your brain evaporated and then, boom, all of a sudden you're all up in my face and I just . . . I don't know."

I lower down into my chair.

"Don't be mad," she says. "Can I tell you something?"

"Anything."

"I'm terrified."

"You are? Of what? Me?"

"No! It's just I've never done this before. The whole be-together-with-another-person thing."

"No way."

She laughs. "Why is that such a surprise?"

"Because I figured you've already had a whole ton of boyfriends, been going out with different guys since like the sixth grade or something."

"Yeah? Not so much."

"I don't mean it in a bad way. More like, how can someone like you be available?"

"Someone . . . like . . . me . . . ," Jamie says with painful slowness. Her eyes narrow.

"Funny! Smart! Pretty!" I say because she's looking at me with a bit of a death stare.

"Oh." She smiles. I love it when she smiles. Jamie's grin covers her head to toe.

"You should've been snapped up a long time ago," I say. "I mean, it's obvious why I haven't been. You're a different story."

"But you're smart and funny too."

"You forgot pretty."

She looks away. She knows it. "You're a guy; you don't have to be pretty," she says. "But I've had crushes. There've been boys I've liked. I've just been too afraid to make a move. Actually, scratch that. I tried once. It did not go well." Jamie lays a hand against her face. Like she's hiding a freckle or something.

"His loss."

"Maybe I'm being too hard on you."

"If you don't want to kiss, then we shouldn't." I fiddle with the armrest. "I figured that since we almost, you know . . . I guess I want too much."

"And what's that?"

To love someone else. To be loved.

That missing spark that I've never had before. I wanted

to be her movie star, and now I'm feeling like the guy sweeping up popcorn and scraping old gum and boogers off the seats.

Jamie holds out her hand. I take it. Our palms meet. Her knuckles skim over mine as our fingers wrap together. "Let's walk," she says.

We go slow enough that I can push with only one hand at a time and not go crooked. When we come to the ramp, I let go and grip the wheels as I use my left foot as a brake, skidding against the brick incline. At the bottom, I look at her and she looks at me.

Our hands snap back together. Hers is still warm.

"This is good," she says.

I nod in agreement.

"Maybe this can be us for now," she says.

"Okay." I frown. If it were up to me, we'd be full-on embarrassing the bandstand because I really want to kiss her. A lot. I sneak a look at Jamie. Her gaze studies the four trees ahead set up like a square, like she's deciding which corner to stand on. It dawns on me, I will stand with her wherever she chooses. And maybe standing together for a little while is okay.

"I hope you don't mind if I tell you that I like you, Dylan," she says carefully.

I could pop. "Of course not! Why would I? I like you too."

"Yeah?" She sounds delighted. Almost surprised. I wish she weren't. I'm the one who needs to hang what she just said on a wall in a gilded frame with a commemorative plaque and everything. "I hope you don't think I'm a total dork if we go slow."

If it means more of our nightly phone calls that've become a welcome habit before bed and more texts in between classes at school, then I'm all for it. I don't want her to be terrified, not by me or anyone else. I can wait. She is worth it all. "Dork is the absolute last thing that comes to mind. I'm too busy thinking how lucky I am." I squeeze her hand and she squeezes back.

We stare at row after row of sleeping roses. They will bloom when they're ready.

FOURTEEN

I am flying high and with good reason. My doctor switched me out from a wheelchair to crutches, and while I'll miss being low enough to hear what everyone is saying, moving around is a heck of a lot easier. While that's awesome, the biggest news is the best news of all. I went in for a checkup after the operation, and Dr. Jensen took a look at my chart and said the most magic words I've ever heard in my life. "I'd like to refer you to an endocrinologist and get you tested for acromegaly."

Acromegaly. Gigantism. Meaning there might actually be a reason why I'm so big, meaning there might actually be a way to stop it. True, my mom is already freaking out because there's a possibility for brain surgery to noodle with my pituitary gland in case there's a tumor on it or something, but I'm like, Sign me up. Here's a butter knife; go get that benign beauty. My dad was filled to the brim with tumors like the ultimate cancer piñata, so who knows if he had acromegaly too? Maybe that was the start, like a domino effect or something.

It's making me feel like I have a chance to nip it all in the bud. The only thing that's bumming me out is I have to wait a million years for my appointment. I had no idea endocrinologists got so backlogged.

Another day ends and another bell rings. School lets out, and JP and I leave at the same time, surrounded by the same guys who generally follow us around.

JP's girlfriend of the week stops by. Bailey is like all the others. She's nice, with long hair, and instantly all smiles once she meets up with him. Which for Bailey is weird. Every class I've ever had with her, and we share plenty, she's like her very own TED Talk. Lots of thoughts about what happens if you can't break through a cellular wall, and how hard it would be to trawl the giant plastic patch in the Pacific Ocean and recycle it. What if? What then? How come? Bailey can brainstorm forever. Under JP's arm, she smiles in proud silence. He's hers. For now.

"Oh man, I almost stepped on that dead banana slug," he says. "Nasty."

"Ew . . . ," Bailey moans.

On the sidewalk, a dried-up slug from last night's rain shower lies shriveled up from the surprise afternoon sunshine. Confused silvery trails twist all over the pavement until they come to a stop under the dead snail without a shell. JP nudges it with his toe, mushing its corpse. "Why do they even bother?"

"Rain forces them out," I say. "Not his fault the sun got him."

JP scrapes his foot on a low brick wall. "Now there's gunk stuck on the bottom of my shoe. He should've saved time and died at home."

"That's nature. You can't expect something that wants to live to give up just because you think it's gross."

"Slugs can be cool sometimes," Bailey says. "They have retractable eyes! And—"

JP snorts. "Who cares? It's not a bug you can use and actually get something out of, like a bee or Venus flytrap or whatever. If that slug had accepted its fate and died like it was supposed to, then it wouldn't have ended up on my shoe."

"All it wanted was to live a happy life. You can't blame someone for trying," I say.

"Shoe," JP reiterates.

"But you were the one who stepped on it," I say.

"Whatever." He stops and stares past my shoulder. "Oh my god, who is this?"

I pivot. "Jamie!"

"Hi!" she calls back. Jamie coasts down into our school's drop-off zone on a shiny pink bicycle, scarf billowing behind her, hair flying. Like she's descending from on high and gracing us with her presence. I feel warm all over.

She slows to a stop and dismounts, flinging the kickstand with her toe. "Hope you don't mind—I wanted to show off my new wheels."

"They're great," I say.

There are no games with us, and I hitch my way over to her. I make a motion that I'm headed for her cheek and she leans forward, meeting me with a smile. I bend down and give her a kiss right on the apple. "Congrats on the new crutches," she says.

"I'm free!" I say before introducing her. "JP, this is Jamie. The girl I was telling you about." Once I had proof, I showed him the text where she couldn't decide what jammies to wear to bed, the pink or the purple. It was cute and goddamn sexy.

JP's mouth is open. He eyes her up and down, lingering on her face, her legs, her hair. That's right, JP, Jamie's frigging beautiful and she's all mine. "Hey," he finally says.

Jamie blinks once she notices him, and I move closer to her. You're here for me, I want to say. Not him. I've seen that melted-ice-cream face on girls once they meet JP. If I see it on Jamie's face, I might die. "Tell us about your bike," I say.

She snaps back to me with her bright white smile. "My dad got it for me last night because he wants me to stop riding the bus. So cute, right?" Pretty cute, indeed. "It's got a basket and tassels on the handlebars and everything."

"It's adorable," Bailey agrees.

"Thanks." Jamie grins at her. "Do you like it?" she asks JP, and I'm pissed. Why the heck does she care what he thinks?

"I don't know much about bikes," he says.

"Oh." Jamie shifts from one foot to the other.

"It's perfect," I tell her, giving JP the cue to take off.

"This has been enlightening." He guides Bailey with him and stares directly at me. "We'll catch up later. Like, a lot of catching up later."

I wave. Thanks, man.

"Have a great time, you guys . . . shit. I mean, you two?" He stumbles backward, turning red. "I mean . . . Sorry, you know what I mean. Sorry. Bye."

"Huh?" I squint.

"It's all good!" JP gives me the thumbs-up. "This is Portland. Keep it weird—live the dream. Let's all go play putt-putt sometime." Bailey giggles and they flee the other way, leaving me and Jamie on the sidewalk.

I shift my crutches and look at her. "I have no idea what that was all about."

Jamie tugs down her skirt. "He was calling me out."

"I like calling you." I brush my finger against her chin.

"Points." She smiles.

We've never said, out loud or otherwise, that we're a for-real duo now. I've been waiting for the perfect time to casually drop it when I'm buying her a cup of coffee or something: And my girlfriend would like . . .

Being with her is like bringing my favorite brain jumping jacks to life. I never know what she's going to say or what we're going to talk about, but I love the challenge. I love the thrill. When we're official, I will tell her just that. I will be that dork who buys her flowers just because it's Tuesday. Although I might have to get a job first.

Jamie numbly fiddles with the tassels.

"You okay?" I ask her.

"Yeah," she says, but I'm not convinced.

"What's wrong?" I take her hand in mine.

Jamie shakes her head. "Sometimes people say weird things when they see I'm trans."

I drop her hand. "What?"

She looks pissed and leans in to say it again. "That I'm trans."

"Transponding?"

"Uh, do I look like a radio?"

"Okay. Trans what, then?"

Jamie rolls her eyes. "Because I'm transgender? Hello?"

I'm not hearing this right.

"Dylan?"

"You're joking—this is a joke," I say. She stares at me, eyes confused and wide. "Did JP put you up to this?"

"What? No! Why would you think . . . Dylan, you knew I was transgender. I said so your first day in group."

The air inside my ears starts hissing.

"You said it was fine, remember? The day we met?"

I am pretty frigging sure I would remember that. I rack my memory, but nothing about trans anything comes up. We had five good things, I shared her five good things with the group and . . . I zoned out. Emily elbowed me and the girls were all glaring at me. I had to say something. Holy shit, I did say it was cool. I can't breathe. This whole time. Jamie's been transgender this whole time.

All my blood slides into my ankles. My pulse is about to explode through my cast. I need to sit down. So dizzy. My stomach fractures and slides like all the melting glaciers on earth into the ocean, raising my internal sea level and drowning me from the inside out.

Wobbling over to the wall, I ease onto it. She's still there. Jamie leaves her bike on the bike rack and stands in front of me. Everything I've ever known from all my mom's nightly detective shows flashes through my mind. Those trans ladies on TV are always prostitutes and drug addicts, and they always get murdered and end up in Dumpsters, and the killers always say they were duped and had no choice. . . .

"Dylan?"

Her face. The angles. No, wait.

His face. I see it.

His knobby knees in a skirt. His big feet in a pair of girls' boots. His eyes welling up with tears.

Oh god, this is happening in front of my school. Everyone knows me here. All the teachers that I need to give me A's, straight A's and perfect report cards—they work here. They can't see this. I can't let anyone know. What if the Rhodes committee finds out about this? They'd never accept such a fucking idiot.

I get my crutches and go as fast as I can down the sidewalk for home, hanging my head so no one can see that yes, I do know that boy.

"Dylan, wait! You knew; I told you." She jumps in front of me and takes my arm. We freeze on the spot, light cold rain sprinkling down the back of my shirt and soaking my neck. "You said it was cool. You looked me right in the eyes and smiled and said it was cool."

If there were something to say, I would say it, but everything inside me feels like bone shards pushing through the surface. Unsorted, wrong. For the first time, looking at Jamie hurts.

She drops her hands and grips her fingers so tight they turn dead white. "Please tell me you were listening to me, please. I need to know you heard me that day."

Slowly, so slowly, my crutches start to move again. I'm two sidewalk squares away from her, five squares, six. . . .

"Then we're over, Dylan," Jamie says from behind me.

Her voice is so cold, I turn around.

"Done," she says, lips clenched. "I feel like everything we ever had was fake."

And it's like a switch flicks and I'm all confused, because what the hell is happening?

"This was a huge mistake," she says. "I thought I was giving you points for being decent, when I was really giving you idiot points the whole time." She lays her fist to her head. "Or no, I didn't give them to you. I gave them to myself for thinking we were real. God, I feel so stupid. Whatever, we're done."

"What?"

"Dylan, I'm dumping you!"

I'm back in front of her in no time. "You can't dump me. We were never going out."

"Get away from me." She edges away in fear.

Just like that, I'm the monster again.

"We were never going out," I say again, louder. Stronger. She can't do this; she can't win.

The tears in her eyes spill over. "I got lost in you," she whispers. "And you were never there."

She flies to her bike and gets on it, riding away faster and faster. "Jamie!" I shout. Because how fucking dare that kid think he can dump me when we were never a thing, and oh my god, I kissed a boy.

I'm left on the sidewalk, rainwater collecting on the tips

of my ears and my nose and dripping off onto my stupid school jacket that pretends to make it seem like I belong somewhere. I wipe my nose, my face, my eyes, and I curse her out, Jamie and her bike disappearing into the afternoon. She can't dump me. We were never a thing. We never made it official. Then, oh god, she was a boy this whole time. I squeeze my eyes shut as hard as I can.

When I open them, I see stars.

She was crying, which makes no sense. "Boys don't cry," I mutter. The world grows dim and I shove off for home.

FIFTEEN

Safe at home, I stumble toward the basement, no crutches and no cane, hopping and lurching deeper down the stairs until I touch bottom. Walking on my cast is everything Dr. Jensen told me not to do, but screw it. If I could go deeper down forever, I would, but this is as low as my house gets, so I stop once I hit the trains.

I forgot about the trains.

Mom said they were for me, but I never wanted them.

I hate them—I've always hated them. Why was he building a train set when he could've been playing with me? Why would you waste what few years you have left on earth building a cheap plastic world? I turn away from the empty town. My reflection stares back at me and I hit one of the mirrors with my bare forehead. It's cold, but I'm so hot, it stings. I want to forget—*Eternal Sunshine of the Spotless Mind* style. Either that, or find out that this is all a big joke and Jamie is a girl.

My girl.

But no girl is ever going to want me. I see that now. Jamie dumped me, and seriously, what the fuck? I got dumped. I knock my head against the mirror hard. I got dumped and we weren't even going out. Then harder. My hand balls up and I punch the mirror. The glass cracks and the reflection of my face is splintered—a crawling spiderweb of broken shards breaks it up into pieces. Jagged chunks of a jigsaw puzzle.

I blow. There's nothing I don't destroy. Glass smashes with each punch and my knuckles bleed, leaving smears of red pooling in the gaps. I kick an old steamer trunk with my good leg so it feels just as shitty as my broken one. So big and huge, huh? These arms that mock me in the fractured mirror, is this what people want to see? They want to see me smash and tear the place down? Fine. Watch me. I am reborn. I am the Beast.

The Beast pulls and yanks a train track off the table and another and another, but it's not enough. The wooden table, it's bolted to the wall. I dig deep and pull a standing leg off and push the wood in half until it snaps like a twig. Breathing heavy, I smash it into the little town. Trains and plastic trees fly. I take the wooden leg and throw it like a harpoon, knocking over a row of old bikes. The smallest Huffy lies there, all dumb and powder blue with red and white stripes. My old bike from when I was little. I pick it up and wing it into the stairs, where it falls into a dented ball, leaving a crater behind. Is this what you want, world? You motherfucking got it. I am that monster under the bridge. I will eat your children. The pain from my leg is amazing. I love it. I savor the agony from my back and my chin and my hands like it's money I'm saving up to buy something great. My leg burns as I tear off the door to the boiler room and I don't care. I don't care.

Metal chunks from the hinges rain down and I let them fall, pointy sides up, on the meat of my shoulders. An old oak desk sits in the corner. My muscles, these big giant things I've always hated and tried to hide, scream as they come to life. I squeeze my hands into fists and lunge for it. Lifting it over my head, I throw it to the concrete floor, where it cracks in half. My bloody knuckles burn and drip on the floor in a pattern. I swing my hand out and the drops dribble from my nails and splatter down in a lazy arc. A canvas. Oh look, I'm finger painting.

My phone beeps. Sucking air in through my nose and firing it through my mouth, I pause. Everything hurts. I don't want to have a phone right now. I'm afraid of what it says. I'm actually drooling. I sigh and wipe it with the back of my furry hand. My fingers look like they've been run through a garbage disposal. Great. Now there's blood and drool on my face.

I am finally what people see.

My future life streaks before me. I'll live alone in a trailer park, be even more hairy and huge than ever, and subsist on cases of beer, peanuts, and old porn. If I ever do have female companionship, it will be the kind I have to pay for. I just hope the future escort doesn't mind escorting herself to the lot my double-wide sits on.

Or maybe I'll just give up and become the hulking football player everyone thinks I should be, and I'll get a big fat NFL contract and bash everyone to death and get a bunch of groupies who'll only talk to me because of my millions of dollars, and they'll go back to my penthouse and fuck me on Sunday nights after the game. On the Lord's day.

Trailer park or penthouse, either way I'll find girls who'll like me for a price.

I slump at the thought and the mirrors mock me.

God knows what Jamie saw in me.

Jamie.

I feel her lips on mine and it feels like slivers of glass from the broken mirror crept into my chest and rolled around. It hurts. Everything hurts.

"Hello?" I hear from above.

Mom's footsteps overhead walk around in confused loops. To the living room and back to the kitchen. I look at the annihilated basement. I'm covered in blood. There's glass embedded in my forearm. I part the thick hair with my fat fingers and try to dig it out.

"You home, Dylan?"

This is not going to end well.

Pondering what to say, I peek in some of the remaining mirror to see just how bad it really is, and I realize I don't care anymore. I am the Beast. Mom will have to deal.

The basement door wheezes open. "Dylan, are you downstairs?"

"Yeah."

Her feet pad down the top steps. "What are you doing?"

"Sitting on a pile of broken glass and bleeding."

Now they run, bang, bang, bang, and boom—she's at the bottom, gasping. "Oh my god." She races to me and kneels. "Did someone break in? What happened? Are you okay?"

"I did this."

"What do you mean, you did this?" Her mouth bobs open and closed like she's a drunk goldfish. "Why?"

"It doesn't matter."

"Excuse me?" She stands up. I shrug. An embedded chunk of glass bites the inside of my shoulder.

Mom's hands lightly sweep over the train set and everything still clinging to the walls. "Something happened," she says. "You didn't just do this for fun."

"Maybe I did."

She picks up a large piece of fake grass and places it gently back on top of a rounded hill, patting it down. "I don't believe you're capable of this."

"Here's proof." I raise my knuckles.

Lunging to my side, Mom seizes my bloody hands. "You need to go to a hospital."

"No," I growl. "I'm never going to a hospital ever again."

"But, Dylan—"

"Never."

"These are deep. You need stitches."

"I'll get a Band-Aid."

"Please." She cups my cheek. I shake off her hand. "Tell me what happened."

"I need you to leave me alone."

"I will not."

"Yes," I rumble. "You will."

"What? Where is this coming from?"

Jamie's face. It sneaks inside my thoughts, and I feel her entire body balancing inside the palm of my hand. She stood in my hand and I held her against the sky. Thinking about it burns. Aches. "Can't I just have a shitty day for once in my frigging life?"

"No!" she yells so sharp, it snaps me backward. "You did not destroy the last thing your father ever made because things didn't go your way today!" She bends and screams in my face. "He was dying! He could barely move! Cancer was eating up all his organs, one by one, and he still dragged himself down here because he wanted to make this for you. He wanted to leave you one thing, just one thing for his little boy, and you've ruined it!"

"I was a baby. I barely knew what a train was."

"That's not the point," she says. "This little village was his legacy to you."

"Bullshit!" I burst out. "I'm stuck in his legacy every single day!" I am my father's clone. Each picture of him might as well be a picture of me in bad clothes. I pitch forward and scramble to my foot. I'm all rickety, bumping around on one leg because my other one can't handle the weight. I pushed it too far. "If you think I'm thrilled about being a carbon copy of my dad, you're crazy."

Mom slaps me across the face, a thousand bees stinging me. "If you become half the man he was, you're lucky."

She rubs her hand and I struggle to see. "That's not what I meant."

"Enough." Mom pounds up the staircase. The door slams. I look at my broken reflections jumping between the shattered shards of glass and I sink back down. The floor is cold. Like sitting on an ice floe.

I welcome the drift.

SIXTEEN

Mom didn't help patch me up, and I didn't ask her. I washed out the cuts, glued them together all by myself with Super Glue, covered them up as best I could with Band-Aids, and went to bed. It's lunchtime, there's a tray of two meatball subs and a bottle of iced tea before me, but I'm hustling to finish my homework before all my afternoon classes.

Every time someone asks me what happened to my hands, I just glare at the person until they slink away. Never been happier to look like an axe murderer. I wish the bandages were invisible. I wish even more that I was.

I don't want to be here. Not when everything is red and infected.

My homework lies limp before me, and I don't want to touch it. Not that it's hard, because it's not, but I've never felt dumber in my entire life and I hate it. Who cares if I can whip out this physics homework in under ten minutes?

Everything I thought I knew has been turned upside down. Am I so fucking desperate that I fell for a boy in a skirt?

Because I did. I fell ass over backward for a boy in a skirt. Hard.

I can't believe I zoned out that day in group. I can't believe I let this happen. If only I'd paid attention, I would've heard her . . . him . . . fine, Jamie is a her . . . say that bit about being trans and been like, whoa. Dodged a bullet. I wouldn't have gotten on the bus, wouldn't have let her buy me coffee. And there's no way I would have frigging kiss—

I can't even finish the sentence in the privacy of my own head.

Everything I knew about myself is effed. All those Lego pieces I thought were clicking together to create my supposed self might as well be moldy avocado pits stacked in a slippery pile. I don't recognize who I am anymore. I liked her so much, felt so good with her. Felt like home. To know I was completely into a boy in a skirt throws everything out the window. Who am I? Am I gay now—is this what it all means? I'm so frigging confused. And worst of all? JP knows.

He knew before I did.

The seat next to me is empty, ready for him. I already chased off Bryce from sitting there, he knows better, and even though I don't really want to be here while JP holds court, I see him coming and brush crumbs off his waiting seat because here comes the king.

He acknowledges tables as he passes, gives a cheap wave here or there to his future girlfriends, before plunking down in his seat next to me. "Hey, man," JP says above the din in the cafeteria. It's so loud in here, you'd think this was the monkey house at the zoo. And I've been there; our cafeteria is way noisier than that. Especially sitting at this table with all these guys fighting to be heard.

"Hey," I mutter.

"Just so you know, I got you."

There is a small flare inside me that he'll let this slide. That he's my friend. We can do this weird thing where I'll vent and he'll listen and then we'll both pledge to never speak about it again. That instead of JP going down his relationship memory lane and listing every girlfriend he's ever had and what was wrong with them, he sits there and commiserates with me that my first attempt at an actual relationship was a cock-up of epic proportions. I mean, shit, between the two of us, I would've been the one to have an actual legit underline/bold/italics relationship. Jamie would've never been just another checkmark in a column, not to me. Then I could've been the one giving him advice. Doesn't that count for something?

It's not like I can tell any of this to Mom. So I'm anxious to hear what he has to say.

"I didn't know that you were . . . you know."

"That I what?" I ask.

"That you had a type."

"I do have a type. It's girls."

"But she is a girl, right? Isn't that the whole point?"

Dear Dad . . . I start a letter. *Now that you're done laughing your ass off at me and what an idiot I am, please help me not cause significant frontal lobe damage to JP. It is most tempting.*

"You've been totally avoiding me," JP says. "I texted

you like a hundred times last night, tried to get you at your locker before almost every class. Look, all I'm trying to do is check in. What's up?"

"Nothing."

"She seems nice?" he tries.

Only eleven more minutes until the bell rings.

"Dylan, did you not know she was tra—"

"Could you just shut up?" I jump at him.

"Oh shit, you didn't. Hey, look, it's really no big deal. My cousin started dating this girl, but then we all found out her girlfriend lived as a dude for the first twenty years of her life. It was like a holy-shit-no-way thing, but you know what? It was fine. She's a really nice person. I met her last Thanksgiving in Kentucky. She likes green olives, hates lumpy gravy, and says 'cool beans' like all the time. They're still together. Lesbians and everything, four boobs, it's all good. At the end of the day, more people will be happy for you guys than not, so who cares?"

"I care." Because I'm a moron who will be alone forever. So yeah, I kind of frigging care.

"If you guys are cool, I don't see what the—"

"I said shut up."

"I'm just trying to be decent here."

Decent? Bullshit. Pouring salt in a wound. All I want to hear is: That sucks, followed by Tough shit, and then Let's move on.

"Dylan, talk to me, man."

The lunchroom rustles to finish up and all around me, kids dump their uneaten food in the trash. So un-Portland of them. They should compost. Not like I compost at school either, but at least everyone's probably done their homework. Mine still sits in front of me, undone and miserable. "I have four minutes to finish physics."

JP laughs. "Not gonna happen. Even you aren't that smart."

"Why are you on my case so hard, JP? Seriously, don't you have a girlfriend to dump or something?"

"Because this is major! And you haven't said shit to me about it, I'm dying here."

"I'm not a sideshow."

His perfect hair tosses off his perfect face. "Aren't you?"

"Then why don't you go run home and tell your mommy all about it? Oh no, wait—you can't because she's drunk."

For once he's fucking quiet.

I hunker down over my homework and try to squeeze off one problem. Just one. So it looks like I've done at least one frigging thing right today.

A slow clapping starts. It grows bolder and louder and I look up and there's JP, standing on top of a chair in the middle of the cafeteria doing this weird rally clap. Everyone joins in. The entire lunchroom claps along with him, like it's primary season and he's running for president. Some morons in the middle cheer, because they'll do whatever it takes to get in JP's good graces. The kids at the far perimeter, the losers of St. Lawrence, kind of hold back, not quite sure what's going on. I feel like one of them right now.

JP settles down the clapping like a conductor. "I know the bell's about to ring, but I want to make an announcement," he booms. "My best friend, right here—you might know him as the Beast—anyway, this giant hairy son of a bitch has a new girlfriend, and I think we should all, like, give him a round of applause because I never thought we'd see the day."

Oh my god.

The lemmings cheer and my heart stops.

"Not only that, not only that"—JP throws his hands out like a puppeteer, and everybody zips it—"I have to give him credit. His girlfriend is real pretty, and it's cool they see something in each other." (The room fucking goes, "Awww!") "And he's finally met his match, because I think it's safe to say he's the only guy here whose girlfriend is trans. So give it up to the most open-minded guy we know, Dylan Walter Ingvarsson!"

My shit is spread out all over the table and I get books and papers sopping wet trying to scramble it into my bag, grab my crutches, and get the hell out of here. All around me is laughter, the evil uncomfortable kind, and for the briefest of moments the only thing I think is, no one deserves this.

Until JP hops down in front of me, and then all I think is, I'm going to kill him.

"Is it true?" Bryce asks me.

"Uh . . ."

JP nods. "True. Met her yesterday. Dylan is ahead of his time."

"I didn't know you were such a fag, Dylan," Ethan says.

"I'm not gay!"

"Not buying it. You have to be gay, because this whole trans thing is bullshit," Bryce says. "I don't care how much surgery or how many hormones a guy does to look like a girl; you're still a guy. You can't change DNA."

"I think I'm gonna throw up," Ethan says. "Like, for real? You're actually going out with a chick with a dick? Do you guys just blow each other all day? How does that work?"

"Look at him. A tranny makes sense. He would smother a real girl," Bryce says.

"Hey, don't ever call Jamie that," JP counsels. "And you didn't say shit when Jason came out, so be nice."

"Yeah, but that's different. We all knew Jason was gay since kindergarten. The Beast humping a dude in a dress is gonna give me nightmares." Ethan makes a gagging noise.

"We're not a thing. I like girls; she's just a person I know," I blurt out.

"What's its name again?" Bryce asks.

"Jamie," JP pops off. "And she's got curly brown hair and wears skirts and rides a pink bike and everything. The whole nine yards."

I give him the look of death.

His arms fold triumphantly. He might as well spray-paint *Top that, bitch!* on the ceiling.

Whatever bubble used to protect me and make me popular by proxy has been obliterated. I can feel it. If JP is magma at the center of the earth, I am now the moon. Even if nobody ever takes me on in an abandoned hallway or whatever, I know it's over.

"Where does it go to school?" Bryce asks.

Ethan laughs. "We should go fuck it up. Make it put some pants on."

"Hold up, you fucking Neanderthals," JP says. "Leave her alone."

"If a girl has a penis, it's not a girl. That's like Biology 101 and shit," Bryce says just as the bell rings, scattering everyone to class.

"Bryce, Ethan! Wait!" I call out to them. Twenty minutes ago, they would've stopped.

JP's about to bolt, and I grab him by the neck. "If anyone hurts her, believe me, you'll get it ten times worse."

He works to not fidget in my grip, and we both stare at each other. I can feel my eyes burning his. I've never hated anyone more.

"They're . . . not gonna do . . . anything . . . ," he coughs out, and I loosen my hand. "They're all talk. They couldn't even remember an empty box for the can drive, remember?"

"Dylan Ingvarsson!" Mr. Copeland calls out from left field. "You release him right now, this second. No choking people. That's a detention."

Oh, so some shitstain standing up on a chair and putting me on blast in front of the entire cafeteria is Catholic-school kosher, but one tiny squeeze of a chicken neck and I get detention? This is garbage.

"Mr. Copeland . . ." I try to plead my case and JP sprints off. Fucking coward.

The slip gets written up, and I stuff it into my pocket next to my phone.

I don't want to go to class. I don't want to be here. I don't want to know these people.

Somewhere in this city, Jamie is sitting in her school and most likely not wanting to be there either. An image of Bryce and Ethan flashes in my mind. I feel sick because I know if they really want to, they'll find her. People talk. I'm all worried they're going to harass her as she's just trying to ride her bike or something. Whatever happened with me and Jamie is one thing, but that doesn't mean people have the right to give her a hard time. She didn't do anything wrong.

Things creak and crawl into place, and before long I have a plan.

I get my phone out and text: *Can we talk?*

SEVENTEEN

I have a secret.

It's foul and dirty and sends me into a death spiral from euphoria to self-hatred every time I do it, but I can't stop. It always happens when no one is home. I start to get idle hands. Everything starts to tingle, and a silent itch demands to be scratched. It sends me to my stash buried in the living room, where I keep the discs hidden underneath the loose floorboard. Once I have what I need (and I hate that I need it), I turn on the TV.

As I sit in my chair, I turn the sound on low so no one will hear and ready myself. Hands hot in my lap and gripping my favorite controller.

I play Madden NFL.

The bestselling football video game of all time.

Once it boots up, all my tension releases and I get lost building teams in franchise mode. I know all the players and their stats and make unstoppable brute squads that annihilate opposing teams. As the players inside the video game make their hits, my muscles twitch. Hours disappear as I play. There is only football. Nothing else matters. It's my guilty pleasure, and no one can ever know how much I actually love football, which is why I fly to dismantle the entire system when I hear my mom's bockety old car slow down and park.

Racing against the clock, I save, eject, and throw it all under the floorboard as soon as her key slides into the lock. I turn off the TV and tear into the bathroom like nothing ever happened. Besides, tonight is an important night. I've been waiting for Mom to get home. We have to get ready for dinner.

I hear her enter and dump her shoes off to the side. Flushing the toilet full of damp TP from wiping my brow, I leave the bathroom with a slightly sweaty face and pink cheeks.

"Hi," I say.

She gives me a weird look. "I don't want to know."

Good. You won't. "Did you get the stuff?"

Mom thrusts a thick paper bag full of groceries in my hands. "Here. But like I said this morning, I think this is a terrible idea."

I'd grumble something about how it's a plan and not an idea, but this is the first time she's said more than "Get up" and "Dinner's ready" to me since I manhandled the basement. "Things didn't end well," I say, trying to justify the cost of imitation crabmeat.

"Sometimes things don't and that's okay," Mom says. "In

fact, I think having Jamie out of your life is for the best. The way you've been acting since you met . . . this certain young lady . . . is not cool."

Ingredients out on the counter, I get to work blending the mix for the crab cakes in a bowl and check the oven temperature. I'm not even hopeful Jamie likes them. I'm on autopilot. "All I'm asking is for you to be nice."

Mom's coffee cup hits the counter with a mad clink. "Be nice? I know a trans person; I work with a very sweet man in accounting. He's short and has delicate hands. That's how I knew when I asked him."

"I don't think that's how it's supposed to work."

"Are we an expert now?"

"No," I mumble. Once I knew Jamie's real deal, as with all things unknown I turned to Google for the lay of the land. "I just don't think you're supposed to go up to someone and ask them. It's pretty much the opposite of your business."

Her finger wraps around the handle. "I work with him every day, I call him Jack when he looks like a Jill. And I'm about to sit through my son's date with a very confused young person, what more do you want me to do?"

"It's not a date," I snap.

"Sweetie, look. It's not that you two aren't perfectly fine people, it's just that I don't think you need that level of complication right now."

I lump the ingredients into little patties and lay them on the tray.

"Did you hear me?"

Don't worry, Mom. I heard you. "You have nothing to worry about."

"You're not attracted to her, are you?"

There's no way I can tell her the truth that yes, I was. A lot. That it still tears me down the middle. How at night I stare at the ceiling I painted blue and wish that Jamie were with me. I miss her so much.

"No," I say.

She sips and sighs. "You met in therapy. And if you were sent there, that means she had a reason to be there too. Keep a distance, is all I ask. Cordial. Hello, how are you, that kind of thing."

I grunt. What Mom doesn't know is I'm going to tell Jamie my plan and then we will finagle the details over crab cakes.

"She is very pretty," Mom says. "But I knew, had that sixth sense. Her voice, her feet, the intangible tangibles. I put two and two together."

My mom, the gender whisperer.

"All I'm getting at is that this is a big change for Jamie, and she's struggling. And so are you. So keep it light."

"Okay, I heard you a million times now." I don't need to be reminded how I was stupid and everyone else knew immediately. "I'm just trying to be a good person." Except I feel anything but.

The crab cakes slide into the oven and I set the timer. Mom helped with nothing. She refused. I wish she'd helped, just like I wish she'd forgive me and start caring again. If the crab cakes taste like ass, that's all on me, but there's not enough time to dwell because the doorbell rings. "That must be Jamie."

Mom heads for the door, but I chase after her on my cane. "I'll get it." I brush past her, my shoulder knocking crooked some dead great-aunt's stupid painting of a fat bunny under a gerber daisy.

Mom fixes it for me—she can't help herself. "Bull in a china shop," she mutters like old times. Maybe she's done being mad at me.

Seeing Jamie is like opening a door in an old cartoon to all the dancing trees and sunlight. Even with her scowling death glare, she's as stunning as always. I want to hug her, but I can't. Tonight I have a job to do.

New Jamie still looks like Old Jamie, the one I remember. The one I felt every scrap of happy with. Except now there's a major something different that I can't get over. I know this is Portland, I know she's not even the first trans person I've met—there's a librarian at our local branch who went from a he to a she and no one batted an eye—but that wasn't the same. That librarian was a snippet from someone else's book. A book you could put down and leave on a park bench because you didn't care. Jamie was a chapter in the one I was just beginning to write.

No matter how much I lie awake at night and think of all our wonderful horrible minutes together, it's like there's this object Jamie's carrying around now, and it's shiny and distracting and it doesn't matter what she says or does. It's the only thing I can think about. Underneath the skirt, she's got guy parts and I fell for it.

Jamie stands there in her coat, arms crossed, with I'm

assuming her equally pissed-off mother. "You must be Dylan," her mom drags out with a sneer.

"Please come in!" my mom chirps, arms outstretched and full of hospitality and joy. The very picture of bullshit. "I'm Anna. May I take your coats?"

"Jessica," Jamie's mother says. She is tall. Just like Jamie said. "Thank you for offering, but I'm afraid I won't be staying. I've been informed I need to wait in the car."

Jamie's jaw grinds so loud I can hear it. "Mom," she says sharply.

"Teenagers," my mom says, and both moms roll their eyes.

"Mom," Jamie says again.

"I know, I know—I'm leaving." Jamie's mom plants a kiss on her cheek. "See you soon."

Our front door shuts and we idle awkwardly in the hallway.

"I made crab cakes," I throw out. "Because they're your favorite."

"That was nice of you." Jamie and I lock eyes.

"They're in the kitchen. For eating." Oh god.

She looks down and slips her coat off. My mom stands there, an eager beaver, hands ready to receive Jamie's coat and hang it up. "I got it," Jamie says, and drapes it on an open hook. "So . . ." She wanders down the hall toward the light, stepping over the threshold and standing next to the refrigerator. "I'm assuming this is where we do the eating?"

"Offer her some water," Mom whispers up at me as she skates by.

"Do you want some water?" I ask once I join them.

Jamie shakes her head, her hair dancing like she's in a commercial. "No thanks."

The oven hums. I hope that means it's busy burning the crab cakes and we can hurry up and throw them in the trash and order replacement pizza as soon as possible.

"So, Jamie . . . Do you have a favorite holiday?" Mom asks, cracking through the silence.

Jamie shifts from one foot to the other. "Um . . . Christmas is always nice."

"I agree." Mom nods. "My favorite is Martin Luther King Junior's birthday. Always has been."

"Since when?" I say.

"Since before you were born," she says. "Except when you've got a little kid you're forced to get all excited for Halloween and Christmas, wake them up on New Year's, et cetera, but for me it's MLK all the way."

Jamie and I stare at her, afraid of what's coming next.

"I just love his message." Mom clears her throat. "To judge someone by the content of their character. Beautiful, just beautiful."

"Please stop," I say.

Jamie's eyebrows shuffle and land on confused. "Okay?"

"Mom was just leaving, right, Mom?"

My mother looks like an angry wombat about to strike, all cuddly until you get too close. "Yes! I was. I'm going to bring your poor mother a cup of coffee while she's waiting in the car." She holds up the decanter. "Does she take milk? Sugar?"

"And how," Jamie says.

"Great." Mom practically throws hot coffee into a new mug, dumps in the milk and sugar, and stuffs her feet into her good house shoes. "If you need us, you know where we'll be."

The door slams, and Jamie and I stand on our three legs in the kitchen. "She seems nice?" Jamie offers.

"She's trying too hard and she's pissed at me. Tricky combination for her to pull off."

"Oh. Well. Thanks for inviting me over." She shoots the smallest of smiles. "Even though this is weirder than weird."

"Uh, yeah. Right, okay. Thank you for coming." The plan, I chant to myself. Remember the plan. "I . . . I didn't like how . . . What happened was . . . You know."

"I know."

"So. I wanted to say I'm sorry for everything." I stick out a hand. "Friends?"

Jamie's shoulders sag. "Yeah, sure."

We shake on it.

I'm not sure I believe what we're shaking on. The way she's slumping into the counter makes me think she doesn't either. It's like we both know our coexistence is futile. We can't just be associates on planet Earth, bumping into each other on the sidewalk to ask each other about the weather. Not without some pretty solid hits to the gut. I have no idea where we go from here.

"I made crab cakes for you."

"I heard."

"They're your favorite."

"Do you want a medal or something, Dylan? Do you

know how hard it is to be here? Why am I here, anyway? Did you have me come all the way here just so you could feel better? You seriously want to just be friends? For real?"

"What's wrong with that?"

"So sticking the 'friend' Band-Aid on everything that happened suddenly makes it okay? I'm supposed to ignore that you were King Asshole and made me feel like the stupidest person for thinking we were . . . Fuck it. Yay, crab cakes." She smudges a spot on the counter. " 'O frabjous day! Callooh! Callay!' "

" 'Jabberwocky.' "

Jamie shoots me a hot glare. "You're not the only one who likes school. Just because my head's not all swollen up like I have hydrocephalus or whatever doesn't mean I don't have a party going on up here too," she says. "Although hydrocephalus is a terrible condition and I wouldn't wish it on anybody."

"Cover all your bases there?"

"Shut up."

It's obvious neither one of us gives a shit about the crab cakes, and suddenly I'm doused in gasoline and she's holding the match. Deep down, there's a part of me that's still into Jamie, that still wants to talk to her all the time. It hits me over the head and I swallow. *Oh, Dad, I hope you hear me wherever you are and make it go away.*

I don't know what to think about this, so instead I bury it.

Peeking at Jamie, I watch her chip chunks of carbon off an old burner, and I realize it's not just her anger I've been hearing, like sonar beeps; it's sadness. For every black look and pissed-off word, there's tenfold within from where she's hurt.

"I am sorry," I say.

"I heard you the first time." Jamie doesn't look at me.

"I didn't handle it well. There's a lot I wish I could take back," I say.

"Well, guess what, Captain Tact, there's nothing I wish I could take back. Other than going through all this without you even listening that day."

"Can you tell me now?"

"Why?"

"So I can listen to every word."

She sighs. "I was telling the group that my grandpa called me my dead name and how my dad corrected him and said, 'Please call my daughter by her real name.' It was a big deal. Dr. Burns asked you what you thought, but it was all crickets. Then you said it was cool."

"That's unfair." I knew Dr. Burns was a piece of work. She was trying to make me look stupid in front of a group full of girls. "A dead name? Like I'm supposed to hear that and be like, Hark! That means Jamie is transgender. Yeah, no. Unfair."

"If you'd been *listening* and had picked up on what Wretched was saying about how well my dad was doing with my transition and how Hannah was asking me about adjusting to my new hormone schedule, then you could've easily read between the lines," she says. "It's my deal, I'm the only one who decides how it's told."

"But why couldn't you cut to the chase and say, 'Hi, my name is Jamie and I was born a boy'?"

Her eyes ignore mine hard. "I'll never say that because it's not true. I was assigned male at birth, but my gender is a girl."

"Look, I know it's bad form for people to barge in with questions, but you can't say we're all a bunch of dummies because we can't read your mind."

"That's so far from reality, it's stupid," Jamie says.

"Why did you never mention anything about being trans? Like, ever?"

"I was as out with you as I was comfortable with," she says. "I'm pretty low-key about it, to be honest. Most of the time I have other things on my mind. Did I forget my lunch money? Why did my dog pee by the back door when she just went out ten minutes ago? Things. Thoughts. You know, life."

"All I'm saying is a little clarity is a good thing."

"When was I unclear? Was it what I wore, every word I ever said? The pictures I took? The stories I told? Being happy being out with you? Who I frigging AM? Because I thought I was opening up to you, more than to any boy I've ever met before. So please, you're so smart, when was I ever hiding who I really, truly was?"

My mouth shuts. I didn't realize it was open.

The timer buzzes. I hop over to the oven and get a mitt. Tray in hand, I let the door slam shut and rest the baking sheet full of deformed patties on top of the burners. I hop backward and we both stare at them, for they are very sad.

"It's fake crabmeat," I say.

"Hmmm. Like our so-called relationship."

Burn. "The diabetes thing," I point out. "That was a lie."

"By omission."

"Why lie about that?"

"Because when you followed me onto the bus, I was scared. You're very big. And we were alone. I didn't want to get into my personal medical business with a virtual stranger, because I don't have to. Ever. And didn't want to risk getting beat up again."

"That other guy knew?"

"Yeah. His name was Colin and he knew. Just like I thought you did." Jamie wanders over to a crab cake and pokes it. She pries off the half-charred corner and nibbles it. "Not bad. But yeah, I used to rule my old school with all the girls I hung around with. We were the law of the land. They thought I was their gay BFF, but I wasn't. I was me pretending to be a gay BFF." She looks at me. "Isn't that nuts?"

"Why is that so crazy?"

"Because as long as I was the catty gay boy who was all, yaaaaas, mama, WORK, you are so fierce," she says, snapping her fingers in a loop, "and went shopping with them and did their hair and makeup, and teased Colin, just like they did, it was fine. Like, normal even to be all, 'Oh girl, would you look at what my favorite piece of meat is wearing today? I see trade!' and then they'd think it was hilarious. Queens of the eighth grade, the five of us."

"I'm afraid to ask, but I need to know. What's trade?"

"Straight-looking dudes who bang gay guys for money," she says. "You'd be rough trade because you're bulk goods."

"Oh." Now I know. "It sounds like you were a very fabulous stereotype."

"Not a stereotype; I copied this guy I knew from a

continuing-ed class where we learned how to use a darkroom. All the chemicals and stuff. He was the most phenomenal human being ever, completely fearless. I admired him so much. After that, I began to act like him too." She shrugs. "I feel bad I had to steal his personality, but it helped cover up my own. So . . . yeah."

"You always knew you were a girl trapped in a boy's body?"

"Nope."

Every clip I researched on YouTube has lied to me. "But . . . that's what everyone says."

"That's fine for them, but I say something different. I had very cool parents growing up. They never minded buying me nail polish and whatever. For them it was like a point of pride. But when I was twelve, I started to realize I wasn't a boy who liked glitter and had crushes on boys . . . I was a girl who liked glitter and had crushes on boys," she says. "That's when things started to go downhill."

"I get that."

"It was the scariest thing I've ever known," she says in a light voice. "It's very practical being with popular girls—they make the rules. They protect you from everything, and that's how I adapted. But then I just couldn't do it anymore. The depression . . . It was bad. So I started wearing clothes I liked and wearing my hair the way I liked. And I started living life the way I felt good. How I felt right. The girls were okay-ish. Two of them did everything they could for me; we're still close. Two of them broke away. One girl even said I couldn't 'do this to her' because it ruined 'her balance.' I mean, what? We don't talk."

"What about this Colin guy?"

Jamie leans next to the stove and grazes on her patty. "We were alone one day and I didn't even say anything near as stupid as before, you know? No messing around like with the 'Would you look at this piece!' stuff. I just had a little crush on him. Nothing major. I wasn't even rude about it. All I said was, 'You look nice today.' That's it!" She shakes her head. "When he knew me as Jeff, he thought it was all a joke. This time, as me, as Jamie, when I was genuine with him, he didn't like it. He let it be known. I thought he broke my cheekbone, he shoved me into the locker so hard." She touches her face. The same spot she touched in the rose garden. "The two girls who broke off teamed up with him and all his crew and they made my life a living hell. My parents panicked that I'd be beat up again, or worse. Transferred schools and that's that."

"Fresh start."

"Hmmm." She chews. "These crab cakes aren't half bad."

"Thanks."

I'm not thinking she looks cute in my kitchen munching away on food I made. I'm not thinking about looking up this Colin person and pummeling him into pudding. I'm not thinking about how much I'd enjoy it, mashing his stupid face into goo for what he did to her. I'm not thinking any of that—nope, I'm not.

"It's weird, you know? I thought you were my boyfriend. My first boyfriend. All that lofty la-la stuff. The walks in the park, trips to the corn maze, holding hands, riding on a Ferris wheel and getting stuck at the top . . ." She sighs, and it thumps me in the ribs. "But that's all gone."

"Right."

"I'm still the same girl, though, and you're the same guy. It's crazy."

"What's crazy?"

"You're not even my type. I'm completely into skater boys." She laughs to herself. "Never thought I'd go for . . ."

"A beast?" I say.

She shrugs, the grin on her face saying it all. I lean against the counter. Standing hurts. And she thinks I'm the Beast. She's just like everyone else. Fine. Bring on the plan.

"I need to tell you something."

"Shoot," she says.

"Word got around in my school that you were trans, and a couple guys said bad things, so I'm going to protect you now."

"I'm sorry, what?"

"I'm going to be your new bodyguard," I declare, puffing up like the untouchable nightmare monster I am.

Jamie brushes crumbs from her hands and the corners of her mouth. "That's nice, but no thank you."

"Wait a minute." I deflate. "I want to do right by you."

"Uh-huh, I bet, and no thank you. I do not need your assistance."

"These guys made a threat. I want you to call me anytime you need me. I'll be there."

She ogles my cast. "You're just gonna hop on over then, huh?"

"Jamie . . ."

"I get it, you're trying to be all gallant, but look." She

reaches into her bag, moves past her camera, and brings up two black canister-looking things.

"What are those?"

"One is Mace and one is a kubaton, like a little hard metal staff. Here, give me your hand."

I stick my hand out and she lays the kubaton right below my thumb and presses down. A burst of pain makes me yelp, and I yank my thumb away, cradling it to my chest.

"I learned that in my all-girls safety class. Isn't it cool that girls need to learn this stuff to feel safe? That was sarcasm, by the way. But that's just one way of using the kubaton; there are loads more. Here, let me see your neck."

"No way, you sadist."

She puts the Mace and evil kubaton back in her bag. "Like I said, thanks for the offer but I'll be okay."

"What if you get jumped?"

"If I get jumped, what am I gonna do—tell the attackers to hold that thought for a minute, I need to call my bodyguard? Be serious, Dylan," she says. "Why don't you tell your boys to chill out. That might be more effective than you finding a white horse."

But what if I want to save the day?

Jamie gathers up her bag and swings it over her shoulder. "Was the bodyguard thing what you wanted to say? That the reason I had to come all the way over here on a school night?"

"I . . . guess so."

"Cool. Thanks for the crab cakes. I got homework now," she says, heading for the front door.

"Do you want to stay and do homework together?"

"Nope. See you 'round, friend-o."

The door opens with a creak and shuts with a bang.

Before Mom has a chance to fly in and get all in my face, I take my homework upstairs and lie on my bed underneath my blue ceiling. *Oh, Dad,* I think to the infinite nothingness beyond our roof. *That did not go as well as I hoped.* And then I wonder, did Dad have anything to do with that?

I wish I knew what his answer might be. It dawns on me I would give anything to have five minutes with him. Just five minutes. To see his face. Hear his voice. Ask him all the questions I ask the air because all I want is to know him.

But I can't. And I never will. So I try to keep moving, keep dealing with stuff and things. Fill my head up, ignore the void. Forget what I'll never have. I take out my stack of five thick books with one hand and drop them on the bed. Homework. Time to do just that.

EIGHTEEN

Another day of epic bullshit; signed, sealed, and delivered. What fun I had pretending people weren't laughing under their breath as I hobbled by. How delightful it was trying to get up the nerve to ask Ethan and Bryce to confirm that they were only kidding, right? They're not really going after Jamie? And oh! How proud I was of myself when I chickened out every time.

I didn't eat lunch today. I didn't know where I would sit, didn't know who would have me. What if the entire school has secretly hated me this whole time and I never knew? I didn't feel like finding out.

This was supposed to be my year, dammit.

I shuffle over to the bed in my room. My pillow waits for me and I smother my face with it and yell. Not loud, but enough. I take the pillow off my face and stare at the blue, blue, blue ceiling above. When I was in the second grade, I wanted to paint it sky blue because that's where my dad was. Up in the clouds.

Hey, Dad.

It's me. I know it's been awhile.

If you're in heaven, you're really tall now, like miles high, so here's a joke I get all the time: How's the weather up there?

If you thought that was funny, ha-ha, me too! I love it when people say that to me, it never gets old! If you didn't, I don't like that joke either. It drives me insane hearing it over and over, right? Except I don't know your thoughts on the matter. I wish I did. I wish I knew what made you laugh, because even though everyone tells me you were a funny guy, that could mean anything. I really don't know what your sense of humor was like.

I want to.

I wish you'd talk to me and help me out, like you do for Mom. She misses you. I miss you too, in case you didn't think I did, because I do. I just pretend I don't sometimes. Like when I shrug off seeing other kids' dads pick them up after school and stuff. It's easier that way, but it doesn't make me miss you any less.

I'm hoping you can help me out, just for a second.

I'm thinking if I was dead inside and soulless, it'd be a really handy way to get through high school. You've seen JP—you know what a dick he is. And I'm stuck because he has the entire school on lockdown. He put me on the outs and that's it for me; I'm done.

So please make me horrible. But not like with Jamie how we used to be horrible, and how we had the greatest days of my life together. I mean really authentically awful, so if I can't be with her, I can at least survive the rest of high school as a miserable stone-faced curmudgeon.

P.S. Please make me stop growing.
And make me six inches shorter.
And a hundred pounds lighter.
And have no back hair.

Thank you.
Bye, Dad.
I miss you every day.

I close the door on my letter to a dead man and add an addendum to the universe: please, someway, somehow, take away my feelings for Jamie.

That has to go in the postscript, because I don't want my dad to know how bad it is. All I want more than anything is a sign from above. Since I don't know what he thinks—what he thought—about any of this stuff, I'm worried all I have is his disapproval. I mean, what if I like Jamie and Dad doesn't? I'll never get that sign. He'll never talk to me.

As if the thought of my dad never talking to me weren't scary enough, I'm worried my clock is ticking too. If my candle is set to go out at the age of twenty-six, just like his, then I kinda want Dad up in heaven to be waiting for me with open arms.

But this connection I have with Jamie won't go away. As soon as the front door shut last night, I knew I was sunk. It's a very strange and uncomfortable feeling because I don't know which equation will solve the problem.

I have these crazy thoughts where I reach my hands into my own chest, through the skin and muscle and past the sternum, and grip my feelings for her. It's like dipping my hands into a barrel full of warm rice, pressing from all sides. Soothing and awesome. I take it, gather up all these scattered grains, each one a different atom of her, and pull them from my heart and hold them. Her wit, her laughter, her jokes. How she surprises me, how I want to hear what she has to say. How I want to tell her things.

They're too wonderful to throw away in the Dumpster, but I'm terrified to put them back.

I can't stop thinking about Jamie. In an aching, need-to-be-with-her way. But if I've learned anything from missing my dad, it's that I'm really good at cramming all this stuff away in a drawer for later.

Or never.

There's a knock at my door, and I slam that drawer shut. Mom hasn't come here to talk to me forever. If there's ever a time for one of her cheesy "You're superduper" pep talks, it's now. I've been missing them, but I'll never tell her that. "Hi, Mom," I call out.

The door opens and I sink. It's JP. "What the fuck are you doing here?" I tear over to him, ready to rip him in half like a phone book before he gets the chance to say it's taco night. Because he's always here for taco night. "Get the hell out, JP, or I'm going to finally do to you what I couldn't in the cafeteria."

He grabs on to the doorjamb, as if that will stop me. "Go ahead, you frigging animal, I'm not here for you anyway. I'm here for me."

I snort and it's bitter.

"What does that mean?"

"Of course you're here for you," I say. "Since when isn't it all about The Amazing JP?"

"Oh my god, you're so up your own ass."

"Are you kidding? You lit me on fire and told the whole school to pour gasoline. You think I'm going to let that slide? I should tear you apart right now, starting with your face."

"Okay, hold up for two reasons. One, I'm helping you guys. You two need my approval so everyone else gets the deal. And two, you're like the biggest fucking baby I've ever met."

"Your approval? I'm the baby? What the shit, JP," I say. He's too busy with his perfect body and his perfect hair and his perfect girlfriend parade to even guess what it's like being me. "Why are you here?" To torture me? To rub it in?

"Because I can't take it anymore and I need to know why you never give a shit about my mom."

My stomach loosens. "I . . ."

Because it makes me terribly, horribly uncomfortable.

"You act like it's this nothing forever, always leaving, always changing the subject, and then when I'm all trying to be like, 'Yay, Dylan,' you shove my mom in my face? Who does that?"

I stand there.

Hop once to check my balance.

"Do you know how cold the tree house is? Don't you know I'd give anything to be able to sleep in my own bed and know everything's going to be okay when I wake up? That maybe she'll be downstairs making breakfast for once?

And not because she feels guilty and orders takeout, but like real food because she wants to feed me. Because I'm her kid and that's what moms do," he says, shaking his head when I say nothing. "Why'd you have to go there?"

"I thought you were here for taco night."

JP nearly slams his forehead on the door. "Are you serious? You and your mom are the only two people in the world I trust with this, and you turn into, like, a pile of bricks whenever I bring it up."

"What do you want from me?" I say. "You're coming over and making me feel like shit and digging up all this business with your mom and whatever, and never not once did you say sorry for embarrassing me at lunch."

"You shouldn't be embarrassed for liking Jamie. She's cool."

"Get off it. You know what you did."

"Maybe."

"Yeah. Maybe."

We both fold our arms at the same time and that's weird, so we both throw them down and then that's weird, so I hunch into Minotaur mode and he head-kicks his perfect hair out of his eyes.

"I dumped Bailey," he says.

"What does that have to do with anything?"

"Just saying. We used to talk about this kind of stuff."

"You talked. I never had anything to contribute."

"Well, now you have Jamie."

"No, I don't."

"You can get her back. You guys were mad happy together," he says. "I could tell."

"Would you shut up already?"

"I'll make you a deal," he says.

"Super fuck your deal."

"We need each other. You and I. How about I make it the best thing—the official best thing ever—for you and Jamie to be together, so no one at school gives you grief. I'm talking social media hashtag campaigns and shit. Hashtag Dylan-LuvsJamie4evs. Like, getting the entire student body cheering when the five o'clock news team comes and films you two all dressed up at the dance."

I ponder the notion.

"You know I can."

I can't disagree. He has that intangible thing that makes people get in line.

"And all you have to do, like seriously the only thing, is get Adam Michaels for me."

"That's what this is about? You didn't get your frigging money?" I blow, honest to god ready to throw him into next week. "It was never about your mom, was it? You've always used it to get me to get the money because you know I can't deal. Get the fuck out of my house."

"Okay-okay-okay, don't hurt me." He zips out of reach and down the stairs.

I scramble for my cane. Plummeting down the stairs, I can hear my mom and JP muttering and laughing. Everyone cheered for Jack after he stole all the giant's stuff and ran back down a beanstalk. No one cares that maybe the giant was trying to get away from little shitstains like Jack.

I hit the first floor and hobble over to them. "I want him gone," I say.

"Dylan?" Mom cries out. "What are you saying? What happened?"

JP stuffs his arms into his coat. Of course it looks good on him. "No worries," he says. "I was just leaving."

My mom rises to stop him. "Wait, what's going on with you two?"

JP silences her with a look.

"Sorry," she says.

"Don't apologize to him," I say, ready to drop-kick him outside.

JP speeds fast out of the kitchen into the darkness of the hallway, protecting his neck the whole time. "I'm going, I'm going."

"Get out." I slam the door in his face.

"Dylan!" Mom charges toward me. "How dare you chase him away like that!"

"News flash, Mom—JP is a piece of human garbage."

"He was scared of you. Didn't you see how he was cowering? He thought you were going to hurt him. What's wrong with you?" She hugs herself instead of me. "I know you two are having a rough patch. And that's normal. All friendships encounter some rocky times here and there. As long as you guys have open communication, you'll be fine."

I want to scream, but I don't. My pillow's all the way upstairs. "Mom, he's using you just like he uses everyone else."

"He is not. I swear, Dylan, you are so selfish, it's infuriating. He comes here for a little piece of comfort and security—he's a very sensitive young man."

"He's a manipulative asshole!"

"His mother is a full-blown alcoholic. Where is your compassion?"

"Mom . . ."

"I'm serious, Dylan, what is up with you these days? Turning your back on your lifelong friend? You two never even play video games anymore." She pauses. "You know, I blame Jamie."

"What?"

"I do! Ever since you met her, you're destructive, you're moody, you insult your father's memory, I don't know what to do with you anymore." She walks back into the kitchen and flings dirty dishes into the dishwasher. "And I know it's Jamie because her poor mother told me the same thing. She's bending over backward for her son, and then once he declares he's a she, her new 'daughter' treats her worse than dirt. Jamie's a bad influence on you."

"What the hell are you talking about? I don't treat you bad."

Mom wraps her fingers together. "We used to be so close, Dylan."

"We still are."

"Do you even want me around anymore?"

"Of course I do. Is this why you can't get enough of JP? Because he's a needy prick and I'm not?"

"Enough! That's Jamie talking; I can hear it."

I take a breath and hold it, letting it out slower than slug trails. "Mom. I need you in my life. I love you. Everything between you and me has nothing to do with Jamie or JP or anyone else."

"But we've always looked after JP. You two used to call yourselves brothers."

"Leave him alone!" I slam my hands on the counter.

Looming over her, I can almost see steam flying from my nostrils. Mom looks up at me with wide eyes. "I see." She picks up her book, steps into her house shoes, and leaves me.

"Mom," I say, hoping to coax her back. Now is the time, I want to say. Shake the Mom-Poms™ and tell me how everything is going to be okay.

"Sleep off your anger, Dylan. Calm yourself. We'll talk about it again in the morning," she says with a dull voice from the living room. The TV clicks on so she can double down on ignoring me with her trashy novel and blaring a hideous crime drama with raped-up little kids and murderers, murderers everywhere.

I catch my reflection in the window. My head hangs low. I touch the top of my scalp. My hair's growing back. Just like the rest of me. Growing, growing, always growing.

I disappear to the basement.

Down in the cool clamminess of the cement walls filled with clumps of pebbles and rocks, I hop across the lost chunks of broken glass still hiding in thin cracks on the floor and make my way over to the trains.

Tiny broken trees and tracks. If Dad was as big as me, it's strange to think he sank so much time into making something so small. I kneel down and come face to face with the tiny town. Flaps of grass and uneven terrain. Splayed wiring tangled in between bumps of fake moss. I nudge a few tracks into place with my fat finger. I smooth a raggedy row of shingles flat.

When I sit in the corner, my pocket doesn't yield. My phone. I get it out. No messages. There's only one person I was hoping to see there anyway. I start a text, but halfway through I stop and make the call. I have to.

"What's up?" Jamie says.

NINETEEN

"I just wanted to talk to someone who understands," I say.

"Then I have no idea why you're calling me." She pauses. "Are you okay?"

I press my back into the concrete. "No."

"What's wrong?"

Everything I want to say is caught in a snare, pulling and tugging against the rope. The trains lie crumpled on a model of a tiny town that looks like an earthquake and a tornado hit it on the same day. I rest my chin against the small world. Everything is chipped and plastic and smells like a musty cabin. "When you and your friends busted up, how bad was it? Like, did they turn the whole school against you? Is that why you transferred?"

"I . . . it was not good. It was partially them, but it was mostly me."

"Why you?"

"I changed."

"Um . . ." Beyond the obvious? Or am I allowed to say that? "In what way?"

"It's hard to say, because you can be like, oh, it's because I stopped doing her hair or she didn't want me to wear skirts because my legs are better than hers, but I guess because I found enough pieces of me that were real. And they weren't fans."

"They sound shallow."

"What can I say? Popularity does weird things to people."

"I get that," I say, but I can't tell her that aside from all the perks I get from hanging out with JP, I still want to be friends with him for some dumb reason. It's just something we're both really bad at. But if I tell Jamie I'm afraid the rest of the school will stone me without JP, she'll think I'm more shallow than people who care if someone wears a skirt. I don't care what people wear, I need them to acknowledge my existence. I hate that I need JP for that. "JP and I had a fight. A bad one."

"That kid I met when I had my bike?"

"Yup."

"He seemed really full of himself. Are you sure it's over?"

"Positive. I'm about to be a leper."

"Whoa. That's pretty bad. What'd you do?"

Let you down, I want to say.

"Okay, let me ask you a different question," she says. "What did he do?"

"Same thing he's always done. It's just the first time I noticed."

"Do you want to know what I learned?"

I nod, but that's dumb. She can't see me. "Yeah."

"That sometimes, friends disappear. They go away. That all the stuff you know about them to be true, they'll never see it. And the best part about it?"

"What?"

"They think equally terrible things about you, and that's why you shouldn't be friends anymore," she says. "You can rehash a million little details, every conversation, every text, but at the end of the day, shit happens. And if you don't like the shit that happens when you're with them, time to mosey."

"Easier said than done."

"Yeah, except I've done it," she says. "It sucks; it leaves holes in you."

I already have this little Swiss cheese thing going in my gut. I hate knowing it's only going to get worse. We're quiet. I fiddle with a switch next to the tracks. Nothing happens when I flick it. "My mom thinks I'm being selfish. She's not on my side anymore."

"Oh, do I know what that's like. My mom and I can't be in the same room alone for more than ten minutes before we're at each other. She thinks I'm going through a phase. I ask you, would anyone really go through this for a bucket of giggles? Yeah, don't think so."

"My mom's mad at me."

"She holds a good grudge?"

"The best," I say. "But it's not like I didn't deserve it."

"What'd you do?"

"I messed up a train set my dad built."

"So help him rebuild it."

"I can't. He's dead."

"What? Oh my god!" she almost shouts. "I'm so sorry! You never told me."

"You didn't notice the lack of a dad when you came over for dinner?"

"I dunno, no, but I didn't bring my dad either, so I figured we were square," she says.

"It's fine. He's been dead for twelve years."

"I'm sorry."

"Thanks."

"I mean it."

"I know *you* mean it," I say. "And thanks." I mean it.

Leaning back against the chilled walls of the basement, I appreciate the empty chunks of missing mirrors. Although what would the mirrors show if they existed? Me smiling as I'm talking to Jamie. Yeah, I'd see a big old globby grin on my face because talking to her is like sunshine in February, and in Portland that is no small thing. All it takes is two minutes on the phone with her and I'm good.

I'm falling for a girl with boy parts. This is weird. Although technically I fell a long time ago. Over the phone, it's better than best. Like a tiny little rectangle rendering us as nothing more than voices. As simply us. She doesn't have to see me and my hideous, hairy-ass self, and I can talk to the person I need the most.

"Hmmm," I hum.

"What?" she asks.

"Just doing better."

"Good." It's curt and short.

"Are you feeling better?" I ask her.

"About what?"

I put some padding back under a fake hill. A gentle swell returns to the meadow. "I don't know—what's bugging you right now?"

"Do you really want to know?"

"Of course I do."

"I want to go to the bathroom in peace."

"Huh?"

"There was a huge beef at school today. They arranged a unisex bathroom for me and I could totally tell when the three teachers who were against it gave me the side eye. It's like walking past a very thin laser. Zing."

"They won't let you use the girls' bathroom?"

"Bingo. I have to walk way the hell back to the designated bathroom, because heaven forbid I make the world's fastest pit stop in any of the fifty girls' bathrooms. That would be SO BAD. And everyone would DIE." She sighs. "It's only temporary. I believe people will change. In time this will be in a history book."

"I never thought about it that way." I try to imagine it and it sucks. You have classes all over the building and can only use one bathroom. I would just stop drinking water. But then you're denying yourself water. Screwed up. "I'm sorry you have to deal with that."

"Thanks." Her voice sounds like she's peering out a window and seeing a very sad face in the glass.

"You know what I hate more than anything?" I ask her. "Going number two at school. I hate getting the pass and then you have to sign in to the bathroom and when you sign out and the monitor is like, ha-ha, well look at you, ten pounds lighter. Hate it. Poseidon's kiss right before English is the absolute worst."

"I'm afraid to ask."

"Backsplash."

"Okay, I just threw up." She laughs. "This is why I never, never poop at school. Never, ever, ever."

"How is that possible?"

"Ever heard the phrase 'scared shitless'?" She laughs, but sounds like she's repeating a bad joke to a tin can. "I didn't for years. I never wanted to go in the boys' bathroom. I held it all the way through junior high."

"Every day?"

"Unless it was a total emergency, then yeah. I did."

"Whoa."

"The whole bathroom thing is dumb. I don't want special treatment and I don't want to go around educating everyone—because it's seriously not my job. I just want to pee." Jamie laughs. "I can't believe I'm talking to you about this. It's so embarrassing."

"To be fair, I'm the one who brought up poop."

"True. You're a terrible influence."

"Horrible."

"So horrible."

I just want to scream, YES! Be horrible with me! Instead I hang up.

I drop the phone on the train set and clench my fists above. "Gah, why this now!" But I know why. The fluttering is here and using my stomach as a bouncy house. "Fuck off, butterflies," I say as I call her back.

She answers. "What happened?"

Nerves. "Um. Dropped the phone. Or something."

"Oh . . ."

"I want us to be friends," I blurt out.

"Yeah, isn't that why I ate a crab cake the other night?"

"You didn't eat the whole thing."

She laughs. "Don't get nitpicky."

"It wasn't good?"

"Moving on. Friends. We've established that. Do you want to get it notarized or something? Because that'll cost us three whole dollars."

"I don't know. I don't want to offend anyone."

"If by 'anyone' you mean me, go back to the days when I was just another girl on the street. No big deal."

That's what I'm afraid of. I stick a wobbly tree back up into the grass, and it falls over again. This is why I love school: I don't have to question anything; I just have to conquer it. "Be patient with me," I ask her.

"I'm trying," she says softly.

"I don't like not knowing what's going to happen. Things used to be real clear. Now I'm not so sure."

"But isn't that on everyone's bumper sticker? We're all growing a little bit more every day and all that?"

I jump. "Can we not talk about growing?"

"Um. Okay. Well, since we're friends and all that, if you want to ever talk about great unknowns or screaming into the void or whatever, you know where to find me," she says. "But I gotta go. Have homework."

"We should do homework sometime."

"NO! I mean, no thanks," she says, scrambling. "I'm real

bad at math. I don't want you to see how dumb I am. I'm practically redoing Algebra I. It's pathetic."

"You are not dumb. Like, at all. Maybe I could help you?"

She thinks on it. "Maybe you could. But not tonight. Bye, Dylan."

"Good night, Jamie."

We hang up and I feel empty.

I don't know why. I should be feeling like my battery is in the green. Every time Jamie and I talk, it's like sitting inside the eye of the hurricane. An absolutely good place to be. Where whatever is swirling around on the outside, like trees and flying cows or whatever, everything on the inside is still. A place to be whole. I don't want to think about it, so I do what I do best.

Bury it. Bury all the feelings.

Problem solved.

I shake with a shiver, throwing an entire day's worth of crap off my back.

My broken leg is still attached to me like a stiff slab of concrete, and with cramps in all my other muscles, hefting myself off the floor is no picnic. The litany of all things wrong with me skips through my mind. Thankfully my blood test is in two weeks. My bigness will have its proper medical diagnosis of acromegaly and I'll be fixed. I can't wait. Shifting upright, I put only the slightest weight on my leg. It's still sore from the last time I was knocking around the basement, and I don't want to mess it up any further than it already is. This cast is my plaster symbiote: it needs me and I need it.

I hop upstairs, one step at a time, and shut the light off on the little village once I get to the kitchen. *Sleep well, Dad.*

The idea is nice, wishing him a good night's sleep and all, but his body is rotting in a box in the ground. If there's anything left, that is. Mom went for an all-natural burial. But who knows, maybe the chemicals from years of chemo turned his veins into plastic, and someone dug him up and posed him like a heroic warrior in one of those traveling body shows.

How would I want to see Dad posed? Definitely not with his torso and legs all carved open like he's a chest of drawers, jeezus. I saw that poor guy when the show came to the Oregon Museum of Science and Industry. Don't think getting turned into something out of an Ikea catalog was what that guy had in mind when he donated his cadaver, but as for my dad? I'd love to see him on a horse. Sitting victorious atop a horse with his abdomen and chest hollow. Clean of cancer.

I try the pose. Like I'm a general, triumphant over all the shit that's trying to kill me from the inside out. Arm outstretched with sword, other hand tucked inside coat. I hold very still. Practicing like I'm dead too.

Past the kitchen, Mom sits, very much alive but in a different kind of stasis, in the living room. I lean on the door frame and stare at the TV over her shoulder. Nonsensical death and mangled bodies and strangely intuitive detectives who instantly know everything.

No one knows everything.

Mom looks over to me. Our standoff thaws. "Hi," I say.

We're the ones left behind; all we have is each other. "You're welcome to come sit, if you want to," Mom says.

I do. I shuffle and hop over to where she's sitting and seat myself next to her. Mom reaches for me and I lean against her. If I'm crushing her, she doesn't show it. She lets me and holds me nearly the same way she has since I was little. There's nothing to say about this stupid show; she and I know I won't be staying long—my homework sings its siren song and I need to go soon—but for now, it's just the two of us with no one knowing anything beyond the moment of now.

TWENTY

Mom drops me off at school with a hug, and I don't stop her. The car door hangs open and it takes me a hundred years to get out, but she's patient. I asked to come early and Mom obliged.

"Group today?"

"No frigging way; I'm fine. It was all a big misunderstanding."

She nods a touch. "Guess it's all for the best. Now you don't have to see that Jamie girl."

Dad? Throw me a sign, please? Anything? Flicker a light if I should tell Mom I talk to Jamie every day now? That we text each other in between classes to say nothing but hi? I scan the length of our well-lit school. Nothing.

"Sure." Jamie said she stopped going to group too, but Mom doesn't need to know that. Apparently Mom doesn't need to know anything. *Right, Dad? But seriously, Dad, feel free to jump in.*

"Have a good day," she says.

I look for good-luck pennies and see none. "You too," I mumble, and she drives off.

The halls are slick and bare, and the rubber tips of my crutches make a squish-punch against the linoleum. I wanted to be here early so I wouldn't have to see anyone, and last night I got a late start on my homework because neither me or my mom wanted to get off the couch. So we didn't, and now I'm behind the eight ball on trig, but I don't mind. Someday, during my interview with the Rhodes committee, I'll tell them that when I was in high school I used to pretend an asteroid was about to crash into the planet and kill everyone, but I solved the impossible calculations to avoid disaster and saved the entire human race in the nick of time.

Thinking about cracking open my textbook and setting the doomsday-countdown clock on my phone sends a little thrill to my heart as I open the door to the library. The place is empty. I've got my pick of places to sit, and I go for the quiet corner. I throw my bag down, but I'm not alone. There's sniffling behind me.

I turn around and there's Bailey. At least, I think it's her, she's all hunched over in a ball, head down and sounding like she's cleaning out a fish tank with her face. "Bailey?" I ask.

Her head pops up. Red, wet face, smudged eyes, and runny nose. Both sleeves of the white dress shirt of her uniform are soaked through. I see skin. "Oh," she says, wiping everything up with her cuffs.

She gets her things together, but I stop her. "Are you okay?"

Bailey's face crinkles up and she starts to cry again. "No," she says in a whisper. "Please don't tell him."

I get her a tissue from a pocket pack Mom stashed in my bag on the first day of school. She takes it and blows her nose. "Tell who?"

"JP," she says, all irritated.

"I won't. But honestly, who cares what he thinks."

She breaks down in a fresh round of tears.

"I know you guys broke up, but it's gonna be okay." I pat her on the shoulder, but just once so it doesn't come across as creepy.

"I don't know what I did wrong."

"You didn't do anything wrong, trust me."

"I told my mom I was going out with the most popular guy in school and she was just, I don't know . . . She was so proud of me because I was actually leaving the house and doing normal high school things."

"You don't need JP to get out and go do stuff."

Bailey's tissue is a wet rag, so I get her a new one. "He dumped me in my own driveway," she says, dabbing everything at once. "He came over and goes, 'I think we make better friends, don't you?' and then next thing I know we're sitting under my basketball hoop and making out. I asked him if we were still together, and he just shook his head no. Then he left. But we made out. I'm so confused."

"That's his way of doing it, I guess."

"He was my first kiss. He said I was like no other girl he'd ever met."

"Look at his track record," I say. I don't want to shrug, but I do. "This is his deal."

Bailey glares at me. "Maybe you don't get it, because you're on a whole different side of the train tracks and all, but in a regular normal boy-girl relationship, we mean what we say."

"What the hell is that supposed to mean?"

"I know what's going on with you and your Jamie person. He told me." Bailey mops up her cheek. "JP said you're into her because she's the best you can get, so maybe you just don't know what it's like in a normal relationship."

I look over my shoulder. No one's around, no one heard, and I'm thankful. It's still too damn early. "Look, Bailey. Whatever JP told you, about anything, pick a topic, is a flaming pile of dog shit."

"So you're not going out with a tranny?"

"Don't ever call Jamie that. I'm serious: that word is not okay."

"But she is, I mean, she's not a real girl," she says.

"Jamie worries about school and friends and all that stuff. She's as real a girl as you are."

"No offense, but she's not. Because she has, you know, boy parts, right? She didn't get them chopped off yet?"

I lean in and whisper back, "Do you dwell on everyone's junk when you meet them? Like, all you do all day long is think about dicks and janes? Is that your thing, Bailey? You can't stop thinking about what's in everyone's pants?"

"No." She throws herself back in horror. "Ew. I do not."

"Then why are you doing it to Jamie?"

"Fine." Her face is dry. She sniffs once more to seal it up. "You did kiss her on the cheek, though. I saw you."

"I did."

"So there you go."

"You of all people should understand that relationships are a bit more complicated than that. But okay, yes. I kissed her on the cheek. Happy?"

"Are you going to bring her to a dance or something?"

"I . . . don't think so."

"Why not?"

Because before I knew, I absolutely would have, but now I wouldn't, and I feel downright shitty about that fact. "Because I hate dances."

"What's her real name?"

"Jamie." I get my books and put them on her desk. "Did you do trig last night?"

"Of course I did."

"Spot me?"

"How very unlike you, Dylan."

"Hmmph." We plow through it, and I thank the crashing asteroid gods our teacher assigned only ten questions yesterday. Cakewalk. We close our books at the same time.

"Please don't tell anyone," I say. "About Jamie." If I need to bury it inside, then I need to bury it everywhere.

"I won't. I promise." I hate that I'm relieved when she says that.

"See you in class?"

"Yeah," she says, but she has no intention of moving. I can almost see Bailey going over every minute she ever spent with JP, dissecting it like the scientist she is and trying to piece it all together. She wanted the fantasy, and JP got out before she saw the reality. He always does. She doesn't know how little she meant to him. I do, and that's an awful thing.

I wonder if all JP's ex-girlfriends feel the same way? Whispering to each other in solidarity and trying to warn girls before it's too late. I hope so. A groundswell might get him to quit doing this shit. I hand her a few more tissues and leave her in the library.

Spread the word, Bailey.

The weirdness people send my way is like a wall of spiderwebs. It's like I'm wading through invisible phantoms. I go to my locker and toss things where they need to go. When I close it, JP's there. "Jeezus," I curse under my breath.

"I need to talk to you."

I hold my hand up. "I wish you peace," I say, getting all my stuff ready for homeroom.

"Whatever," he says. JP shuts my locker door. "Come with me."

"I really don't want to."

"It's about Jamie."

We go.

We weave through the hall, him high-fiving various wannabe bros and me following. Whatever attention I get from trailing JP is tenuous, and I drink it in while I can. I admit, it's nice being popular by association. I lock eyes with everyone I pass. Remember me. I'm decent. I'm okay.

JP ducks into a narrow hall next to the auditorium. This better be quick; the bell for homeroom is going to ring any minute. "What is it?" I ask.

"Ethan and Bryce found Jamie online and they didn't come to school today."

"So? You yourself said they were idiots and weren't going to do anything."

"They changed their minds."

Yellow light barely bounces off the bricks around us, but all I see is one nightmare scenario after another. What they do to her, what I do to them. "Where are they?"

"I don't know."

I land against the wall. "Oh my god."

"Dylan," JP says. "I'm on your side. I'm being legit—I don't think you and Jamie are weird or anything. Quit being so embarrassed. Let me get Bryce and Ethan to come back to school, I'll talk to them. No one will bother either of you ever again."

"Then do it. If you're such a good guy, what are you waiting for?"

JP draws a huge breath. "Adam Michaels. I need you back. He never paid up."

"No."

"But this is what we do, Dylan. I make the deals, you get the money. This is our thing."

"Not anymore. How about you call Bryce and Ethan and get them to leave her alone right now because that is what sane normal people do."

"I know and I will, as soon as you visit Adam Michaels."

"My days of beating people up for you are over. I did it to make you happy. Don't you get how screwed up that is? I'm done. Like, over and out forever, done."

"Bryce and Ethan are out there."

His face blurs and we're two feet shorter. He's covered in freckles and I'm not covered in hair. We're in the fourth grade and he's got this amazing new Hot Wheels to trade if I only go stand outside on a ninety-five-degree day and save him a tire swing until he can get to the park. He doesn't show up when he says he's gonna, and I get a sunburn.

We're slightly taller, shaggier, starting seventh grade, and fitting all these new teeth of ours into retainers and braces. He's telling everyone at camp how cool I am and I feel so good, I never notice that I'm the one pushing aside little kids because he asked me to get him the last granola bars on the table.

We're taller. But really, I'm taller. We're only freshmen and I'm taller than everyone else, including all the sophomores, juniors, and seniors. I can't fit at the tables, the desks; nothing fits. Except when I'm around JP. I know what to do, where to go, how to be. He jumped right into the high school flow without a single hiccup, turned around, and said, "Follow me." So I did. I did everything he ever asked as long as there was a place where I fit.

"JP . . ." I look at him. Maybe for the first time. "Have you ever been my friend?"

"Dylan, we've been friends since we were practically babies."

Except I'm not talking about how long we've known each other.

JP brings out his phone. "One text and these two idiots are back at school and no one from St. Lawrence ever bothers Jamie for the rest of forever. Do we have a deal or not?"

"What is wrong with you?" I lunge for the phone, desperate to do it myself. "She's a person, not some pawn in your stupid game."

"I have no choice!" He slides the phone down inside his front pocket, where I'm definitely not going. "Adam Michaels has missed every deadline to pay me back. He's up to three hundred and fifty dollars."

"So what? Why do you need this so bad?"

"It's all I have! This is what I do; this is my thing."

"This is how assholes are born."

"Shut up. I run this school. I'm the guy in charge, not you. This is what I control."

"I'm not doing it."

"I can't let everyone see I let Adam Michaels slide. This is not some Robin Hood situation here. There are at least two other kids who owe me that much or more. If they see I can't collect, then I'm out like over a thousand dollars," he says.

"How can you say you're all supportive of me and Jamie with a straight face and then blackmail me into beating someone up?"

"I'm a businessman."

"You're a back-alley loan shark."

"Take the deal."

I scowl at the wall just behind his head. Notches and dings line up inside these faded rusty bricks, and I'm listening so hard for their stories of how they got there because I can't believe what I'm hearing in real life.

"Dylan, take the deal," he says. "My dad . . . I haven't seen him in almost two months. He's gone."

That sucks, but I knew that. His dad still wires him money whenever JP asks him. "Sorry about your dad."

"So you'll do it?"

"How about you help keep a fellow human being safe."

He shakes his head and sucks in air like I'm asking him to dig another Panama Canal. "I can't. I just can't. Adam Michaels needs to pay up."

"You'd rather throw Jamie to the wolves?"

"I . . . I need Adam Michaels. And if Ethan and Bryce aren't the ones who find Jamie, it'll really suck when someone else does."

"Are you saying what I think you're saying?"

He stares at the closed door down the hall instead of me. "She's a real nice girl too."

"You frigging piece of shit. You win." I leave the hallway on my crutches. He goes one way, I go another. The bell hasn't rung yet; Adam Michaels and I can go outside and be back in class in like five minutes.

I round the corner of the senior wing and there he is, collecting his books like a good little student. I button up my school jacket because blood on a white shirt is always a pain to get out. "You," I say.

"Back again?" He drops his bag on the floor. "Not so much a cripple this time."

"Never was."

He looks at my leg and crutches. "Whatever. Let's go."

We find the busted emergency door that everyone props open with soda cans and go outside onto a barren, cold patch of earth and glare at each other like two dogs.

I am the bigger dog.

My fists bunch up, looking like two hairy medicine balls, and there is nothing I want to do more than break this kid's fucking nose. Hear that crack, get that adrenaline high, because I'm frustrated as shit. I want to hate JP, but I don't. I'm just sad. I want to hate Jamie, but I don't, because it's hard to hate someone you want to be with all the time.

"Hope you know I'm just humoring you." Adam Michaels circles the yard, gets closer to me. He shouldn't do that. "Kinda want to hear you cry like when you broke that thing. Don't worry, I'll be quick. All it takes—"

I lunge, grab his shirt so fast all the threads pop, strike him up and in his gut, right on the solar plexus, and throw his sorry ass on the ground. Mud flies and hits me in the chin. I'll take it. It's better than blood. Adam Michaels lies there in one pathetic heaving pile because all the nerves in his celiac ganglia are spasming the fuck out.

"Do you know who I am?" I lean over him, pushing him hard on his gut so it burns. "They call me the Beast for a reason. Time to pay up."

My fist reels back. His eyes snap wide.

Do it for Jamie. Do it for Jamie.

I can end this kid and he knows it.

But I can't.

My hands fall open. Adam Michaels takes his first actual breath. "Work out a payment plan," I say. "Tell JP you'll pay him . . . what can you afford?"

"Um . . . m-maybe ten dollars a week?"

"Tell him you'll pay him thirty-two dollars and eight cents a month for a year. That's a ten percent interest rate, and don't borrow money until you know you can pay it back."

"Whoa, you're really good at math."

"I know. Now get out of here."

He crawls through the door, doubled over and covered in mud. Back in the hallway, the bell screams over my head. If I were more social, I'd have Ethan or Bryce's number, but I don't because all these years I relied on JP for everything. If I didn't have the need to branch out, I didn't, and now I'm kicking myself. Instead I call Jamie. She doesn't pick up and I have to leave her a message: "I'm worried about you. I need to know you're okay, like right now this second."

I hang up.

I realize that might've been a little overdramatic and call back.

"Maybe not quite that bad, but whatever. Call me as soon as you get this message." I hang up, stand in the corner, and wait.

TWENTY-ONE

The closest midway point we have is the mall. I keep expecting all the teachers to call truancy officers, but nothing happens. We turn heads in the mall on a school day for only obvious reasons: I am an almost-seven-foot-tall hairy dude on crutches sitting in the food court next to a girl who makes everyone do a triple check. A pretzel lies half-mauled on a skimpy napkin in between us as I pull my hat down and Jamie takes another billion pictures.

"Jamie . . ."

"Don't worry, I'm not posting anything to the Internet. No one will know we're here right now," she says. "It'll be a latergram."

"No, you're not taking this seriously. Ethan and Bryce are transphobic idiots, and JP is really dangerous. I don't know what he's going to do anymore. He said some real scary shit."

"I get it. I heard you the first sixty times," she says sharply. "And you're starting to sound like my mom. No amount of expert opinion can convince her that I'm not going to be the target of some insane plot. So I'll tell you the same thing I tell her: I'll be fine."

"I know, but I'm afraid they're going to come after you and hurt you, and you're brushing it off like they accidentally changed the red dye in their Froot Loops or something."

"Are you done?"

"You're mad at me because I'm trying to look out for you?"

"Maybe I'm sick of hearing about my imminent demise. Despite everyone's well-intentioned concerns, it's quite nice being me," she says. "Seriously, my own mother thinks I'm going to end up a prostitute and get murdered by a john, so I don't need to hear it from you too, okay?"

"She does?"

"No, not like really officially hooker, just 'her biggest fear' for me and whatever."

"I'm not saying you're gonna be a hooker. I'm trying to tell you I do not know what's going on and I'm afraid." Because you mean so much to me.

"And I heard you; now please hear me. I'm done with everyone thinking that me being alive is an open invitation to bigots and weirdos who want to do awful things. I am way past over the lectures. It sucks, okay? I just want to live in peace." Jamie tears a hunk off the pretzel and chomps down with an angry bite. "Don't worry. I can take care of myself."

Her teeth roil and grind the doughy thing into soup. She's so pissed, but I can't help it.

Dad . . . Even if she's mad and can't stand me right now, give me a sign to reach out and hold her hand. Send the okay; send the all clear. Like someone dumping their tray in the trash in the next three seconds.

I wait.

Okay, five seconds.

Still nothing. Crap.

I glance over at Jamie and in spite of my best efforts, I smile.

"What?" she says.

A daub of yellow spots her cheek. "You got some mustard here." I point to mine, locationwise.

Her tongue flares out but misses. "Did I get it?"

"Nope." I reach out with my thumb and wipe it away. The napkin is a wreck, so I lick it off instead. She smirks and looks to her lap. Now I have to ask. "What?"

"Nothing," she says. "I think it's adorable that you still want your prince fantasy."

"My what?"

"Your bodyguard thing—how you want to be my prince in shining armor. It's sweet."

I laugh so loud, everyone at the food court twists to see. "I would make a real shitty prince." Let's just stick to the Beast, thanks. Much easier. "Besides, I don't think it's some massive gesture to warn you about stupid people. That's just normal friend stuff."

"Maybe I watch too many stupid movies where the guy comes in and sweeps the girl off her feet. Carries her away and they kiss in the rain. You know the ones I'm talking about?" She waits for me but I shrug. "Anyway"—

she ducks her eyes low and blushes—"I don't know. I love those movies. Have you ever wished you were in a movie like that?"

A slab of pretzel gets stuck deep in my molar because of course I have. With her.

"You think I'm being a cheesy dork, I can tell," she says.

"Nah. You're a romantic."

"I am." She sighs. "What about you?"

The mall is packed. I try to make eye contact with a stranger. A lady over there waiting in line for a Venti peppermint pumpkin mocha white squall. The lady looks up, catches my eye, and shudders. She grabs her drink and runs.

"I'm a realist," I say in a dull voice as that lady flees.

Even if I got the sign of all signs to pick Jamie up and sweep her off her feet *(Dad, how about someone tripping on that spilled strawberry shake right now? No? Dammit),* I don't know if I could be the type of boyfriend Jamie wants. I just don't look the part. She's into all those romance movie guys and their swoony gazing. I'm way more suited to standing in front of her and smashing the oncoming world to bits. Besides, I've already tried to be a movie-star guy with her, back in the rose garden, and she shot me down hard.

So I guess it's good to officially know Jamie will never go for me. I can stop worrying about us and me and her and all the rest of it and just be. Maybe we can be friends.

"Yeah, I suppose I'm a realist too. Everyone kinda has to be at least a little bit," she says in a similar monotone. "Since you loved group therapy, with your whopping one session and all . . ."

"Two!" I laugh. "I showed up for the second one, I just didn't go, remember?"

"Semantics. Anyway, here it comes, ready? Pop psychology. You're a leading man in a movie, like action or horror or thriller. Which one are you and why?"

"A lead? What does that mean?"

"Like an actor. How about classic Hollywood? If I'm doing me, I'd kill to be Sophia Loren because oh my god, but since it's obvious I'm more of a Katharine Hepburn, that's not a bad deal either. You get to pick between James Dean, Paul Newman, and Marlon Brando. Spoiler alert, I'm bringing home Brando from *A Streetcar Named Desire.* Oooh, Stanley."

"Jimmy Stewart," I say. I'm the guy saving the town and coming home to my family on Christmas, my wife and four kids smothering me with hugs and kisses. Ill-fated suicide attempt and all.

"Oooh . . . I like it. The Everyman. Oh, hey! *Rear Window!* He has a broken leg in *Rear Window*! That's perfect."

"I guess so." He's also super paranoid and sacrifices his girlfriend to go head to head with a murderer, so there's that.

"Grace Kelly was so pretty in that movie. Her makeup was flawless." She peers across the food court. "Can we stop in Sephora?"

"Out of pineapple lip gloss?"

"You remembered."

Some things you can't forget. She gets up, I do too. We chuck the sad remains of our pretzel in the trash and there's nothing I can do but follow her into a store that smells like

Play-Doh doused in rotting Sharpie markers. "We have to go to Sephora, huh?"

"You're my BFF. You of all people should understand." I am despising the descriptive term "BFF" because it has one too many Fs. "Help me pick out some colors. I need a new nude palette," she says.

"A what?"

"Eye shadow. Don't worry, we'll get you up to speed by the time Pride rolls around."

"Why do I have to go to Pride now?"

"Well, I usually go. We make it a party—to me it's like a birthday almost. My day, I love it. But if you're not into it, that's okay."

"It's in June, right?" Maybe I'll be ready by then.

"Uh-huh, June." Jamie takes my hand and gives it a squeeze. Feels like she's made of fireflies and it lights me up. "I keep forgetting this is new for you, sorry." She drops my hand and picks up a box with some girl's slick and shiny cheek on it. "Only if you want to. Pride's not going anywhere. What do you think of this moisturizer?"

"I don't," I say. I drift into the aisle and glance at the wonderland. I don't even know what half this shit is. Lipstick? Okay, that's easily identified. But lip gloss, lip balm, lip tar, and lip stain? You only have two lips. How many boiled dinosaur bones do two lips need? I grip my disgusting crutches, the rubber all split and cracked with wear and tear. When I look up, I have a heart attack. It's my mom. Staring at her phone and ambling into Sephora. I duck down and almost crush Jamie. "Hide!" I tell her in a whisper.

"What?"

"My mom's at the mall, she's in the store, hide!"

Jamie jumps and turns and stops, waiting for me. "Aren't you coming?"

All I can do is shake my head. "I'm too big." Hiding, like crouching into a ball or something, is stupid. The only thing I can do is stand next to a wall and hope my mom doesn't see me.

Mom is still staring, staring, staring at her phone. Please keep reading all those emails.

Jamie gives me a sad look and resigns me to my fate as she darts off behind a row of colors wedged in plastic containers. I lean against a post next to a bunch of tubes and tubs and wait, peeking from behind the brim of my hat. Mom comes in, finishes up a text, and looks around. Be small, I command my entire body, and it just goes, ha ha ha, sucker. . . .

Mom sees me and gasps so loud everyone's head in Sephora snaps along for the ride. "Dylan Walter Ingvarsson, what are you doing here?"

"Hi, Mom." I look across the store. Jamie is invisible. It's for the best.

"I want answers. Now."

"I was . . ." I don't know crap-all about any of this. I grab the nearest thing. "Shopping. For Mother's Day. Here's some lip . . . stuff."

She peers at the black plastic tube of goo. "It's November."

"Christmas, then. But now you spoiled the surprise." I put it back.

"Not buying it. Why aren't you in school?"

Struggling to come up with something, I've got nothing. I shut my mouth.

"That's what I thought." She tugs at one of my crutches to get me moving. "You're going back right this second, mister."

"Wait a minute. Why are you here?"

Her mouth pops open. "I . . . had a feeling this is where I needed to go."

Dad! Dammit, how does he keep doing this for her? I don't get it. Why won't he talk to me?

"And I have a coworker who's retiring and I wanted to pick up her favorite perfume." She reaches behind me and snares a box. It's all pink and loopy with little white birds on it. "So now I have it, let's pay and go."

Mom marches me toward the cashier behind a counter and alternates between watching where she's going and shooting me *the look,* just so I know I'm still in a very large amount of trouble. Got it. "That lip gloss wasn't even my color, Dylan. I have more of a peach complexion."

"Um, okay." I sneak my head around. Jamie's still hiding better than a baby deer.

"It was a good choice for you, though. You've got your dad's pink cheeks. Wait." She stops us both. "Were you shopping for yourself? Or Jamie?"

Now *the look* has shifted to *oh no, what does this REALLY mean?*

"Honestly, I saw you coming and ducked into the nearest store."

Relief smooths her edges round. "Thank god. For a second I thought we had our own Jamie situation on our hands. Not that this negates all the trouble you're in, mister." She gets moving again and plunks the perfume on the counter. "Ma'am, do you have children?" she asks the woman behind the counter.

"I do," she says brightly. "Two girls and a boy."

"And what's your strictest punishment for a kid who skips school, like my son here?"

The woman behind the counter looks up and up at me. "That's your son?"

"Yup."

"You poor woman," she laughs. "You must've cracked open from the pressure."

Mom smiles along. "Ten pounds, eight ounces, I demanded a C-section."

They get their full jollies on and I stand there while they laugh at me. "Good lord, he's a beast," the woman says. "When he came in with that girl, I was like—"

"What girl?" Mom demands.

I eye-yell at the woman behind the counter to say no more, but she's Team Mom. "She's young, tall, and pretty. Think she had a camera?" the woman says, and I'm instantly screwed.

Mom tears away from the counter and storms through the aisles one by one. I catch a glimpse of Jamie trying to make a break for it, but Mom spies her first. "Jamie!" she yells. "Young lady, you and I need to have a talk."

"Mom," I interrupt, throwing myself between the two of them. "It's not what you think! Don't take it out on her, take it out on me." If there was any way to bargain, to plead, to steer her another way, I'd do it all, but once she saw Jamie, it was over.

Jamie holds on to a display and grips her heart. "I didn't mean—"

My mom bucks around me and gets too tight with Jamie. "I don't know what kind of agenda you have for my son, but you will leave him alone from now on," she says in a low tone. "Understand me?"

"Mom, it was my idea, not Jamie's. She's innocent."

"You." She switches her sights to me. "We're leaving. Go."

I look over my shoulder and see Jamie holding it in. "I'll call you," I mouth.

Jamie nods and lays her head against her clinging hands holding on to the shelf, and that's the last I see of her as Mom drags me by the arm through the mall, like I'm some belligerent five-year-old. I don't want her to touch me and I yank my arm away.

"Ow!" she cries, and rubs her wrist.

My gut sinks. I've done this before, hurt her by accident. I'll move too fast or turn a corner too sharp and completely take her out. "I'm so sorry, Mom."

She pushes back the sleeve of her coat, and underneath her whole forearm is red from where I wrenched her off me. "You've got to be more careful," she mutters.

We find the car in the garage and get in. Our doors slam shut, and I wait for Mom to start in on me. Start tearing me a new one about ditching school and how bad I'm punished. To go off on Jamie, the whole nine yards. But she doesn't. It's as quiet as a coffin. The streets slip away and it starts to rain. Blocks tick by and the car wends its way up to the front entrance of the school. The wipers swish back and forth, and we both sit in the car.

"Just . . . hop out." A thin layer of tears sits heavy in her eyes. "I'll see you at home."

"Mom."

"You wrecked the basement, you threw your best friend out of the house, and now you're skipping school to go to the mall with Jamie, and I'm supposed to sit here and take it? What's next? Drugs?"

"We're not on drugs."

"I don't know what to do." Her gaze follows the windshield wipers. "I met with my boss this morning. They want to send me to Pittsburgh for a meeting. I've been killing myself to get a promotion and if I do well, this could be it. We need the money. College is coming. This is my moment, but I don't know if I can leave you for two days."

"I'll be fine. I can take care of myself."

"Not if that girl's in the picture."

"She's a friend. You said there's nothing wrong with having friends."

"I don't think Jamie is a healthy influence."

"She is." I'm doing my best to protect her from JP, and if that means having my mom mad at me forever, so be it. "You just don't like her because she's trans, is that it?"

"Don't start with that. Her being trans has nothing to do with it. I'm lying awake at night because you are going through a really hard time right now, and the last thing you need is some confused individual with a complicated history to throw a wrench in the works."

"You make it sound like I'm a cotton gin."

She grits her teeth. "You fell off a roof, Dylan. You said it was all an accident and a misunderstanding and you were fine. I'm starting to doubt myself in letting you tell me what you needed."

"But that's got nothing to do with Jamie!"

"I'm not fond of Jamie because you, of all people, are skipping school to see her."

I can't tell Mom why. She'll never believe that her precious JP, who said grace with her at every dinner, has turned into a full-blown asshole.

"I'm going to tell work I can't go," she says.

"Don't. You work really hard. Get your promotion."

"A promotion's not worth it if my kid is falling apart."

"Look at me," I say. She does. "Do I look like I'm falling apart?" Strong like bull, sturdy like ox, ain't nothing bothering me, nope. Everything is HUNKY-DORY. I add a smile because I'm the only one who can sell it.

Mom looks like a gigantic balloon five days after a Thanksgiving Day parade. Everything about her has gone poof.

I already feel like lukewarm crap; it's best if I leave. I crack open the door and try to get my crutches on the sidewalk without getting my cast wet. I don't worry about my head or jacket getting soaked. No one uses umbrellas in Portland unless an ark is floating by. "You've left me for business trips before," I say. "It'll be same as ever. I'll eat, I'll do my homework, I'll wake up, and I'll go to school. No big deal."

I'm out of the car and up onto the brick steps leading up to St. Lawrence before my mom can pull out into traffic. My brain is supposed to be gearing up for physics, but it feels more like scrambled eggs. I hang back in the lobby until the bell rings, hoping I can slide into the day like nothing happened. It's still early. If anyone asks, I'll tell them I had an appointment with my orthopedic surgeon.

Which is almost true. I'm meeting with him next week because I grew another inch, oh my god, someone please rip out my pituitary gland with their teeth, I'm begging you. The blood test can't come fast enough.

Ten minutes tick by. The bell shrieks and I ease back into the current. There's three things I want out of this day to make it substantial, decent, and tolerable. No JP, no JP, and no JP. That's it. I head toward my locker and something is off. No, it's worse than before. Everyone is staring at me. I can feel all their eyes burrowing into me like festering ticks.

My stomach sinks.

They all got the go-ahead to hate me, say the terrible things, reduce me to anecdotes that make them feel like they have the right to do whatever idiots do. JP gave them his blessing. I know it. And the son of a bitch confirms. From the far end of the hallway, where he just left English, he sees me. A smile lights up his face. He points at me and starts to walk over. One of his minions laughs along with him. The one laugh attracts more guys and the group grows larger. They all look at me and laugh.

JP makes like he's merely passing me in the hall, as if it'll ever be that simple again. "Bad news, Dylan," he says my way. "I don't take payment plans."

If I could, I would run.

TWENTY-TWO

This past week has been hell. The only thing getting me through is nightly phone marathons with Jamie telling me to turn the other cheek, to forgive, to be patient . . . all the things she tries to muster up every day and all the things I am currently failing at.

Thanks, JP. Now I'm everything I never wanted to be again. I'm the kid not picked for dodgeball or volleyball or to represent Mrs. Martin's class in the first-grade spelling bee, even though I can spell the second and third grades under the table. Heads turn away from me. Like I have leprosy, Ebola, and plague all in one. It used to be I couldn't go anywhere without a robust "BEAST!" thrown my way as I went by. Now the sea in the hallway parts with a trail of snickers made under their breath.

And really, for what? Because some sniveling little jerk told them to? Because they think it's weird I kissed a trans girl on the cheek? So what, big deal. Lots of stuff is weird. I'm no fan of ketchup, but Jason Harrington practically drinks it with a straw. I might not hold hands with a dude but I didn't give him shit when he brought a guy from his traveling basketball team to the dance last year. No, I was cool about it. I was like, oh wow, good for him for getting some palm-on-palm action because I—the sweaty, heaving ox over here in the corner—will never find someone to hold my hand. Hoof. Paw, whatever. So I'm not too keen on Jason following JP's orders by throwing me a bunch of ketchup-swigging judgmental smirks these days.

There are a few smiles. Little quick sympathy grins from the girls in class. I only notice because I'm trying to not stare at their assets as they walk by.

I'm still mad.

Mostly I sit and eat my lunch in the library and pretend I'm Gandhi. Which is bullshit because I can guarantee if Gandhi hadn't been on a hunger strike, he would've had friends to eat with him. Plus, I want to pick up JP and throw him into the whirling, twirling engine of a jumbo jet, and I'm very sure that goes against everything Gandhi preached.

Every time I see JP's face, I think of Jamie. I wish you peace, I chant in my head. "I wish you peace," I say now as he's at my locker trying to "touch base."

"I really want to talk to you," he says. "Please? Just for one minute? You can time it."

"I wish you peace."

"Stop fucking saying that."

I lean over him. "I will say that until I'm purple because if I don't, you will be literally—not figuratively, not metaphorically—dead, and I have no desire to go to prison. Not my scene. I wish you peace."

While pushing off my locker, I "accidentally" knock him on his ass. Not super hard, but enough to end it for today because I can't handle adding another ball to the juggling act I'm trying to pull off. No matter, he's off to his new girlfriend's house so he can go molest her in a quiet corner and she can coo and feel special that he chose her for the day. I'm alone again. But hey, this is great. I'm totally not feeling like ground-up slug on the bottom of someone's shoe as I get into my mother's car, which is waiting for me in the drop-off zone because she doesn't trust me to get home by myself anymore.

I slam the car door shut.

"How was school today?" Mom asks, her attempt at sunshine falling short.

"Awesome. I made a lot of new friends, and everyone picked me to represent our class in the school spelling bee."

The car pulls into traffic. "They still have spelling bees?"

"Uh-huh. And Becky and Suzie made me friendship bracelets at recess too."

"Okay, enough." She sighs, about to begin again. "You know, Dylan—"

"Please don't," I say.

"All I'm trying to say is—"

"Mom, not today, okay? Please." Because I'm having a shit time and if you're going to say anything, say I Love You. That's it. No advice. No wheedling about *my attitude.* No momsplaining to me why JP and I need to go back to Square One and be bestest buddies for life. No opinions on my friends or lack thereof or school or grades or my imminent future. Just I Love You. That's all. Done.

"We're having some trouble, you and I. It's obvious."

"Mmm." Astronauts can get the gist of it from space, so yeah.

"Maybe we need a break. Some time apart. Come back together in a stronger place."

My ears perk up.

"I've decided to go to Pittsburgh," she says, and I want to jump out and do the cha-cha.

"Really?"

"One of my coworkers ran into the same problem with her teenagers, and she said it was a breath of fresh air for everyone," Mom says. "But there's a but!"

"There's always a but."

"You have to follow the rules. You must answer your phone at all times. You must check in with the Swanpoles across the street when you get home from school and before you go to bed. You must do all your homework and you must go to school. You can hitch a ride with all the kids from junior high, I already called the lady who runs the buses. They'll pick up on the corner of Going and 77th." She draws in a breath. "You must not make me regret leaving."

"Got it."

"You and I need a reboot," she says. "We both need to order some room service and watch a movie. Come home and everything will be back to normal."

"I think it's a good idea."

A real good idea. A Nobel Prize–worthy idea. Some time when I can sit and eat as much food as I want without anyone reminding me how much it costs and play Madden until my hands are raw. She fills me in on some basic details, and after I wolf down a snack of three peanut butter and jelly sandwiches, I'm upstairs in my room to call Jamie and tell her all about it.

She answers immediately. "Did you get your blood test? When do we find out Dylan the Giant has a posse?"

"Blood sucked out Friday, but I have news."

"Tell me."

"My mom's going on a business trip to Pittsburgh."

"This sounds promising."

"Honestly, I'm just excited to have the house to myself," I say. "She's only gone for two days, one night, and I might as well wear an ankle monitoring bracelet, but it's thirty-six hours without Mom. I'm psyched."

"I'm so jealous."

"Don't be. It's going to be me and about thirty of my closest pizza-shaped friends."

"And maybe a little something else."

My eyebrows raise. "Go on."

"Let me ask you something, how fast can you grow a beard?"

"A full beard, or some scruff? I can do scruff in a day."

"Good to know. How long for a full beard?"

"Like three days. Why?"

"When's your mom going out of town?"

"Next Thursday."

Jamie's grin fires across the phone lines. "Start growing that beard on Monday."

TWENTY-THREE

It's Friday, and a sweeping breath of calm fills me as I pick good, clean clothes to wear to the hospital. White cotton button-down shirt. Clean jeans with the leg cut out for my cast. A navy blue sweater. I comb my hair, not that it does more than tickle a scalp full of stubby follicles. This is a baptism. *Dear Dad,* I start to dictate in my head. *It's time to learn the truth. We have the thing. That spark, that flare, that tumor that makes us (made, in your case, sorry) grow way too big.* This is the day I take my first deliberate steps to getting to the bottom of whatever the hell is wrong with me. I'm on the road to my diagnosis and I can't wait.

It's an ungodly early appointment, but I don't care. Mom's saying things and they float around me, creating a bolstering cloud of security, because this is it. I've googled the snot out of acromegaly. I'm ready to join the parade.

The blood test today will look for an overactive hormone and I've already checked nearly everything off the list. Enlarged hands and feet? Yup. Everything is enlarged, it all counts. Coarsened facial features? You bet. A deepened, husky voice? You've been listening in, haven't you, you sly devil? There's other stuff that doesn't line up with the list from the Mayo Clinic, but there's enough right there to say oh hell yeah, it's gigantism. I've already signed up for the acromegaly mailing list. I'm ready to be the state of Oregon's chapter president.

Someday, when I'm being interviewed for *Nova* or *60 Minutes* because I'll have cured cancer by then, they'll ask me about my formative years and I'll say what a shitstorm my life was until I got my diagnosis. And once I was a legit medical giant I was no longer ashamed to tower through the halls. I had a genetic ailment that no one could take away from me. My pituitary gland produced too much growth hormone; it's not my fault. Perhaps there's surgery on the horizon for some benign tumors causing trouble, but once they're gone I am in the clear. I stop growing.

I fasted overnight. I haven't had any breakfast. Let's do this.

Mom and I get in the car. Back on the road again and we're off to the hospital. It's a different room in a wing on the right I've never been to. Everything is fresh and new. Even the magazines have better pictures of bikini-clad ladies over here. Doesn't matter they're illustrating some weight-loss bullshit; still counts. The lab tech calls me in for the blood draw.

"Why you smiling, baby?" she asks.

"Nothing." Everything. "How much blood are you taking today?"

"Eight pints."

"Really?"

"No, you'd be dead." She laughs. Gotta love phlebotomist humor. "Couple vials, baby, and you're on your way."

The needle goes into my vein. Vials are filled. She releases the purple elastic around my bicep, presses a cotton ball against my arm, slaps some paper tape over it, and I'm free.

TWENTY-FOUR

The shelves in bodegas and corner mom-and-pop shops always make me smile. It's a hodgepodge of stuff they ordered once but didn't sell, so they let it sit on the shelf with all the other items to turn yellow and fade under the fluorescent lights. I straighten my sports coat and chuckle at one package of generic diapers, next to a pile of wrenches, next to some old travel bottles of shampoo, next to some faded boxes of birthday candles, and a box of off-off-off-off-brand teeth whitening strips left to die next to two bags of Acme kitty litter.

It reminds me of my head. A pile of random shit crammed together. I almost want to buy the teeth whitening kit just to bring it home and give it a proper burial. Maybe I'll add it to my list, which is pretty brief. The only thing on it is Beer.

Two six-packs and a pack of gum from every corner store we go to.

Because I am a bit of a math nerd, I actually looked into how many ounces of beer it would take for someone my size to get drunk, and the answer is a lot. Since we don't want to be caught, we figured that if we buy two six-packs and some random gum at each store, no flags are raised. If we hit up enough stores, we slide under the radar, secure plenty of suds, and have a lovely long constitutional whilst getting said brews.

Jamie has to wait outside as I browse in my man drag, select beer, and buy it. We already know it works because we stashed a brown paper bag from the last store under a row of scrub bushes, but I'm still sweating like a pig. No one seems to notice. Why would they? We scoured all the closets at both our houses and found usable man things. Thankfully her dad is real tall and doesn't seem to be missing his scratchy brown-plaid sports coat. Jamie and I worked up my everything real good before we left. Gave the coat some Professor Huffinblad patches on the elbows that her mom had been meaning to add forever but never got around to, and with my wire frame glasses to boot, it's all complete. Jamie swiped them from her grandpa, and as long as I sink them down the bridge of my nose and look over the top, my eyes don't kill too much. She said that was a perfect touch because it makes me look like I need bifocals and I'm too stubborn to get them. Good for the age range we were going for.

In addition to the khaki pants and the respectable socks and loafers, she sliced a rigid line through my hair with a fine-tooth comb and parted it to the side. Flecked with scattered gray hairs at the temples that she individually painted. Put together, but not too much. Casual. I look like a banker approving a loan for a pot farm.

The *pièce de résistance* is the beard.

It's thicker than it should be after three days and covers everything. Neck, high up the cheeks, and almost under my ears. I hate it. It's itchy and looks stupid. Jamie laughed her ass off while she painted about seventy-five hairs on my chin gray. So of course her laughing at me made it better. Just kidding, that sucked.

The girl behind the cash register is older than I am, but not by much.

"Excuse me, sir," I hear behind me.

I spin around on my crutches and glare at Jamie. "You're supposed to be outside."

She holds up a box of Only Dudes hair dye. "I was wondering if you could help me?" She tries so hard not to laugh. "See, my dad is the same age as you, old as hell, and he's turning gray and sagging into his shoes too. Do you have a preference when selecting cheap hair dye for old men—and by 'old,' I mean actually-pay-attention-to-boner-pill-commercials old—to pretend they're still in the game?"

Jamie shimmies with glee. This whole beer excursion came from one long exploded dare with one another. "I'll do it if you do it" became "Let's do it." Turns out we both always entertained the thought of getting blitzed but never had the opportunity. And now we do. Thanks, Mom!

"Young lady, you are quite a hoot."

"Thank you, sir. I like to think so too."

I check the clerk behind the counter. She's not watching us, and I give Jamie's shoulder a little bump. "Dork," I whisper under my breath. I was excited about getting all this beer, but it turned out it's just us doing what we do best, and that's my favorite part.

"You look great!" she whispers back.

She gives me a shove. I give her a shove. She bumps me with her hip. I turn around and knock her with my butt. Jamie bounces into the teeth whitener. We glue our mouths shut because whoever laughs first loses, so we snort up a storm.

"You're horrible," she says.

"No, you're horrible."

"We're both so incredibly horrible," she says, and I'm like, oh hell yes, we are. Forever and always.

Jamie walks away and I tap her lifting heel with my crutch, making her trip. "Don't blow your cover," she shoots back with a huge grin.

"You started it," I rumble back.

She situates herself by the sodas and I scan the store for people. We're waiting for someone to check out and I'll stand behind them, so it looks like I'm just another man buying beer and gum before going home to the wife and kids.

Some guy comes in and I'm relieved. He's gotta be like eighteen or something, but I bet he'll buy an energy drink and I'll look crazy old by comparison. Then I lean against the beef jerky because I don't like looking like this.

Having this thing on my face feels exactly like that time I

got trapped under my grandma's thick wool blanket when I was four: I can't breathe. I can't get out.

Stop. Focus. I breathe. It's just a beard, not a death sentence.

I need something else to do in the store and decide on examining shoelaces. My choices are brown, black, and white in either twelve- or twenty-inch lengths. Twelve seems too short, but the twenty looks too long. One of the laces isn't wrapped properly at the end, and the end is fraying. The store should offer it at a discount. A ruckus hits my ears.

The guy has Jamie pinned in a corner.

He's in her space, her back against the wall, and picks up a lock of her hair. She smiles, a fake one, and twists her hair away as he laughs. I'm there before her hair hits her shoulder. "Leave her alone," my voice booms above him.

The dude turns around and faces me. "What's it to you?"

"Get what you need and go," I say, stepping in between him and Jamie.

"What if I'm in the middle of getting her number, huh?"

I look at Jamie. Her head shimmies no, just enough for me to see. "Is he bothering you, miss?" I ask her.

She clamps her lips down. "I'm fine; you can go."

"You heard her," I tell the punk.

"No, you," she says.

"What?"

Anger slips across the way from her to me. It's so strong, I almost want to hold on to the shelves. "I'll be fine. You don't have to be here," she says, as if she just found out I drowned all her new puppies in a sack. Then warmth comes over her and she smiles at this fuckfaced jerk. "Hey," she says to the guy. "Thanks, but no thanks. And you, sir," she says to me, suddenly cold again. "I'm good. Okay?"

"You heard the girl, bro," the guy says to me. "Step off."

"She told you the same thing. Take a hike."

The guy shoves me with his pointy little fingertips. "You got something to say on this hike of yours, tell me outside. I always wanted to take on the Man."

Hold on, I'm the Man?

I have been a bully. I don't think I want to be the Man.

My reflection in the dim light of the window is everything I don't want to be, because that's not me. That's what I might be. I'm not some old man in a sports coat; I'm a kid. I should catch a glimpse of some thin-shouldered twerp in a ratty old T-shirt and beat-down hoodie with acne all over his face.

Jamie called me sir, but not in the fun jokey way. Feels like I'm the bad guy now. She stands firm and I have no idea what to do. My only talent is growing bigger, so I wish she'd just let me chest-bump this dude all the way to Idaho.

The punk looks me up and down and all over, hands flexing in and out of fists because he can't figure out what's next. He wants to take me on—I can smell it, hear the blood rush in both our ears. I step back, I want no part of this. He gets tighter in my space. Daring me. Jamie watches us from the side, her hand sneaking out to grab the neck of a glass bottle, just in case.

Out of the corner of my eye, Jamie creeps back many steps. Safe.

"She's not interested," I say in a low whisper.

"Let her be the judge."

"You guys . . . ," Jamie says.

"She already said no thanks. You got a hearing problem?" I say. "In case you do, I'll talk real clear. She's underage. She's off-limits. A real judge would throw the book at you for trying to get with a minor."

The jerk's got nothing after that. He slinks out of the store and finds his bike, riding off into the night. I turn to Jamie just as she puts the glass bottle down. "Are you okay, miss?"

She nods but doesn't say anything.

Please look at me, I ask her without words.

She does. *Why'd you have to do that? I was fine. Everything was fine.*

How could I not?

I'm so pissed at you.

Why?

You're not my fucking bodyguard, okay? she says back as she stares at the ceiling.

Oh. "Let's go," I whisper, turning to leave.

She pinches the fabric of my sleeve. "Get the beer first." *I need to get shitfaced. I was kinda joking before, but I'm for real now.*

I can't be the prince, can't be a bodyguard, definitely do not want to be the Man, and now even being a friend feels all shot up with holes. Don't quite know what that leaves me, but it feels like nothing.

Jamie stands fast, not moving until I get more beer. Opening up a cold door, I get another six-pack and walk to the front. The counter girl's phone is like a barnacle on her hand, practically burrowed into her skin. She was texting so hard, she never saw anything. Perhaps searching for the perfect meme GIF was involved. I hope she found it. The beer settles evenly on the counter and I wait for the girl to do something.

Card me. I dare you.

She gives me the slightest once-over and scans the bar code with her plastic wand. It beeps. "Eight dollars and seventy-five cents."

I don't budge. I'm fifteen years old, card me. My wallet flops open to my school ID. It's me, only with no beard. I push it toward her. "Don't you want to card me?"

She flips a hand. "Nah, you're good."

I take off the glasses. I tug at the acrylic paint in my beard and let several tiny gray tubes fall to the ground.

The clerk is oblivious to the point of pain. "Sir?"

I don't want to be called sir ever again. "You shouldn't be selling me this beer because I'm only fifteen years old."

"Right. And I'm the pope." She snorts with laughter. "Eight dollars and seventy-five cents?"

"Your Holiness." I throw down a ten, grab the beer, and crutch as awkward and fast as possible out of the store.

Jamie sneaks outside right behind me. "One more store?"

"No. I'm done."

TWENTY-FIVE

There is a sun setting above us and we do stare at the wonder of it all, but it's been entirely silent between us. The incident at the store looming large. I'm afraid of bringing it up, because what if she says she doesn't want to hang out anymore? The longer we don't talk, the more nervous I get, and I'm starting to wonder if we should just call the whole thing off and get her home before it gets any colder out.

I make one last shot.

"Knock, knock," I say as we walk through the chilly streets, glass bottles clanking in our backpacks.

"Who's there?" she answers. The first words we speak in like twenty minutes.

"To."

"To who?"

"To *whom*." She laughs and I do too.

"Cheesy goodness," she says.

Then it's quiet again.

"I think . . ." My voice breaks across the cold air. "I think you're a really brave person."

"Ugh." The groan comes from her gut and goes way long. "You sound like that girl who stopped me in the lunchroom at my new school and was all like, "I think it's great you're trans. You are so brave," and all I could think was, I am so hungry and you are blocking me from my food."

"I can't think you're brave? That you're a warrior?"

"A warrior? Have I been drafted into battle or something? Where's my cool armor; who's at the gate?" she busts out. "Seriously, Dylan. You don't have to hurt yourself. I'm not mad at you."

"You sure acted like it in the store."

"No, I didn't. I wanted to just enjoy myself a little. Is that so crazy?" She stops dead on the sidewalk under a frigid tree. Tiny drops of mist and rain collect and drop on and all around us. Winter will be here soon. The rain threatens. "Maybe . . . ," Jamie says, not looking at me. "Maybe I like it when a guy gives me a compliment. Even if it's a creepy dude saying gross things like how he wants to lick me like a lollypop."

I wince in disgust.

"I know! It's ick times infinity, I know. And I know I shouldn't say anything like this because it's conceited and all the rest of it, but . . . I'm pretty. And I like hearing it."

"But did that guy say you were pretty?"

"Not verbatim, but it was like—hey, I find you attractive

and I'm going to inform you in only the most gross way I know how."

"Jeezus, Jamie." Bubbles simmer. "That's so wrong, I can't even."

"And you're the expert? You have the inside scoop on what to do when someone says you're hot? Because I'm thinking no one's ever—" She stops herself.

The gravel under my feet. It's all I can study right now. There are no books.

"I'm sorry," she says.

"It's okay."

"I'm sorry, that came out really wrong."

I look at her. "I just don't want anyone to hurt you."

"Why is that the only thing I hear from everyone?"

"Because we read the news. Because I have a 'transgender' Google alert now, and shitty things are always in the feed. Because people are crazy." Because we care about you.

"I have the same google-fu as anyone else, and the majority of the stories are good. Trans professors, teachers, parents, lawyers, actors, actresses, models. You name it and all totally conquering the world. I am happy being me. My glass is half-fucking-full, I do not exist to be your tragedy," she says. "I'm not stupid. I knew what to do. If that guy hadn't taken no for an answer, I would've hung out next to the girl at the counter until he left."

"But what if he was waiting for you outside? What if he had friends with him?"

"You're worse than my mom," she says. "She worries all the time. It's all I ever hear. 'What if, I'm just saying, you're not thinking . . .' Look, you see these boots?" She tips her beat-up knee-high leather boots my way. The same ones she was wearing when we met, back when they were shiny and new. "I'm wearing the heels down from stomping all over town because when I'm frustrated or mad or whatever, I'm off. I walk. I clear my head. I bump into people. I make eye contact. I go on my way. I do it alone. When I walk, I feel free." She puts her foot back down with its twin. "Let me enjoy being myself."

"Okay" is all I say.

We start moving again.

"Maybe it's different for you because—"

"Because I'm ugly as fuck?" I spit out. "Maybe it is."

"No, no, no. I wasn't going to say that, anything like that, I swear." Jamie holds my arm. Her fingers are freezing, I can feel them through my coat because her touch is electric. "Maybe it's just you're so big, you don't need to be afraid."

Bullshit, I want to scream.

Bullshit.

But of course I say nothing.

We stop walking and pause. The ground is thick with wet leaves glued to the edges of the sidewalk.

Operation Tattle Ye Not, Neighbors has begun.

Once out of the park, we land in a gully that steers the rain runoff into the sewers and walk along the drainage line until we hit the alley of unfinished road that runs directly behind my house. Mostly gravel and dirt with giant muddy potholes, which is good for us. No cars, not ever. We walk side by side, quiet again but with concentration, until we hit my backyard. I pick up Jamie, my massive bag full of glass bottles that I've been lugging like a pack mule, and help her and the beer over our chain-link fence and into the wet lump of turf we call a yard, then we split up for tactical reasons.

I go all the way around the block, pop out of the alley, turn right, and keep going until I cruise up my front walk, take out my key and open the door. No harm, no foul. Hi, Swanpoles. I'm home by six o'clock. Text that to my mom.

So funny, the last thing my mom said before she left for Pittsburgh was "It's a school night. If you're going to binge-watch something, keep it to only four episodes." That and "Shave that thing off; it looks ridiculous."

And now that Jamie and I got the beer, shaving my beard off is the only thing I can think about. Not that I have anything to compare it to, but it was the shittiest beer run I've ever been on. I go to the back door and let Jamie in. She's just as cold, if not freezing. That skirt has to be drafty.

It's weird: a month ago the only thing I would've focused on is what's underneath the skirt and now I don't care. I'm only worried about whether or not she's warm enough.

I leave Jamie in the kitchen to unload the beer and aim for the bathroom. "Dylan?" she calls after me. "Little help here?"

"Be right back," I say as I head straight for the box nailed underneath the mail slot. I pick through all the letters. Nothing but a bunch of junk mail. How long does it take to check some hormones in a blood test? Seriously. Takes forever apparently, it's been five days. Five. I leave the mail in the box and shut myself inside the bathroom because I can't stand my beard. I need it off my face. Time to get rid of this itchy, scratchy reminder of everything I don't want to be. As soon as I close the door, I exhale at my reflection in the mirror.

I throw the glasses off. They hit the bathtub with a clunk and skid rattling into the drain. I turn on the water in the sink and lather up.

I'm fifteen years old. I want to be carded.

My face sheared, I breathe a little easier and pat dry with a towel. I slip off the sports coat and plunk it on an empty hook. Jamie wedges the door open with her toe, two bottles in each hand. "Oh no, your beard is gone."

"So?"

She hands me the full bottle. It's cold. Ice cold. Every ad I've seen since I was a baby has made beer in glass bottles out to be nectar of the gods. It's amazing, the happy music and bikini girls won't let you forget it. You will drink it and have a party. So, here we are, our plan executed to perfection, and I don't want it. It's unearned. I put it on the bathroom counter and leave it there.

She puts her unopened bottle next to mine.

The chill in my bones from walking through all that frigid slop makes me sink. Jamie glances about the room, but not in an "oh wow, I really like the tiles, they're so beige" way. It's more of a maybe-I-should-leave face. Perhaps she's already mapping out her escape route and the mileage she's going to put on her boots walking home.

I don't want her to go. I never do. The thought that she might sucks.

Corroborating her observations might help. That always

worked in biology lab last year. "I do know I'm hideous. I just don't know what to do about it," I say.

"Oh come on, Dylan, don't make me feel worse, I know what I said was mean," she says in a blur. "It's a certain look and you make it work, I swear on a stack of . . . whatever's not blasphemous."

"It's okay; I am aware." I gesture to myself, trying to laugh and holding up my hands, furry side out. "What I want to know is what do I do with it all? My whole everything. I'm a throw rug. You might think it's dumb, and maybe it is, but I hate being so hairy. It's everywhere. The last time I saw my skin, it was screaming red and scaly from a bad wax. And that's just one thing that bugs me."

"You don't like being hairy? That's the big deal?"

"It's mostly just gross. Feels like it's endless."

"It's not a death sentence. If there's something you don't like, work it out." She scans the room, thinking. "Let's fix it right now." Jamie grabs my electric razor and clicks it on with a bzzzz. "Shall we?"

My neck tightens. "I don't want you to see my back. It's disgusting and I hate it."

"But this is such an easy tweak, it's stupid." She shakes her head. "Besides, confession time, I'm mildly curious what you'd look like without a pelt. We're friends, right? So it's no big deal."

We're friends, we're friends. That word is starting to tick me off and it shouldn't. Friends hang out, friends get beer when their mom is gone. Friends shave each other's backs. Oh my god, what are we doing?

But I trust her.

I stare at the buzzing razor. "You know how to use one of those things?"

"Let's just say the one I got for my thirteenth birthday is legs-only now."

"Right. Okay." I fumble with the buttons on my shirt and dump it in the hamper. Reaching behind my back, I grab my undershirt and pull it forward, folding it over the side of the tub. I look up at Jamie. This is the first time she's seeing the full effect. Everything is thick. Dense. She flinches. I want to hide. "I told you it was bad," I say.

"No, no. It's all good. Friends help friends." The razor comes down and cuts a swath from the back of my neck to my shoulder blade. "See? Going great."

A disgusting blob of back hair falls on the floor. "Nope." I reach for my shirt. "This is too gross, no way."

"Don't look." She makes another pass. "It'll be fine. We'll get the Shop-Vac later."

I pretend it's completely normal to watch clumps trickle down like deformed little black snowflakes. That all kids our age do this when no one is home. It's not sex, drugs, and rock and roll that teenagers seek in the abandoned dusk of twilight; it's a guy sitting on the side of a tub while a girl kneels on a toilet and shaves his back.

Halfway through, Jamie sighs and drops her yellow scarf on the sink. "Getting hot in here," she mutters, and taps the head of the razor clean. In the mirror, I see her wipe her brow and grimace. Determined to finish the job and attacking my shoulders, my arms, my sides, like I'm the biggest hedge in her yard. She dumps her jacket and steps out of her boots. Her hands skim the width of me. Gliding as she works. By the time Jamie's done, she's glowing and pink. Hands on hips and satisfied.

"Done," she says, winded. "Honestly, I didn't mind the way you looked before, but don't mind it much now either."

I stand up. She did a great job. Pivoting in the mirror, I nod my approval. This is way better than when I got waxed for Splish-Splash. Looks natural. Just the right amount of chest hair, arms no longer look like a flattened family of squirrels. On my back I have two distinct scapulas. Pretty cool. "It's so much colder," I say.

Jamie blots her forehead with the corner of her scarf. "Yeah, well, I'm a sweaty mess. Enjoy until we need to do it again."

"You'd do that?"

"Sure. I'll shave your back, and you can . . . Hmm. We'll figure something out."

I hold my hands out. There's a freckle on the back of my hand I never knew was there before. The hand is topped by clean fingers and knuckles. They wiggle and I move my arms through space. Up and down, like I'm pushing something high above my head and pressing it low again. Bending my elbows, I twist side to side to check my biceps. Everything is bare. Air hits my skin like molecules of ice. Little goose bumps erupt and I shiver. When I look up, Jamie's staring intently at me. "What?"

She swallows. "Just happy to be here."

"I'm jealous."

"Why?"

"Because you're happy. I mean it when I say I think

you're a warrior. I don't think I could just stomp through the world and be like, fuck it, I'm taking a walk. I stomp because I am big and have nowhere to hide," I say. "Can I tell you something?"

"Always."

"There was no football," I say. "Up on the roof. It was never there. I opened the window and got up on the roof and stepped off." I look down because as much as I love her face, I hate seeing pity on it. It's happened before; not in the mood to see it again now. Instead I fiddle with tossing off my one loafer. Easier said than done, and it ends up crammed sideways under the sink.

When I look up, there's no pity. No sadness. Just Jamie. "I know."

"You did?"

"It wasn't written in stone or anything. But I knew," she says. "You claimed you hate football, hate people thinking you're a football player, but you were trying to get a football off the roof. Didn't add up."

"This doesn't shock you?"

She comes near me and pulls up her sleeves. Raised thin scars line each arm, like razor-edged spiderwebs. "When I say I know, I know. This is me getting my football." She tucks her arms back inside her sleeves and folds them around herself.

"You cut up your arms."

"Well, I mean, it was more like, I don't quite know what to do; maybe this will help," she says. Jamie rubs her arms like she's cold, stopping on one spot and sweeping it with her thumb. "Here's where I thought about going all the way down, letting it all run loose, but I chickened out."

"God, Jamie." I hold my hands out and she rests the back of hers in my palms. My thumbs lightly run across the ragged lines. "I'm so sorry."

"It's okay. I didn't want to be dead; I just didn't want what life was offering at the time. It was like opening hundreds of tiny release valves with an X-Acto," she says. "My mom found out. She walked in on me when I was getting dressed one morning. She saw the cuts. Some of them were fresh. It was not a pretty scene. She flipped."

"Because she loves you."

"It's true, she does. My dad too. It was the worst, darkest time in my life, but they got me help immediately. We began talking about our family. What does it look like? Like they were worried it was going to change me forever, somehow. And I said it looks like every picture we ever took, the ones hanging on our walls in all these cheesy, shiny frames from HomeGoods. Me in the middle. Mom, Jamie, and Dad."

When we met I had no sympathy for the girls in group who hacked themselves up. It made no sense. They were too pretty to have problems. "I never knew."

"You and I didn't go to therapy to swap recipes," she tries to joke.

"I just always pictured you as above it, I guess."

"Above what? Pain?"

"No, like you conquered it. All the things that bother people because you fuck-it stomp it out. Like you're fearless and strong and brave and all of that."

"Don't say that and not see me," she says. "No one lives without fear."

I'm not here, I'm not leaking in front of her. I'm not being some sob story in a bad song performed by untalented douchebags. I'm not falling into the hole I've been stepping over my whole life—I'm not. I don't come up for air. I press it back inside my eyes and blink in my palms.

She finds one of my arms and holds it.

I release my own self and tug the spool of toilet paper, tearing some odd squares and mashing them into my eyes until all I smell is paper fiber and I have to sneeze. "It's okay," she says, after I mop up my slop.

"I'm afraid of myself," I whisper. "I don't want this. I keep growing and growing. I'm a tumor."

"You're not a tumor."

"Then what am I?" My face rises up to meet hers. "Because I'm not a normal fifteen-year-old. I never got to be a kid. I never got to be free. I've always had to deal with being big." I shake my head. "And I just keep getting bigger. I'm going to grow out of control, just like my dad. I'm a living, breathing tumor with a GPA. My body is going to eat me up from the inside out and kill me just like my dad's killed him."

"No, it's not. I looked it up too. Gigantism can be controlled. You'll be fine," she says.

"I'm going to get cancer and be dead at twenty-six, just like my dad."

"Well . . . I hope not." She pauses, standing over me as I sit. "But no one knows, you know? We could walk outside, smell the effing roses, and get hit by a bus. That's life."

"That's life." I rest my head against her hip. She wraps an arm around my shoulder but can't cover the whole of it and settles for the soft spot below my neck. I pick up her wrist and hold it against my cheek. In the quiet of my bathroom, where there's no one in the world but us, I can feel her heartbeat on my skin. She's here. Alive and kicking and I'm so happy she is. I don't want to let her go.

But I do, kissing her scars before her wrist slips away. Sniffing the drips up my nose, I sit upright. She lays her palm against the side of my face, cradling my ear. "Do you think I'm a failure?" she asks in a small voice.

"Never," I say. "Why would you even say that?"

"Because I don't think I'm brave or any of that. I try and try. Do my homework, feed the dog, hug my mom and dad, join the clubs, do all the things, but I'll run into one of those shitty alerts on Google News and it's like, will I ever be enough?"

"You're a good person. That has to be enough."

"Most of the time I brush it off. Get all snappy and stuff, but the tank is only so full, you know? Sometimes I don't feel like talking. Because talking always feels like defending and I'm tired of asking for permission to exist." Jamie rubs behind her ear, scratching the back of her earring. "It gets hard because I like myself, I like my body, and then when someone shits all over it, it feels like I have to start all over. You don't know what it's like to have people actually come up to you and ask, 'What are you?' I mean, what am I supposed to say to that?"

"Don't say anything. Punch them in the face." Despite it all, that's still my fantasy.

"Right, because that solves everything," she says. "No offense, Dylan, but your only major hang-up is about being very big."

"And ugly," I remind her. "And being potentially riddled with lots and lots of malignant cancer that metastasizes to all my bones and organs."

She cracks the smallest of grins. "Okay, fine. But you don't have to field questions like 'Did you get it cut off yet?' And 'You're too young to be making such a big decision. What if you change your mind?' I'd like to think I know myself a little better than some lady at Whole Foods." Jamie tugs on her hair, twirling the same lock of hair the guy touched. "It's why I was pissed at the store when you tried to chase off that creep. He was being gross, but he was honest. Then you charged in. I can't go through life getting rescued."

"I'm not going to apologize for chasing that guy away. I would've done that for any girl in the same situation."

"Really?"

"Really. All we can do is be and hope someone else gets it."

"Someone will love you," she says quietly.

"Someone will love you too."

"You think so?"

"I know so."

Her eyes well up and she turns away from me. Jamie takes some things out of a small zippered bag inside her big bag on the counter and dabs where her mascara's pooled into slick black rims. She catches me watching. "Touch-ups."

I miss her hands. "Do me next," I say.

"Are you serious?" She smiles. Then she pounces. Her

fingertips caress my face, rubbing my skin flat, exploring. "What do you want? A smoky eye?"

I don't care as long as she's touching me. "Whatever you want."

"Let's do swarthy pirate," she declares.

She's up close, her face near mine, and I write a last-ditch letter.

> *Dad—Let me know this is okay. Give me a sign, because I can't take it anymore. It's one thing for me and Jamie to talk until we're blue, but I don't want to talk anymore and this girl is centimeters away and soft. I can smell her. Vanilla and honey. I could tilt my head and brush her chest with my mouth. Please tell me this is okay, because I want to. Tell me I'm normal and this is something that can happen and you'll still be my dad.*

My eyes get gently contorted like clay, but I don't care. Her fingers are warm. I follow all the commands—Blink. Look up. All the way up. Blink. Look down. Look left. Look right—and I want her. I want to grip her hips and pull her down onto me, tear off her shirt and find my mouth on her skin, but I wait. I need my sign. I lick my lips. She licks hers.

"Okay, look," she says.

I swivel my head and burst out laughing. "Oh man . . ." I laugh more. There's black lining my eyes, and mascara, and my eyebrows are all combed and pressed into place. I smolder. My cheeks are dewy and I've even got lip gloss on. It's pineapple.

"You like?" she asks.

I nod. "It's something else."

Jamie takes a step back. "I mean, woof, Dylan. This is a surprise. You are no longer that hulking beast in a wheelchair, no sir."

There is no sign, there may never be one, but I can't wait anymore. I stand up and hold my nose to hers. She holds a hand on my chest. "What are you doing?"

I slide a hand up her spine. "Is this okay?"

"Yes. It is. A lot." Jamie bites her lip. "I didn't want to get my hopes up."

"I kind of always liked you."

"I kind of never stopped." Her hands creep across my bare skin. They settle on the small of my back and lock like magnets. All the atoms fly from the drawer and sink deep inside my chest where they belong as I stare into her eyes.

We kiss.

We kiss and stop, our noses a paper's width apart. Barely a touch, but I want more and I dive into her neck. She gasps, fighting my lips up toward hers. This is the only sign I need. We crash like waves.

There's everything else and then there's Jamie.

TWENTY-SIX

A race. That's the best way I can put it, we're both in a crazed race and I have no idea what the finish line looks like. My hands are all over her, hers are up and down my front and my back and when she skims the sides of my ribs, it tickles and I laugh.

"Sorry," she whispers, a grin inside her kiss.

"Don't be." I kiss her back. And again and again and one more time before I wrap my arms around her and lift her high. We're still in my crappy bathroom. We can't jet off to Tahiti or Paris, but I can whisk her up to my room. She weighs nothing. Either that, or I can't tell what she weighs because I'm so light-headed.

We launch into my blankets. Jamie kicks and giggles as I pile on top of her. My shirt's long gone and now hers is too. The lights are off and the only way we can see each other is with the dim glow from the streetlamp flickering through my threadbare curtains. I look down. Jamie's skin looks like colors of the fading day. She reaches up and touches my cheek, her palm warming me to my bones.

She is beautiful.

I don't want to stop kissing her, so I won't. This is how we'll be forever, tangled up in lips with long kisses and short kisses. Chaste ones you'd do in front of a librarian. Deep, punishing ones you save for when he's off restocking the shelves. Like now.

We're alone. The night is ours. There's no stopping us.

All this amazing skin we have, brushing and colliding together, hot fingertips and sweaty tips of our toes, it's like unlocking a hidden door you never knew existed and finding a path littered with bread crumbs. Once you taste one, there is no way back. You can't forget this. We're never coming home.

In the midst of making out and gripping our shoulders, arms, backs, we go further. Like, further south. Jamie's thumb peeks below the waistband of my boxers. Her painted nails dip inside. She finds me and with one touch, it's like being hooked up to a car battery. I explode.

I'm mortified that it took so little, but Jamie kisses me. Her teeth tweak my bottom lip with a wink. "That was hot," she murmurs.

"Are you sure?"

"Oh yes."

We shift in the bed. Now she's on top, her hair spilling down across my chest as she kisses my neck. It's something I never knew I needed. It's especially incredible now that my entire system overloaded, burst into flames, and is being rebuilt one caress at a time.

As Jamie starts to rub against me, everything of mine is still raw nerves. Her skirt shifts up. I see our matching equipment and I jerk back. Jamie panics a little, tugging down her skirt. "I'm sorry, I was afraid this was a bad idea, it's just, I don't want you to think—"

"Don't apologize," I tell her. "For anything. Come here." And I bring her back so her hair dances across my chest again.

There's only one thing I want right now, and that's to do for her what she did for me, make her feel like the length of her skin is dancing inside a star.

Her eyes spiral up to the blue ceiling I painted for my dad and blink as she shudders. "That was amazing. Like riding a horse without a saddle," she says.

I laugh. Of everything I never expected to hear, that has to be at the top of the list.

"What? I always loved horses; lots of girls love horses."

"I know. I read an article once about how girls transfer their childhood love of horses, because they're big and filled with muscle, onto boys once they get older." I flex my chest and shoulders. "So I guess you've come to the right place."

She groans with a smile, diving face-first into my sternum. "You would bring up some random factoid right now, wouldn't you?"

"At your service. My brain never stops working."

"Hmmm." Jamie leans up and nuzzles my ear. "But it did for a moment."

"An embarrassingly very brief moment, yes." I kiss her. First a kiss that would make your friends gag from too much PDA in the halls. Then I follow it up with one that would be acceptable before saying goodbye at a train station. I am getting good at this.

"What would you do if I made you pancakes?" I ask.

"Eat them."

"Let's go."

TWENTY-SEVEN

She sleeps. I don't.

Up high in my room, under the covers of my bed and beneath my silent blue ceiling, trying to force my eyes to close. It's not working. When they do close, the last nine hours go on instant replay and I pop back awake. Sleeping is not an option right now.

I'm still figuring out all the drifting puzzle pieces. Fragments scattered on the floor in the shape of our clothes. Lying here in the dark and trying to sort it all out is harder than actually messing around. In the moment, all I wanted was her. And I got it. Long after we're exhausted and filled with pancakes, I can't help but dissect the night as I would a frog. Slicing it open with precision and gently peeling back the layers until the guts are exposed.

What I keep going over and over is the one question she asked.

We were deep in the middle of round two. Post-pancakes and back in my bed. Kissing. It was dark and hot under the sheet and she's having fun with me and I'm having fun with her and she goes, "Want to?"

"Want to what?"

She stroked my cheek as she smiled. "Do it?"

Everything ground to a halt. Pebbles and rocks went over the ledge in a cloud of dust. She lay underneath me and peered up, her hair on my pillow in a wave. I can't count how many times I've dreamed of this moment. A girl in bed wanting to do it with me. Instead, a weight sank my stomach. The truth is the truth.

"I'm not ready," I whispered.

"Okay."

"Do you think I'm a loser?"

"No." She shook her head.

"Are you sure?"

"Completely." Her fingers dragged down my back. "Kiss me."

I stopped. "Am I hurting you?"

"Dylan, if I'm ever having a bad day or whatever, just come over and lie on top of me," she said. "You don't even have to get naked. I just want the weight of all things real pressing into my bones. It's intoxicating."

"You're intoxicating."

Jamie arched her back, pushing into me. "When you say that it sounds like thunder."

So I kissed her. More and more. After we watched a movie and went back to bed way after midnight, Jamie drifted off to sleep and I tried to join her.

Since I can't sleep, I watch her and beg the sun to stay away. Give me more time to watch her breathe, to be here where nothing else matters.

Moonlight threads its way in through the blinds and dresses her shoulders in silver. She stirs. I shift back to give her space, and Jamie awakes with a start. "Oh!" She rubs her eye. "I forgot where I was. I was dreaming."

"What were you dreaming about?"

"I have this one dream. It's always the same but different," she says, gradually coming round. "I'm on a plane, but sometimes there's no plane, and I land in a place where I'm supposed to take pictures. Like, dreaming about my dream job, you know? And then I get off the plane. Sometimes I don't know where to go. Sometimes I do. But tonight was different."

"How?"

"You were there when I got off the plane. Then I woke up."

I kiss her on the forehead. "Sounds like a good dream."

"What about you?"

"I haven't been to sleep yet."

"What? Why?"

"I don't want this night to end."

"Aw . . ." She snuggles into my chest. And this is why.

We're quiet. Doing nothing but listening to our heartbeats bounce.

"What are you thinking about?" I ask her.

She lifts her head up and the moonlight coats her face in thin light. "Us."

"Is there an us?"

"I think so," she says in a hush. Jamie turns toward the window to check the night, and I see the vestiges of her XY chromosomes sneaking through but only because I'm making myself look for them. I see it in her bones. I never saw before the day she told me, and I don't really care. Not here with just the two of us in my room, anyway.

If we went away where no one knew us, we'd be free. We could hold hands wherever we wanted and not care what people think, because we're just like any other couple, which we are, but we wouldn't have to answer any questions. We'd get married and adopt some babies. She can go and take pictures, and I can stay at home with the kids while I study and teach classes as an adjunct professor in England. "Come with me to England."

"I'm sorry, what?"

"My dream, my waking alive real dream, is to get the Rhodes Scholarship," I say. "And I'm going to Oxford to get my master's and study, maybe doctorate too."

She laughs with the corner of her mouth. "In what?"

"I have this crazy idea that the spread of cancer has similar wavelengths to historical outbreaks of evil. Like hysteria. And I wonder if it can be tracked down and pinpointed to one gene or one cell. Was it Tituba, the possessed teenage girls, or the people who believed them that began the Salem witch trials? Can you nail down Hitler before he invades Poland? That kind of stuff."

"So you want to give human thoughts to cancer cells?" she says.

"No, I think they already have them. Which is why you

watch people do terrible things in history. The creep of being bad starts slow and builds. Like one idea that people latch onto and let it get this almost magical thinking mentality that they use to excuse what they're doing, you know? And then only after the fact, people are like, oh yeah, that whole Nazi thing was really bad. But the Nazis didn't think so while they were in it. The teenage girls in Salem thought what they experienced was real, but if you break it down, the women who got hanged were mostly widows. The minority," I say. Jamie watches me intently. "Just makes me think that must be what cancer is like. The spread. You start with some cells and end up taking over whole organs and bones. There has to be a connection."

"Whoa." She lies back on the pillow. "That's quite the thing you've thoughted up."

"Thanks. And I love books, so I might do something with English, but nothing serious because all I want is an excuse to read."

"Naturally."

"We can get an apartment, or a flat, whatever they call them, and you can fly to Europe and take pictures whenever you want," I say. "It'll be amazing—come with me. We'll go over and live together. We'll get a cat—"

"We need a cat?"

"I've always imagined studying at Oxford with a cat. Dogs need to be walked; won't have time for that."

"If you don't have time to walk a dog, how will you have time for me?"

"Who said I won't? And besides, you'll be right next to

the rest of Europe; you can zip over through the Chunnel and go to Paris whenever you want. Go to London, hit up the National Gallery. It'll be perfect."

"So I get to be a tourist for four years." Jamie's forehead wrinkles down. "What about our parents?"

"You can't stand your mom. It'll be fine."

"I never said that," she says, all defensive. "All I want is for her to stop worrying about everything. Maybe we can come home after you finish up at Oxford."

"No, we need to stay in England."

"Hey, let's go crazy and play the What Does Jamie Want game because that's fun too. Okay, ready?" Her hands flare. "I want to go roller-skating with you. I want to get pretzels and walk through pretty, lit-up neighborhoods at Christmas. I want us to hold hands and walk down the sidewalk on a sunny day with nowhere to go and no place to be. Just walk."

"Okay. Well. Maybe you can go to college in England the same time I'm there."

"And what if I don't want to go to England?" she says. "What if I want something completely different, like to go to RISD like my idol, Francesca Woodman?"

"What the hell is a riz dee, and who is Francesca Woodman?"

"Rhode Island School of Design. She was a photography major and her work is flipping unbelievable and I love her, but my parents hate that I love her, because she killed herself and that's become a bit of a touchy subject around the house."

"Since when do you have an idol?"

"I've always had one; you never asked."

"Why can't you be England's version of alive nonsuicidal Francesca Woodman?"

"Why England?" she asks.

"Because that's my dream. That's my goal."

"To go write papers on the dangers of magical thinking in cancer cells."

"Do not make fun of me," I warn her.

"I'm not! I love magical thinking. Listen, do you remember when we met? Remember in group I said I made a wish on a shooting star?"

"Yeah." That I actually remember.

Her hands play across the broadness of my chest. "I wished for someone who wanted to just be with me. That's all. To just be."

"I want to be with you."

"Do you?" she asks. "Or do you want to set a course for college that ignores everything else? Because I'm excited about applying and all that stuff, but the path is littered with bodies and I don't want to be one of them."

"It is not that serious."

"Maybe for you, but most people can't sneeze and get an A."

A+, I want to correct her. "But you're smart too," I say instead.

"Lots of very smart people get bad grades. It's intimidating to think your entire life depends on a pop quiz in Spanish. I can't keep up that pace," she says. "So I pick petals from flowers, saying, 'He loves me, he loves me not. . . .' I make wishes at 11:11 and when I twist the clasp of my necklace right side up. And when I see the first and only shooting star in my whole life, I wish that I'll meet someone who just wants to be with me. I made the wish and then I met you the next day." Jamie stares at me, her eyes lighting up all the shadows of mine. "Is it you?"

"Of course it's me."

"Then be here and stop thinking of England."

"But I'm already lying down."

She laughs. "I knew you'd go there."

"That's why we're perfect."

"You think so?"

"I know so," I say. "That's why we'll work it out when we go away to England. Maybe we'll travel and be vagabonds. Fill up passports like crazy. Jump from country to country where nobody knows anything about us and we'll be free."

"Shit."

"What?"

"I should've known this was about me being trans," she says.

"It's not." It kind of is.

"Are you afraid to walk down the street and hold my hand?"

I will walk down any street in England with her; I just don't know about tomorrow here in Portland. "It's just, I had a recent round of crap at school from . . . knowing you."

She covers up the flicker of sadness with a big beaming smile, and I feel like the bottom of a garbage can. "Welcome, straight white boy, to the tiniest taste of the other side of the coin. Unfortunately, explaining that you are the expert on your own life to dumbass ignorant people is a thing. Like, oh hey, not that it's any of your business, but no, just because a guy is dating a trans girl, it doesn't mean he's gay. It means he likes a girl. Is that some of what you got?"

I nod.

"Are you going to leave the coin heads up for all the world to see? Or are you going to flip it to heads down?"

"Heads up." I forbid any more words from escaping because there's a slight possibility the answer is What coin, where? Because I can barely handle being myself, I don't know if I'm ready to be a poster boy for dating a trans girl. Only because of what happened under the sheets. It's a little different and I'm not used to it yet. This is a whole other level of being with another person. We were flipping golden at talking and texting and laughing and hanging out. Then tonight happened. Not what I expected for a first time getting physical with another person. But all recent experiences are too raw to thoroughly examine, so off to the drawer they go.

Everything about her furrows. "Hmm."

"Don't hmm. What's the hmm for?"

"What if this bed were front and center at the mall?"

"People would ask why there's a bed at the mall."

"Ugh," she groans in exasperation. "I meant with us in it."

"What? Why do we need to put on a show at the mall?"

"It's not a show, it's us."

"I'm not getting naked at the mall."

"Who's asking you to get naked?"

"You are."

"No, I'm not."

Now I groan. "Why are we arguing?"

Jamie gives me a little hug. "Maybe that's what boyfriends and girlfriends do," she says. "Besides, I don't want to waste a minute. I really want to be with you, so let's leave it. We don't have to worry about college anytime soon."

"Oxford is another six years away, though; RISD is only two. Maybe we could talk to our parents about going abroad for the last two years of high school and—"

"Dylan," she interrupts me. One leg straddles my body. Hello. "It's three-thirty in the morning. Do you want to talk about college or do you want to make out again?"

I pull her down on top of me and answer this question as best I can.

TWENTY-EIGHT

I wake up covered in hair.

Not mine for once, Jamie's. It's everywhere. Strewn across my chest and my shoulders that have just been shoved and shoved hard.

"There had better be a damn good reason there's beer bottles all over the kitchen and you're in bed together," I hear my mom say.

My heart stops. "Oh my god." I snap wide-wide awake. "Jamie, wake up." Elbowing her, I hope she keeps the sheet clamped down tight. There's a whole lot of dermis under here.

"Mmm?" she murmurs, bleary and crusty-eyed. Then Jamie pops up, clutching the sheet to her chest, seeing my mom standing in the room. "Oh my god!"

I yank a portion back to cover me. "Even he cannot help us now," I whisper.

"You need to get dressed and go home, Jamie," Mom says in a low voice. Her feet slam out of my bedroom, and she yanks the door shut with a bang. Oh shit.

"Are you grounded now?" Jamie sits up and fumbles for her bra.

"No, I am dead now."

Jamie flies out of bed—the bra that took me twelve tries to remove clipped in place with her one practiced snap—and scans the floor for her shirt and skirt. Lucky her, her underwear's on. Mine is hiding and I creep upright, gathering the sheet around me like half a toga, to get a new pair. I've been as naked as I can possibly be with Jamie, and yet I don't want her to see me in broad daylight. I'd like to think everyone has this reaction the morning after, but I don't know.

All dressed, Jamie throws her head down to her knees and shakes her hair out, combing it with her fingers. She stands and it tumbles down her back. Ready to go, she waits for me. "I'm scared," she whispers.

"Me too."

"My parents are going to kill me."

"Maybe we can go to each other's funerals."

"Here's hoping," she says, and reaches up to kiss me goodbye.

I kiss her back. "See you soon?"

"That would be awesome, but I'll probably be on lockdown for the rest of forever."

"Send me a pigeon."

"I will. You too." She heads downstairs and turns into the bathroom. Her things gathered and back on, Jamie pauses in the foyer long enough to take one last picture of me before my execution.

"Very funny," I say.

She winks, opens the front door, and escapes.

"Dylan! Downstairs!" Mom immediately yells.

My knuckle jumps into my mouth and I bite it. Fuck. I'd rather have a roomful of cracked-out monkeys rip each and every hair out of my entire body, one by one, than go downstairs and face my mom. There's no postponing this. Only thing I can do is go downstairs, get yelled at, get grounded, and wait for it to be over. And maybe sneak out to see Jamie a couple hundred times so I don't go crazy missing her.

By the time I land in the kitchen, Mom has paced an oval in the floor. Stuck in her very own racetrack.

I sit in a chair. "I thought you were coming home tonight."

"As if that excuses what you've done." She sniffs and grabs a crumpled tissue from a pile on the counter. It doesn't go to her nose or her eyes; instead she squeezes the life out of it. "You didn't return my texts and I knew something was up. I just knew it. I came home early."

"What about your big meeting?"

"You're more important than a meeting. The promotion can wait."

My shoulders sink with guilt.

"I tried to give you space, tried to take a step back, and I come home to my son in bed with a transvestite, no, wait, she's . . ." Mom looks tired. Her eyes flick high as she thinks. "Transgender. I'm sorry, I get confused. Bottom line, you're grounded."

"So it's worse because she's trans?"

"I would ground you no matter who was in your room last night, because you lied to me," she says, simmering. "You said you were going to order pizza and watch TV by yourself, and clearly that didn't happen."

"Fine." I rearrange my face to look more conciliatory. I'm already embarrassed as shit and feel bad she missed her big moment. Just chew me out already.

"Go ahead, be flippant. You are not equipped to deal with this."

"What the heck does that mean?"

"She's a very confused young person with a complicated history—"

"You keep saying that," I interrupt, risking more jail time. "If Jamie were your definition of a girl, would you still say she's confused? Would you keep saying she's complicated? I don't get it. We're no different than any other fifteen-year-olds."

"You have no idea what the world is like." Her fingertips fly to her temples and press so hard, her nails turn white. "And Jamie looks like a tall, skinny boy made out of spindles and wearing a skirt," she attempts to mutter.

"No, she doesn't. She's amazing."

"I'm sorry. You're right, it shouldn't matter. I'm just worried you two will never fit in. It's hard enough for you, Dylan."

"So what? I already know plenty what it's like to fit in nowhere. To make people run away, to have everyone think you're dumb because you can hang a hat on your teeth, to grow up without a dad."

"Don't you dare bring your father into this," Mom shoots at me. "God only knows what your dad is thinking about this up there."

"What would he think?" I ask, barely scraping the air. He had a front-row seat from my blue ceiling.

All she does is shake her head, shake her head.

"Mom?"

"He would not be pleased—that's putting it lightly."

Feels like a knife through the chest. My broken bones throb along with my heartbeat, ricocheting up my spine. "Okay" is all I say.

"It's not okay! Dylan, please, what is going on?" she erupts. "I know you don't have any condoms in your room, so we'll—"

"Waitaminnit, you've been in my room?"

"What can I do?" She throws her arms up. "You're not talking to me; you gave me no choice. I have to look out for you."

"What the hell, Mom?"

"Well, you've officially shed your cocoon, unfurled your wings, and had one helluva time," she says. "There's beer in my kitchen, enough hair all over the bathroom to make a yak a wig, and you just had sex with a girl who has a penis. What else am I to think?"

Dear god, make me a bird, so I can fly far. Far, far away.

"We never drank the beer." It's the best I can do. Jamie and I didn't drink one drop.

"You and I are going to be proactive." Mom clasps her hands. "This isn't how I pictured it, but I guess we'll pick up a carton of condoms now. Maybe they have cases at Costco."

"We didn't have sex," I say.

"You didn't?"

"No."

"Oh thank goodness." She heaves. "I don't mean that in a bad way, I mean it in a you're-still-fifteen-years-old way."

What we did was different. Nothing worse than a hundred million stories I've ever had to listen to at lunch. And I wasn't a hundred percent thinking about it while we were doing it last night, but in the glaring light of day and underneath my mom's microscope, it's starting to shift. Maybe it was wrong. Through my memory, I see Jamie's face in the darkness. In the sunlight, it begins to fade.

My dad. The blue ceiling above us the whole time.

She starts pacing again. "Sweetheart, I love you. Talk to me."

I . . . can't make words.

"I stopped communicating with JP; I'm doing my best to respect your wishes." Leaning against the counter, she looks down at me. It's a strange rarity. "I wish you'd do me a favor and confide in me."

But I don't know what to say. I'm already guilty, I'm only here for sentencing, but Mom is dragging this out and it's making my skin crawl.

"Well." Mom inhales and exhales way slow. "Jamie is really good at doing makeup, you look great the morning after. That's how you know someone has skills."

Oh my god, the makeup. I grab a fistful of napkins and rake them across my eyes.

Mom gets a dishcloth, runs it under the tap, and drips a few drops of soap from the dispenser on the sink. Buffing it together until little bubbles rise, she hands it to me. "Here. You need real soap and water to take off that stuff. Just shut your eyes tight so it doesn't sting."

I don't want to take the dishcloth down. I rub and rub and when I do pull it away, I stare at the black tar ground into the cotton. My eyes burn and I blink. Wiping with the dry side, I don't want to look up. Mom reaches for her bag on the floor and pulls out a book filled with colored stickies and flags. I read the title and want to run, no, fucking swim to the bottom of the ocean and drown.

In bright neon orange letters on a slick electric blue background the title screams, *Be Their Greatest Ally: Navigating Your Child's Sexual Identity*. "So I have this new book that was recommended to me after I found you two at the mall," she starts.

"I'm leaving," I say, and get up from the chair.

"Dylan, wait!" she commands, and stops me from charging out of the kitchen on one leg. "All I want to do is help you."

"You read that on the plane?" What if someone I know saw her reading that?

"I read it everywhere. It's how I knew what 'cisgender' meant, I feel so with it now."

"Oh jeezus."

"Talk to me. Please. I love you for who you are. Always have, always will," she says. "What are we working with here? Are you genderqueer? Bisexual? Is this situational sexual behavior? Are you feeling"—she flips to a giant yellow sticky and the book flops open—" 'the pressures and constraints from heteronormative gender roles'?"

"I . . . yes? I don't know? I'm a fucking big huge man and no one lets me forget it, so maybe?"

"First of all, language. Second of all, you are not a man. Not yet."

"Tell that to the world."

"Okay. Let's try this angle: has possessing these physical attributes made you turn to trans girls?" Mom grips this stupid book like the Bible and won't let me leave.

"That doesn't even make sense." Why can't I just like Jamie? "How long am I grounded?"

"We'll get to that."

"How long am I grounded!" I yell.

"Sweetheart," she says softly.

"Mom. Please." I don't want to talk about this. Definitely not now and after last night, probably not ever.

The metal clang of the mail slot yanks our heads toward the hallway. It's something we're both anxious about, and the rubber nubs of my crutches squeal in a race to get there first. An assortment of envelopes huddles in the box and I snatch them all. Bill, bill, junk mail, letter from the hospital addressed to me. "It's here," I say.

"Open it!"

My results. The answer to all my problems. All this mindless psychobabble from Mom's book can rot in hell; all I want to know is when's the date of my MRI and subsequent surgery. I want to put being the fucking Beast behind me forever.

I read it. I read it again.

Mom tugs at my arm. "What's it say?"

"There are no elevated levels of GH and IGF-1. We can therefore con-

clude there is no biomedical confirmation of acromegaly." I can't believe it.

"What does that mean?"

The letter slips from my hand and trickles to the floor. "I don't have it," I say. Dull weight pulls me down. "I'm not a giant. I'm just . . . big."

She throws herself on me and squeezes. "Oh, thank god!"

"I need to sit down."

We get to the stairs, and my head sinks as far as it can go in between my knees. Mom tells me to breathe, but all I can hear is a loud high-pitched ringing. She blankets me in a hug and it's too much. I'd move, but I don't want to take the chance of accidentally hurting her again. Mom says things. Disjointed, unfortunate things that make no sense.

There's no surgery. There's no benign tumor. There's nothing to blame. I wanted acromegaly. Even if Jamie or my mom tells me I'm fine the way I am, I still wanted a culprit to point to. I wanted a Most Wanted poster with the word CAPTURED scrawled across my pituitary in bright red ink. I didn't get my wish. It's just been me all along and I will only get bigger until the day I magically stop. When I broke my leg, Dr. Jensen said I still had a bit more growing to do because my epiphyseal bone plates had yet to ossify. To which I said, well shit.

Rising to my foot, I'm careful not to jostle Mom. She's asking me to sit, to talk, to hear, to share, to do all these things I am not capable of right now, so I apologize and leave. There's only one place in the house to go and that's where I head, down the stairs to the basement, where I hop across the floor of hidden chunks of broken glass. Stabbing and piercing and I don't stop until I get to the train set, where I collapse to the concrete and wedge myself in a corner laced with cobwebs.

The village is stagnant. Nothing's changed since I was last here.

My dad built this.

My dad was six foot, seven and three-quarter inches tall.

I measured myself last week as a last hurrah and I was six foot, six and a half inches tall.

I've almost caught up to him. Mom was so proud we're almost the same height. I think it's a punishment.

Last night Jamie said she doesn't care how big I get. She said she's excited that she can wear whatever heels she wants and she'll still be the short one. Thinking about it now makes me smile. And then not smile.

I lean against the wall.

Before I kissed her last night, I asked my dad for a sign. I didn't get one. He never talks to me the way he talks to Mom. But maybe he knew what was coming and he backed out of the picture a long time ago. Maybe he saw what happened and he's disappointed.

"Dad," I whisper in the shadows. "Please, please give me a sign if I did something I shouldn't have. Please: now."

I wait and listen. I count to ten.

I'm about to give up when a loud bang hits the kitchen floor above my head and my eyes fly up, heart racing, to stare at the spot.

"Sorry!" Mom calls out from above. "Dropped a pot. You want some raviolis, sweetie?"

"No," I yell up. The spot above looks hollowed out and frozen from where the pot hit. It sends a shiver down my spine that doesn't come from the cold basement wall. My dad is disappointed in me. That's why he doesn't talk to me. Maybe all along he was saying, *Don't do it.*

But we did.

And now I've lost my dad.

TWENTY-NINE

My parents didn't kill me!

I told them I was with a friend, not a lie, and then we fell asleep. Also not a lie!

I'm grounded for a week b/c I didn't call and tell them I was staying over and I'm grounded for another week b/c it was a school night.

How about you?

Dylan? Was your phone taken away?

You must be grounded way long.

It's been four days. I miss you so much.

I'm telling myself you're in the biggest trouble ever and have no means of communication.

Not trying to be a needy gf, I swear!! It's just been a week and I haven't heard from you.

I'm afraid to go to your house.

Can I come over?

I'm coming over.

It's been a little over a week since Jamie and I have spoken. She texts me at least ten times a day, but I don't respond.

When the doorbell rings, I'm not surprised. It takes a while for me to hear it from all the way down in the basement. I get up from the train set, pick up my crutches, and go to the storm window that gives the slightest view of the sidewalk. I think I see some bike tires sitting patiently in the early winter rain. December's a miserable month. Always damp and cold. The doorbell rings again. A few minutes later my phone beeps. I check the message.

Are you home? I'm outside. Can we please talk?

Wiring for Hobbyists. It's a good little book, very thorough. Can't quite say it's a page-turner, but it's been helpful. The electrical system still won't make the jump from one signal box to the other, and I can't figure out why.

As I read and Jamie waits on the front step, I tell myself a series of half-truths:

1. Mrs. Swanpole never leaves her house and will tell my mom if I answer the door.

2. I'm still grounded. (Mostly.)

3. I didn't hear her knocking until it was too late.

My pliers are too small and these wires are missing their coating; I can't tell which is which. Fingers are aching down here in the frigid basement. I still can't believe my dad built all this and it pushes me to turn the page in the book and read about adapters. Maybe it's the adapter.

Putting the book down, I rub some heat back into my hands. I take a sip of black coffee from the mug I found buried way back in the cupboard that says WORLD'S GREATEST DAD and marvel at this tiny town. Wiring a train set shouldn't be this hard, but it is.

I get another text.

My heart, it says. *It's breaking.*

I glance around the spotless basement. My home of late. Everything is clean, I made sure of it. The door to the boiler room has brand-new hinges; it's perfectly hung. All the broken glass is swept off the floor, and the larger pieces from the cracked mirrors are neatly placed in piles waiting for their proper disposal.

The wooden table the train set sits upon is repaired. Dad's tiny town has all-new grass with little trees and flowers. It's perpetual spring. The landscape is way more full than before because I added more hills. Bucolic and stuff. Underneath, I constructed the sheets of cardboard and glued them together like a cake before shaping them into a rolling meadow, just like my dad did.

He's watching.

I can feel him these days. Hovering just beyond the borders.

I'm doing everything I can to get Dad to send me a message. He helps Mom find me in the middle of a city filled with thousands of people; he sends her to the mall. He should be able to send me one stupid sign. A lost ball, a bird, a talking cat, whatever. I don't care. I need help to understand.

A line I never expected to see was crossed, and I need to know why.

It's not that I didn't have a great experience. It's that I don't know what to do with it.

Aphra Behn, the British writer who wrote the poem that broke up my English class, "The Disappointment," would approve. Jamie had just as good a time as I did. I can see Aphra on her perch in the heavens, nodding proudly.

That's all fine, but it's my dad up there in the stratosphere that worries me most. He's up there turning his back on her and looking down with disappointment. It's starting to eat me up. His approval, however empyreal, is important to me. I always figured my dad would be on my side, but I can't break through to him.

I know my dad is dead, but it feels like his silence speaks for him. Maybe the minute Jamie touched down on my thigh is when my dad officially gave up on me. I don't know. That night has become very confusing.

Mom wants to welcome any and all of my relationships. She's seen the light and is prepared to proudly support me in any number of various sexual inclinations as I see fit—just hand her the right flag.

There is no flag.

It makes all the zesty conversations Mom's dying to have remain unspoken. Which I'm sure frustrates her no end. Seems like all she wants to do these days is talk about her gay/bisexual/lesbian/pansexual/queer/intersex/intergender/asexual/binary/nonbinary/cis/trans/genderless/hyper-sexed/skoliosexual/third-gender/transitioning son . . . if only he would pick something.

But I don't have to pick anything. I am what I am—a straight guy. Same as always. Only difference is now a lot of items on the Firsts List have been checked off with Jamie.

Mom's relentless need for clarification pushes me deeper into the basement. It's like she can't accept me being straight and finding Jamie under the covers with me. She wants a reason she can cross-reference with her book that she walks around with all the time. The more Mom talks, the more I want to listen for the quiet voice of a dead man. I can brush off all the dumb shit at school (mostly) because those are people who don't know the whole story. All they've got is I kissed a girl on her cheek who was assigned male at birth. Big deal. Scandal wears off after a month when nothing else happens.

But more than that happened, and I need to know my dad is still with me.

And I wonder what might be next because honestly it scares me.

I can't stop beating that night to death. Over and over. Every time I think I'm overreacting and I should just pick up the phone and call Jamie, I get hit with another round of the same worry, the same fears. I mean, she was ready to do it and I wasn't. Will I have to have sex with her just so I don't have to do other things that I already know I won't be okay with? Or should I just get on with it and act like this is normal? Makes me wonder if burying that night and never acknowledging its existence is the way to go, because it's one or the other. Take it, or leave it. Can't be both.

So instead of facing her or my mom, I come downstairs and spend hours in a cold and dark room alone. I need my dad's approval. As improbable as it sounds, I need his advice. Mom doesn't understand that the only way he can talk to me is through the train set.

Two feet wearing boots walk slowly down our front walk and hit the kickstand of a pink bike with a basket and tassels flying off the handlebars. I stay down here and wait. My ears and eyes are open. I'm listening.

THIRTY

I joined the football team.

Two reasons. One: Who gives a shit? It's okay that I publicly admit I like football. Just because the world sees me and instantly associates me with football doesn't mean I'm not allowed to like it and play. Scholar-athlete. I can be both.

And two: I joined the day after I overheard my mom talking to my grandma in hushed tones about how leaving her big meeting in Pittsburgh set her career back and she won't be able to ask for a raise for a while and she doesn't know what to do when college comes around. Then she asked Grandma for some money and I felt like garbage. So I went straight to Coach Fowler's office the next morning and he jumped up and hugged me.

Now I have somewhere distracting to be every day after school, and our weight room more than lives up to its name. It is a room and it is full of weights. Machines that you sit on and push and pull things that get progressively heavier the more reps you knock out. In addition to housing beat-to-hell pieces of equipment with chipped white paint and a faded banner that reads STATE CHAMPS 1994, the entire room smells like endless crusty-sock miasma. After a while I don't notice the stench but I'm not sure yet if that's a good or a bad thing.

My leg's still frozen in a cast, so I'm doing upper body. Three days a week, Monday, Wednesday, and Friday. Tuesdays and Thursdays I'm in Coach Fowler's office watching film and getting tutored with the playbook. He gave me a list of names of guys who went to the NFL from the Ivies. He made it abundantly clear there are lots of great colleges out there, but I have tunnel vision and he honored it. I got nervous when he couldn't promise I wouldn't get a concussion, but he said he stresses no helmet-to-helmet contact and that as long as I lead with my shoulders and chest, I should be fine. Besides, my brains aren't my only asset anymore. I'm very much looking forward to hitting someone. Like, a lot.

Offensive line. That's pretty much what I figured, and that's where I'll be for next year's season. Maybe if I get good feet, I'll move on to defense, and that's where I'll really get to murder people, but start slow. So all right, that's what I'm doing. Dr. Jensen reinforced the bottom of my cast with a flat, textured grip, so I can start to put tiny amounts of weight on my leg. I'm supposed to still use crutches and go easy on it, but it doesn't stop me from adding another twenty-five pounds on either side of the three-way row. Everything situated, I lean into the incline.

At first I hated the idea of doing weights. I mean,

seriously, why do I need to build mass? I come pretty close to having my own gravitational pull. But it's really frigging hard. I'm always out of breath. Turns out, I am in terrible shape from sitting on my ass and doing nothing for years.

Coach Fowler says if anything, football is going to help me be the right weight, so okay, I can deal with that. If I have to be the Beast, I might as well do it correctly. It makes me focus on getting through these sessions. I do it for me, I do it for my mom, and I do it for my dad. Maybe he can look down and help us win some games or something. Maybe after I make a tackle, he'll materialize in the stands and poke the guy next to him and say "That's my boy" right before he vaporizes back into nothingness.

I'm done with a set of ten and I take a break. There's a bunch of noise outside and my stomach tightens. People approaching. When there's other guys in here, I can feel them watching me bench out of the corner of their eye. It's weird. One senior said he would kill to be as big as me.

That was weird but I nodded and said, "Thanks."

The din gets closer and the baseball team comes in as one. They're getting ready for spring. I grab my towel and move because I don't want to see JP for anything. Been working overtime to avoid him for weeks, but I'm not fast enough. "Hey, man," JP says, coming over. "What are you doing here?"

"I joined the football team."

"But I thought you hated football?" he asks.

"I have a latent predilection for violence."

I move over to the chest press and add more to the puny amount already stacked. Two hundred and fifty pounds. I give JP a look. There's no way in hell he can do that if he tries. I sit down and do two sets of five. "I have more reps to do. Later."

"So . . ."

What the hell, he's not leaving?

"How's things?" he asks.

As if he cares.

"Got any new games?"

Of course he would ask that; he has no concept of living on a budget. Yeah, no, dipshit. No new games.

JP leans in way too close for comfort. "Can I talk to you?"

"What do you want, JP?" I say, low as I can. "You want to use me? Feed me a load of shit so I do something dumb for you because some poor kid didn't pay you back? Well, guess what: those days are over. Whatever you have to say is pretty fucking pointless these days."

"Whatever, dude." JP slips away and I'm alone again.

Fine. He's got nothing. He wants to talk? That's nice, since he's nothing but talk. There's no way he has anything relevant to say, it's him being full of shit as per usual. I keep my head down and steady my hands on the machine. I start to go through the motions and count one . . . two . . . three . . . four . . . , but the background noise deep inside my head wonders what he wants.

THIRTY-ONE

The holidays at my house are always lonely.

In a lot of ways, I blame said house. Mom didn't want to leave it when Dad died, and twelve years later the mortgage is still sucking her dry. It's more important to her to keep the house she picked out with Dad when he was an upstart young engineer than it is to move somewhere else more affordable. So we stay permanently house poor. Some days it seems like a tent on the side of a highway would be most prudent. We don't travel. We don't get on planes and visit relatives back East often, if ever. It's me and Mom and the ghost of a dead man that only talks to her.

She loses it, reliably, either Christmas Eve or Christmas morning, which is the worst because it means the rest of the day gets a shroud draped over everything until at least dinner.

Unfortunately, this year it's Christmas morning.

I knock on her door when she's not up yet, a cup of coffee for her in my hand. After a feeble go-ahead, I enter.

The blinds are drawn and she sits on the bed, sinking into the middle like a bowling ball. "Merry Christmas," she says in a dull voice. Yup, this is Christmas.

"You okay?"

"Yup."

She is not okay.

"I brought you coffee," I say.

"Thank you, sweetheart."

I sit down next to her and we stare at the wall. I've learned it's best not to say anything. In time, Mom sips the coffee. She doesn't need to bother blowing on it; it's plenty lukewarm by now. She does the same thing she always does: turns her head, smiles at me with all the joy of an old shoe left in a puddle, and says, "Just miss him, you know?"

"I know."

"We've been chatting, he and I."

"What's he saying?" Because I don't know. Because it feels like I will never know.

"Afraid that's between me and your dad," she says.

"Does he say anything else?" That no matter what happens, I'll be okay?

"You know you can always ask him anything, sweetie."

Merry Christmas. Here's a punch to the gut because goddammit, I've been asking him things for over a decade and looking for signs in every dead crow and lost penny I see and always coming up with nothing on top of nothing.

She gets up, I follow, and we go into the living room to open presents.

I got my mom a garlic press for Christmas and some new slippers. She got me a gift certificate to our local bookstore, a new pair of shoes, some extra wiring for the train set, and this amazing salmon jerky from a place we like to visit in Astoria. It's seriously fish candy, but it's pricey as hell, so I know what a treat it is. Someday when I'm rich, from football or being brilliant or both, I'm taking my mom to the smoked-fish shop and we're buying the whole store.

It's a good goal.

I have a lot of them now. They are short and don't involve much more than do this, get a small reward. Like a scientific experiment. If you floss today, you get ten extra minutes with this book. If you look ahead and do five problems from tomorrow's homework, you get five more sets of push-ups. Stupid stuff like that. Doesn't matter what it is—it serves a purpose: don't think about Jamie.

We have a few tapes of Dad. I watch them on holidays and my birthday. Not too often. Like if I watch the tapes too much, they'll turn to dust because that's what Mom told me when I went on a bender in the sixth grade. Even though we had them digitally transferred after that, I'm still afraid to take my chances.

I boot up my computer to see him. The clips. Nothing movie length. Nothing longer than five minutes. But there he is, taking up the whole screen. Laughing. Talking, listening. Eating an entire ham in a time lapse and then dabbing his face with a napkin, pinkie up. The ones my mom shot are hilarious because the camera is aimed as high up as it can go and he chuckles because she's still so tiny compared to him. But they love each other, that much is clear. This is why they can still communicate. It makes me feel disastrously whole. And then immediately empty.

The clip of him I secretly did and didn't want to see comes up. There's his buddy goofing around in their frat house at college. Clear and brown bottles and empty red cups lie across the dingy old couch, the coffee table, and the windowsills, and even on top of the curtain rods. Greek letters on the wall. My dad takes up three-quarters of the couch, and his drunk friend tries to crawl across him, misses, and his ass breaks the window. Dad hollers with laugher and states, clear as a bell, "That's so gay."

I pause the clip and rewind. Watch it again.

Was it condemnation? Turn of (stupid) phrase? I can't tell.

I leave the screen frozen on his face, full of life and laughing at his friend's rear end hanging out a cheap, single-paned window.

In time, I turn it all off.

I don't know if I want to see this one when I turn sixteen.

After Mom's perked up long enough to throw a turkey into the oven, I check my phone because if I don't, even on a major holiday, I will curl up in the fetal position. When I check my phone, I imagine a rat in a lab somewhere getting a little pellet every time I click. Today the rat is hungry. I look at the screen and blink. Four texts from Jamie. She wrote to me. I tamp down the leaping in my gut and pretend I don't have all the anticipation of someone else's Christmas morning.

Hey, it's me. I wanted to wish you a merry Christmas.

I left you a present on your front step.

If you take it inside and eat it, then you still think about us.

J.

I get up from the couch and head to the front door. The air is cold and sharp and floods the hallway as I pull it wide. On the front step, as promised, sits a little package wrapped inside a napkin. I peel back the layers. Inside is a pretzel.

The street is still as death. No strange cars, no movement aside from an occasional gust. I look everywhere for Jamie, for her bike. I leave the house and hobble down the front walk, risking a lecture for leaving the door wide open, but Mom's still too steeped in her seasonal depression to notice.

I pick up the pretzel and it's stone cold. Maybe Jamie waited until she was long gone before texting me.

Dad. Now. Give me a sign now.

I rub my arms and look around. I wait for a leaf to smack me in the head or a sudden storm to slam a tree into a telephone pole. Nothing. It's quiet. Maybe there's a delay between here and the afterlife. I decide to make it very formal.

Okay. Here goes.

Hey, Dad, it's me.

I need to know a relationship with this girl is okay because I feel like I've already screwed up by not talking to her and waiting for you and all the rest of it. But you're my dad and you're very important to me, no matter your current somatic state, so if you could please send me a sign in the next ten seconds. Preferably something I can't miss, like a ray of sunshine at my feet or a transformer exploding. Your choice. I'll be right here on the front step you carried Mom over when you first bought the house. I really like Jamie.

There. I said it. I am officially coming out to you; now you know I like her. Tell me you love me. Tell me I'm okay. Tell me we're okay. Give me your blessing.

I count to ten and nothing happens.

No sunshine. No overloaded electrical wires. No sirens, no fires, no fluttering leaves.

I peel off a piece of the pretzel, almost exactly half. One half I put back into the napkin and the other half I bring inside the house. The front door is once again shut and locked behind me and I climb the stairs to my room, where I put the pretzel on my desk.

When I get my sign, I'll eat it. Even if I have to wait forever. Except I didn't hear from my dad, so the pretzel sits.

Maybe he's busy.

THIRTY-TWO

I'm back in the old weight room. Go figure. But as far as stuff to do after school is concerned, it's nice to be a part of something. The guys on the team that I've met so far seem real happy about next season, and now I have a whole new thing to worry about: sucking at football and letting everyone down. No pressure.

My stomach freezes up when I think about it, but I'm trying to look at it like anything else school related. Go to class, do the work, study. So I'm sitting on a rank fold-out plastic mat and trying to touch my toes in the name of flexibility. This is seriously the worst thing ever. Well, almost. Debilitating confusion trumps all. And my dad still won't give me a sign.

I stretch forward as far as I can and graze my shin. If the dead harbor emotions, do they do it daily? Like, is my dad watching and going, *Way to go,. kiddo—those hamstrings are almost as loose as cinderblocks!* or is he like radar, so he can only respond with direct contact from approved earthly residents? I've been beating myself up about this forever now, but I still can't get over why Mom and not me? The train set is perfection, my grades are impeccable, I know the difference between an off-tackle and a slant. I should be every father's dream son. Other than the obvious (he's extra super dead), I don't know why I can't get one single frigging clear sign from above.

People come in and out of the weight room all the time, so I don't notice when the door swings wide, or even when someone sits on the same row of mats to stretch. "Want a towel?" JP asks.

My head jerks toward him. "No."

"Look, I'll show you a trick we learned at baseball camp." He takes a towel, lassoes the balls of his feet, and holds on with two hands. "This works real good." A few minutes pass, him bent in half and holding on to the towel, before he grunts with a finish and sits upright. "Here." He holds it out to me.

"Thanks." I take it and put it down.

Everything about him is round as a pill bug. All tucked in and hunched. "New Year's came."

"Does that every year."

"What'd you guys do?"

"Me and my nine thousand friends? Nothing." Rub it in, asshole. You're the guy everyone loves and you threw a huge party at your aunt's house, and tons of people came and told you how awesome you are. Just like last year. I was there.

"I meant you and your mom," he says.

"My mom? What do you want, JP?"

His perfect hair shimmies as he shakes his head. "Just saying hi. Trying to." He cracks his legs wide forty-five degrees and leans forward. "I hate this—it fucking burns."

"It's not supposed to burn."

"Oh yeah?"

"If it hurts, you're doing it wrong."

"Shit," he says.

"Are you being serious, or are you messing with me?" I ask.

"See? You can't even tell I'm for real, that's how long it's been. Come on, man, look, January came and went, and I made some resolutions. One of them is catching up with you."

I stare at him. "Whatever."

"I miss hanging out."

"That's . . . nice." If it's sincere. I sneak another look at him. Maybe he is? He's all slumped over and hangdog forlorn. Could be an act but I can't tell. I honestly have no idea who he is anymore.

JP gets to his feet, stretches his quads, one-two, and goes near the lat pull. "How does this one work?"

"You sit on it and pull the handlebar down." Rocket science.

"Let me see you do one."

"Nah, I got to stretch."

"Come on, help me out. Spot me. My coach says I need more power at the plate."

I don't move.

"My season starts in like two months. Help a fellow St. Lawrence Lion out."

"Fine." I get my crutch and hike up to my good foot. One more day and I get this cast off my leg. Just one more day and I can take a real shower and a real bath. JP waits on the machine and I amble over and put fifty pounds of plates on. I have no idea what he can pull, so let's start small. "You sit, like what you're doing, yeah. Grab on, and pull down," I say. "Bring your chest to the bar, like that, and keep your elbows pointed down. Pull from your armpits."

We go through the rest of the gym. I show him everything I've learned, all the form and stuff I'm working on. Lats, biceps, triceps, neck, stomach, and he does okay on all of them for his first pass. When he's done, I actually freaking smile at him. Can't help it. Old times sneaking in. Maybe the resolutions he made are working.

I sign off with Coach Fowler and hit the locker room. JP massages behind his neck. "I'm going to be so sore tomorrow."

"You get used to it." Popping my locker open, I stall at taking my clothes off the hooks. Years of him laughing at my back, my arms, my legs, you name it, ring in my ears. I seize the clothes and get dressed. Fuck it. Let him laugh. He's right: things are going to change. When scouts come to St. Lawrence, they'll be coming to see me. Not him, me. Starting left tackle, number sixty-five. The Beast.

I slam the locker shut.

When I get my crutches and stand, he's there waiting for me. "What?" I grumble.

"Nothing. Wanna go?"

Maybe I am being a dick. JP and I leave the locker room and head toward the lobby. We tread silently through the dark mezzanine and down into the foyer by the double doors leading outside. It's one of those days where the gray sky is blinding. No rain, no sun, but the threat of both. Light streams through the glass windows above the doors. JP punches the doors open. It's like walking into a klieg light while my eyes adjust.

My eyes water as I blink, scrambled rods and cones struggling to adjust.

A voice I will know until my last living day gasps. "I don't think I'm ready for this," she says.

"Jamie," I say.

Her bike clatters to the sidewalk.

"Oh, good. You're here." JP skips down the steps, lighter than cotton candy, and slings an arm around her shoulder. "How was school?"

THIRTY-THREE

Jamie's eyes are as big as mine.

We stand opposite one another in shock, my crutches shaking inside my hands. It's her. I'm happy, I'm panicked, I want to hug her, I want to hide, but it's too late now. We're locked in the same square concrete grid on the sidewalk. She inches backward, wavering on her toes to run. The only thing that stops her is JP clamping her in place.

His arm around her, her camera with a new purple strap. For Christmas? A present? I want to punch him into next week. "Are you two together now? What is this?"

"Seriously? That's the first thing you say?" she asks.

I swallow a blob in my throat. "Hi, Jamie."

"We're not going out." JP releases her and they take a step apart. "We found each other."

"He found me," Jamie clarifies.

The weather changes and mist starts to fall. I want to wrap

her up and breathe inside the crook of her neck, but I can't. Those days are gone. Seeing her kick-starts every ache I've been pretending doesn't exist and they explode all at once. My fists spasm and I have to squeeze them together like I'm clutching two Ping-Pong balls to my stomach. There's so much I want to say to her, but all that fades like winter sunshine. I can't bring back what's gone. Jamie stands next to him, beautiful as ever. She catches my eye. We stare at each other a good, long minute.

"JP and I are friends," Jamie says.

"I call bullshit. He wants something."

"Huh?" he says, all innocent.

I ignore him and talk directly to Jamie because if I so much as see him in my peripheral vision, I might just go to prison after all. "JP never does anything without trying to get something in return. It's the only thing he knows."

"Not anymore," he says. "Like I told you in the weight room. New Year's. I made resolutions."

A thousand pounds of shit in a JP-shaped bag. "Jamie, can I talk to you? In private?"

"Not without JP," she says.

"What?"

"Don't you 'what' me, Dylan, because I swear to god, you're lucky you have one person willing to fight for you, because I'm done."

"That's not what you said," JP whispers to her.

"Yes. It is," she shoots back at him under her breath.

"But you're here," I say, stumbling with shock.

"Yeah, she is because she's fucking awesome as shit," JP butts in. "Look, dude, you can be mad at me forever, but what you're doing to her is frigging stupid. And like seriously, when you're all straight up miserable like this, you're a black hole of suck. You're bringing down the whole school. One giant, kinda literally, downer fest. It's obvious you like her, you'd do anything for her. Everyone knows it; we can all see it. Just get the hell over it and apologize for treating her so shitty so we can be all good again."

Fuck JP. She's here, and I talk to her and her alone. "Jamie, you and I—"

"There is no you and I!" she yells. "Did you know I couldn't speak for days? How I fell to my knees in the shower and cried so long, my mom came in because she thought I drowned?" Jamie bites down so hard, dark purple dents dot her lower lip. "You have no idea how much I tortured myself over that stupid pretzel. Who eats half a pretzel? What the hell am I supposed to do with that? I should've never gotten that stupid thing. All it did was make me cry all over again."

"I didn't know what to do with it."

"So you split it in half to mess with me? I didn't know if you would call or not, if you wanted to see me, talk to me. Why did you only take half?"

"I needed some time."

"If you need some time, then you sack up and tell a bitch."

"It's just that—"

"You're all rambling on and on about the genesis of evil in cancer, like it's some Nazi plague with its very own Hitler or something, and then you turn around and pretend we never happened?"

I want to tell her about my dad. "I didn't—"

"Oh yes you did." She hugs herself. "I thought there was more in you. I trusted you. But it turns out you're ugly, inside and out." Jamie tilts her eyes toward the precipitation and tucks her camera safe and dry into her bag. "This is a nightmare. I'm going."

"Wait, wait, wait!" JP jumps in front of her, stopping Jamie from picking up her bike. "You said you'd give me ten minutes and we have six more to go."

"What the fuck is going on?" I bark at him.

Jamie walks a wide circle around JP and stands toe to toe with me. She reaches inside her bag and hands me a postcard, a black-and-white photograph of her lighting a piece of paper with Russian and Chinese and French and Spanish words scrawled all over it. The only one I recognize is *amor,* a smoky haze all around her head in a fog. I flip it over and read:

Jamie McCutchen
A One-Girl Show
February 12–20 at Café Crossroads

"I have a show coming up. You know, for all those photos of mine you never asked to see. Maybe once you get your head out of your ass, you'd like to come. JP paid for the mats, frames, and everything."

"Her photographs are amazing," he says.

"Wait, what? You've seen them?" For some reason this greatly pisses me off.

"Hey, you had your chances. It's not like I was hiding the

fact that I'm really into photography. JP at least showed an interest in what I do."

"JP did all that so you'd come today; do you not see how effed up that is?"

Jamie stares a hole into my head.

"Her pictures really are amazing, no joke. I just . . . I don't know any other way," JP says. "I had to do something. The past forever has sucked. Sue me, but I miss the old days."

"I don't believe a word you say." I want to spit, the taste in my mouth is so bad.

"You really should hear him out. Of everyone here, JP is the only person willing to make it work with you." Jamie goes to JP's side and stands with him. "He's a really good person."

"She's a really cool girl," JP says. "And the happiest I've ever seen you is when you were with her, even if it was just on that one day for like one minute. I thought if you saw Jamie one more time, you'd get a second wind or something."

"This isn't a boat race. You're only making things worse," I say.

"Oh, because you're the hero in this scenario? Yeah, okay. Sure," Jamie says.

"You can be bought," I tell her. "So you're no better than me."

"Don't try that holier-than-thou crap with me. You're the one who went around breaking faces. I'd never ever go around beating people up for candy and controllers and whatever else."

"That was a long time ago. I don't do that anymore."

"I can't believe I fell for a bully."

"Whoa, hold on here. This is not how it was supposed to go down." JP dances in between us, cutting the air up with his hands. "You were supposed to finally say all those things you were dying to tell him. He was supposed to say he was a dumbass and ask for forgiveness, and that's supposed to ignite the flame, get some sparks back, so you guys are both happy and Dylan and I get to play video games and hang out again. I'm bringing you two together. That was the plan."

"That's not what you told me, not even close," Jamie snaps. "You said Dylan had a revelation and was too screwed up to text me. Obviously he had no idea I was coming."

"It's true, I didn't. If you guys are gonna be best buds, then get used to him saying a whole lot of mixed-up, twisted shit, Jamie. . . ."

"Look, I'm trying to be better, I swear," JP pleads. He touches his perfect face, his hair, his chest. "I know what I look like and how to use it. I'm locked inside a box I didn't ask for."

"Oh, boo fucking hoo," I say. "How sad for you, JP, being so goddamn pretty. Must be so tough when the world throws itself at your feet; you must stub your toes all the time."

"Go ahead, laugh it up. You think I've got it so good? Everyone's got problems. I know how easy it is to just frigging smile at someone while you're asking them to do something. And then they do it? It's like this weird superpower."

"For a super villain," I add.

"Whatever, fine. All these tricks—I can't unlearn it in a day. Give me a chance."

"I never should've let you talk me into that pretzel idea," Jamie mutters.

"Wait! The pretzel was JP's idea?"

"You refused to talk to me!" Jamie shoots back. "I didn't know what to do. At least JP was there and listened to me, heard me out. He was a friend; where were you?"

"Yeah, man, you can't treat girls like that," he says.

"Oh my god, I can't even, my ears, I'm hearing things," I ramble. "You're telling me how to treat girls? Am I in an alternate universe? But okay, fine, I do want forgiveness, I do want—"

A timer goes off. "Yay, I'm done," Jamie says, hitting a button on her phone. She gets her bike and whirls it around. "Are you coming?" she asks JP.

"Even after everything you know about JP, you want to go with him?"

"He's at least trying."

"And I'm not?"

"Stop. Just stop," she says over her shoulder.

"You don't know what you did to her," he says.

My forehead's all damp from the flying mist that's finally letting up, and I flick the water to the ground. "Yes, I do. I broke her heart."

"Oh, Dylan . . ." Jamie laughs. A hollow, empty laugh. "You were always so worried about people hurting me. Then you go and hurt me more than anyone in the entire world. You didn't just break my heart; you stabbed me in the kidneys with rusty knives so that every time my heart pumped, it sent nothing but toxic shit through my veins. I can't even stand looking at your face."

"You can stand it for ten minutes so you can get a show at some café. And this one?" I point at JP. "If he changed, even the littlest bit, he'd sponsor your show because you two are the most awesomest awesome friends ever. Not because he needs a favor."

"Dylan, wait a minute. . . ." JP hops near.

Years of backed-up anger comes pouring out. The miserable things I did just so I'd have a place in this world. "Just be quiet." I get over him and leer down. "You treated me like a dog my whole entire life. I do a trick so you throw me a bone. I hate your fucking guts, JP."

He covers his neck and Jamie separates us. "Leave him alone. He said you choked him in the cafeteria. You can't do that. Like, ever," Jamie says.

"Oh my god." I spin in a stupid circle, cursing up at the sky. "Yeah, I did almost choke him. Did he tell you why? Because he wanted to embarrass me for being with you."

"JP said he was publicly supporting our relationship in front of the whole school."

I can't even look at him. "That's what you told her, JP? Neat. You know what, Jamie? You got a real sweet deal here. You get a piece of your dreams fulfilled. I have memories of busting kids' faces for the rest of my life."

"Get over yourself, Dylan," she says. "And do shut the fuck up."

JP stands torn between us. Looking at me and then looking at Jamie. "Seems like this was the king shit of all shit ideas," he says. "I thought we could all figure something out. Seems like I was way wrong. About everything."

He follows Jamie and they leave together.

"Wait," I say, wanting to stop her.

Jamie slowly turns around. "You know what I think when I look at you, Dylan? How can someone so smart be so stupid?" She grips her bike even harder. "Let's go play video games," she says to JP.

I lean into my crutches and watch them climb up the slight hill next to the football field. In all this shitty mist, I feel like the world is taking a cold, wet dump on me. I'm this close to running. She thinks I'm the asshole of the universe. Fine, I deserve that, but she got to say her piece and I never got to say mine. About how much I missed her and thought about her every day. She needs to know. Launching myself after them, I race on one leg to get there and do something, say something brilliant, to keep her from going home with him, when the sky changes. The sun sneaks just enough through the clouds and my mouth drops.

"Motherfucker," I mutter.

Careening over them, in a big, happy bank of color, is a rainbow. A bright, shiny, and twinkling-with-every-meager-speck-of-light-in-the-spectrum rainbow. My sign from above. After all these weeks, Dad finally sent me THE SIGN. *Let her go,* he says.

So I do.

I turn around and head for home.

I let her go.

THIRTY-FOUR

My room isn't as warm as I'd hoped. My back hurts from dragging home mountains of homework and I'm cold and wet. Not to mention, I have nowhere to put all the things clamping my arteries shut with emptiness. I don't know how else to explain it: it's like all my blood stopped moving. Which explains why I'm freezing, I guess.

But I finally got my sign, so it's time to shut up now. I'm going to do the same things I've done for the past several weeks. Eat, sleep, do homework, try to forget Jamie, and lift shit. Only bright side will be getting my cast off tomorrow.

I exhale.

That's honestly the only thing I have to look forward to. After that, I don't know. Maybe taco night.

Night falls and I try not to think about them. I can only hope JP has a heater on in his fort while they play video games. It's getting kind of cold and I want her to be comfortable. There's all kinds of thoughts bubbling up. Me showing up out of the blue and Jamie flying into my arms, the two of us running away. Jamie realizing it was all a mistake, me telling her no, I made the mistake. I want so bad for everything to happen just like that, but I can't run.

Dear Dad, I'm letting her go.

I turn on my computer and update my podcasts. Ooh, the Dyatlov Pass Incident. That sounds interesting. I click on that and collapse on my bed. Five minutes in, I'm hooked. A possible paranormal modern-day incident with likely scientific explanations? Yes, please.

Lying on my bed, I am being as apathetic as possible because if I actually acknowledge things, it will be painful. So I zone out and play a stupid game on my phone. My fingers are too big to do much damage, but I like to beat my mom's score when I can. I'm halfway through Level 5 when my phone beeps. An alert to update Settings. Whatever, that's a quick fix and I'm already losing this game. Might as well do it now. I swipe out of there and into the updates. Security, check. Games, check. Privacy . . . Wait. Hold on. What the hell is uGoiFindU, and why is it buried in the Privacy folder?

I leap up and google it. The first link I find fills me with cold rage. *Install on any phone and track an individual's whereabouts via your device. Does not show on their screen, virtually undetectable. Perfect for parents of minor children!*

It comes up as a cough. My eyebrows cinch together as I stare at the computer. Scattered laughs choke my throat because oh my god. This whole time I've been begging a two-dollar-and-ninety-nine-cent app to talk to me. To love me and tell me everything is going to be okay.

And then I'm furious because are you shitting me? I slam my phone down on the bed. It was never my dad. Mom freaking lied through her teeth! Pacing my room in the ragged remains of my stumpy cast, I'm furious. My mother used a dead man to cover her ass. Telling me my dad can help her find me in the middle of a city with a tin can and a string from his cloud in the sky? This is bullshit. This makes everything I've been waiting to hear from my dad a freaking waste of time. Mom doesn't have a direct line to heaven; she has a shady phone app from the Apple store.

He's not talking to her any more than he's talking to me, which means I don't have to listen to any fucking rainbows.

It was never about fallen power lines and random penguins. What I should've done is freaking talk to Jamie.

When it finally, fully occurs to me, it's like a slap in the face. No, a punch.

I grab a warm sweater and write a Post-It, then leave my phone on the bed with the Post-It slapped on it and head out for the tree house. I can't draw for shit, so there's no picture of a giant middle finger, just a simple sentence for Mom: *Nice try.*

THIRTY-FIVE

Irvington is miles away, no exaggeration. The mist—the freaking miserable, cold-ass mist—won't stop, but by now I'm used to it and I don't care. I have a mission. Get to the tree house. Say things I want to say. See what happens after that.

My crutches slip in the thin puddles and the back of my neck is slick with water, but I keep going. When the houses start to get a little ritzier, I know I'm getting closer. These houses are nice, dream houses even, with two stories and urban farmstead backyards, framed by tall fences whimsically full of reclaimed windows from old houses that bit it long before theirs will. Ideal places to plant roots of all kinds, but they're not Irvington.

Irvington, Knott Street in particular, is full of semi-mansions with three stories and people wearing NPR pledge-drive T-shirts, peering out of double-paned windows and pretending not to judge you. Makes nodding pleasantly at the lady walking her goldendoodle and gripping the zipper of her North Face anorak as you pass along the dimly lit sidewalks a fun experience. Hey! I want to tell everyone. Don't worry, I'm a fifteen-year-old kid. Not gonna club you on the head and rob you blind.

I get to JP's house and stop. It's a corner house. Three stories and fenced in by a stone wall. Taller than me by at least half a foot and every twenty feet a wrought iron light graces a post. I mean, shoot, it's lovely. I want one just like it someday. Except looking at the few lonely lights feebly suggesting the house is a home, I definitely don't want what's inside it.

Stuck on the sidewalk, I'm faced with a dilemma. How to get to JP's fort up in the big oak tree on the other side of the property. I could conceivably ring the doorbell and risk asking his mom, but that's not super appealing. She's either passed out or will scream and throw things. I've never asked him which variation of his mom he prefers. An inkling of pity trickles in for him, but I crush it down.

I'm not here for him.

I try to keep inconspicuous so neighbors don't get all eyeballs on what I'm doing. Last thing I need is for the cops to get called. Surveying the house, I guess I can go in through the garage. There's a code on the door, and I think I remember it, but then again, I don't want JP to hear the beeping of the buttons. He might think it's his dad. I sure as hell don't want to get his hopes up that his dad actually came home. That would suck. The window above me is the kitchen and I could go through there, but I might break something.

Then I laugh because fuck it, I'm the Beast and I can do whatever I want.

I jump up and pull myself up over the wall. Swinging my legs over the side, I jump down. There. And my leg doesn't even hurt, so multiple bonus points all around.

His dad had the sweetest tree house in Multnomah County built for JP in the third grade, and JP's pretty much lived in it ever since. It's insulated and has electricity and its own router for Internet. I stand on the ground underneath it and look up. The lights are dim. I hear them talking. Then not talking. They're up there and I'm down here, but not for much longer.

The ladder is pulled up, just like Rapunzel's hair (aw, how cute . . .) but I don't need some stupid ladder; all I have to do is climb. I grip the branches and knobby burls of the old oak tree and hike myself up until I land at the front door with a thump. "Did you hear something?" I hear Jamie ask.

I undo the wooden latch and push the door open. "Hi."

They both drop their controllers and Jamie screams. "Oh my god! You scared the crap out of us. What are you doing here?"

"I need to say two things and then I'll go. You'll never see or hear from me again."

They stare at me with uncertain eyes.

"I don't want to hurt anybody," I say.

Jamie snorts. "Too late."

"That's why I came. Because I know it is too late and I know there's nothing I can do about that, but then I saw this rainbow today."

"You climb up here like King Kong because you saw a stupid rainbow?" JP says.

"Well, yeah. Because I thought it was my dad."

They hold any snarky comments that were percolating and listen. I'm thankful.

"I can't really explain it more than everything just *crystallized* on the walk over here. It's so clear to me, I don't even mind that JP's here and listens to all this," I say, looking at him. "Don't get me wrong, you can sincerely still go screw yourself, but I'm in a very peaceful place right now."

"That's past unfair," he says. "Between you and me, I'm the one who's made an effort."

"That's up for debate. But, Jamie, I was really confused after, you know, our night," I tell her. "I didn't expect it and I didn't know what to do with it. I was scared."

"You treated me like I was dead because you were afraid?" she says. "That's bullshit."

"It's worse than that. I treat dead people better than the way I treated you," I say. "I treated you like you never existed. I know that."

Her face twists and she looks away. It guts me.

"Like I said, after this I'll leave and you'll never see me again," I say quietly. "But I wanted you to know that I never had any doubts about you. It was me I was afraid of. It's going to sound stupid, but I was looking for a sign."

JP laughs. "A sign?"

"From my dad." I ignore JP and look at her instead. "Because yeah, I was up my butt. I thought for my whole life that I'm a freak. I mean, who am I really? Am I violent because I'm big? Am I angry because I'm so ugly? If only I had someone to talk to about all this—oh no, wait, he's dead." The two of them sit snug together, looking like a billboard in Times Square advertising secret things for beautiful people. "I'm sure there are problems with being really stupid good-looking, but I'll never know what they are. But I wasn't becoming a freak; I was fumbling at being a better person, which as you know is a somewhat freakish state for me. I don't need signs. I only need to do the right thing."

JP squints at me.

"I mean seriously, what is a man?" I say. "A guy with a beard and chest hair and a deep voice? Big deal. If that's all it takes to be a man, I was one in the seventh grade and I was a total little shit back then. Now I know. Being a person has nothing to do with the packaging. It only has to do with being good. I wasn't good to you, but I hope I get a chance to be in the future."

Jamie smiles to herself. "You were horrible."

"I know I was. . . ." My eyes fly toward hers. "I was horrible."

"*We* were horrible."

A warm light flares inside my chest. It dims when she lets me go and her eyes drift back to the controller in her hands. As if that's more important. "We were," I say to myself. "I wasted all that time waiting for a sign. The sign was, I should've opened the fucking door and returned a text message. But I didn't."

No one says anything and I sit, my eyes gazing down at the ground below. My broken leg dangles above slick blades of grass glinting in the lamplight. I sense it's time for me to go. "Well . . . I didn't come here to get you back. But I do want to be the kind of guy you'd be proud to be with," I say. "Because the best thing I've ever held was your hand in mine. And then you in my arms."

She drops the controller. Her fingers twist around each other, gripping knuckles with knuckles. My eyes flick to see her face, but it's hidden. She doesn't look at me. So I stop looking at her. "Even if I never see you again, I'll still do my best to get the Ethans and Bryces of the world to understand better. I'll put my weight behind it. So you can take your pictures and go to RISD and be a mom and do whatever you want in peace."

"Yeah, about Ethan and Bryce," JP slowly says. "They were never going to do anything to Jamie."

"What does that mean? Because I was totally aware of those idiots and doing my best to steer clear," Jamie says.

"I made it up."

"What?"

"I just wanted Dylan to . . . you know. Get some missing funds back from Adam Michaels. You were never in any danger from those guys."

"Jeremiah Phillip Dunn!" Jamie yells at him. "You turned my safety into a game? That's disgusting. You said you were my friend, my ally."

"I am your ally! I was the one totally in favor of you guys being together in the first place. Between me and Dylan, I'm the good guy here."

She scoots herself the hell away from him. An opening!

"If you want, I'll walk you home, Jamie," I offer.

"No, Jamie, stay here," JP says.

She stares at me, stares at JP, stares at me again. "I'm going."

Yes!

"By myself," she says.

Shit!

"I don't know what it is with you boys, but it feels like I've spent the past couple months locked up in a world-class fun house of jacked-up emotions, and I need to go find mine again. I don't know what's true anymore." Jamie edges out of the tree house and brushes past me as she scrambles herself, her bag, and her camera to the door. Her foot rests on the first step down, and she regards the two of us. "I don't want to see either of you. Not for a long, long time. If ever. Don't follow me. Don't call, don't text. Just—don't."

Right before she's halfway down the tree, JP calls out, "What about your show at the café?"

"What about it?" she hollers up. "Are you going to take back all the money just because I think you're unhinged? Cool. You two are seriously made for each other."

Jamie vanishes, and JP and I are left behind like chumps.

The gate slams shut and he turns to me. "None of this went the way I wanted. This is hard—like, for real."

"What's hard, being honest for once?"

"Well . . . yeah."

"Jeezus, enough already." I get my frozen butt cheeks in gear to leave. Not to catch Jamie, but to go finish my homework and go to sleep because I know I've lost her forever. He grabs me.

"I have nobody," he says in a rush. "I said I was sorry. I apologized, like, so many times. When you left, I realized I have nobody. I just want to hang out again, that's all."

"Groom a sycophant."

"Can we start over?"

I blink and we're in third grade again. He's changing the world with a wave of his hand and I'm jumping as soon as he says how high. No thanks. But then like a bad connection, the video of us stops loading on our grade school years. Back when we played all day. Then it hiccups to middle school, when we went to Cannon Beach and all we did was walk to and from tide pools and talk about cool stuff. Back when I never felt more trust for another person that wasn't my mom. "JP . . . ," I say.

When people get hurt, what do we do with the past?

"Dylan."

"I'm sorry I never wanted to talk about your mom and I always ignored it," I say. "It's real shitty you have to live in a tree house."

"Thanks. For finally saying something."

"But everything else? I just . . . I don't know."

And I leave too. When I get back over on the other side of the wall, my crutches are gone. Fine. Be that way, universe. I'm going home. By the time I get home, I'm frozen to the core and the house is quiet. Our car is gone. I open the front door and there's only one light on in the hallway. "Mom?"

She doesn't answer.

I shuffle into the kitchen and see a note on the table.

If you get this note, I found your phone on your bed and I'm out looking for you. Please call me so I know you're safe!

I love you. Mom

I pick up the note and stick it on the fridge under a magnet, wondering if she's out there driving around in circles and really asking Dad for help. I wonder if she feels as helpless as I do when I hear nothing in return.

I drag myself up the stairs and toward my bedroom window. It slides open with all the ease I remember and it's just as difficult as the last time to get out onto the roof. I mean, even more so because I've grown almost six inches since I broke my leg. No wonder the somnabitch is taking so long to heal.

Ah well. It's all good.

I sit on the moldy shingles and swing my feet over the side, embracing the cold dark night in February and waiting for the sun to rise again.

THIRTY-SIX

I sit up there, on my roof, and watch tiny sparks of gold tickle the trunks of the trees as the sun rises. Hazy pinks and yellows gradually waking up. My street is quiet. All the nosy neighbors still sleeping. I keep thinking it's my turn to sleep too, but I don't want to. My eyes are heavier than me and yet they refuse to shut. The sun compels them to stay open. Just a little while longer to watch a new day dawn.

When her car rounds the corner around 5:15 AM, I wave. The car speeds up, parks, door slams, and she sprints around to the side of the house below where I'm sitting enjoying the sunrise.

"Dylan!" she shouts.

I raise my finger to my lips. "Shhhh . . . people are sleeping."

"Oh my god." Mom races to the front door and I hear her clambering up the staircase and opening my bedroom window as fast as her almost-forty-year-old self can go. "Dylan." She squeezes out through the frame and onto the shingles. "Sweetheart?" I'm jealous of how easy it is for her. She slowly crawls toward me and crouches on her knees. "Please don't jump, please, let's figure it out, let's talk about it. Just don't jump, okay?"

"I'm not going to jump." I kinda don't want her to be up here with me, but I'm tired. It's been a long night. I feel a little punch-drunk. She can sit if she wants to.

"Oh, thank heaven." She exhales. "What are you doing? Where have you been? I've been up all night, worried sick, driving around looking for you. What happened?"

"I had to do some stuff. Then I came home," I say. Everything is opaque, my eyes are so tired. "Have you ever had that walk-into-traffic, but just-kidding, but not-really feeling?"

"Dylan." Mom grabs my arm. "You're scaring me."

"Don't be scared. I'm not talking about for-real walking into traffic. Just like, I don't know, that blink-and-you-miss-it wave of zen shit. Like a peace treaty inside yourself."

"I don't know what you're talking about."

"But you've felt lost, right?"

She loosens her grip. "Of course."

"You have that unbelievable failure, the kind that smells like burnt hair, and it's awful. But then it's over."

"Have you been burning hair?" she asks with concern.

"No. I haven't slept in twenty-five hours and I'm loopy as hell. Indulge me on my shitty metaphors." I laugh. "But like, that place where there's no fighting. There's nothing to fight over. Everything is done."

Mom frowns. "Then I suppose you're lucky to have reached that point. I have not."

"You haven't? Ever?"

"No, everything is burnt hair for me," she mumbles.

"Nuh-uh," I say.

"I'm a thirty-nine-year-old college dropout and a single mom with a son who wants to wander into traffic. Obviously things are not okay."

"You've got to trust. And not bug phones."

"Oh." She pats me on the knee. "So that's what this is about. Well, I won't apologize for that. I need to know you're safe. And you better believe if I see that little blue dot of yours standing still in the middle of I-5 in the future, I'll come running. That's that."

"Take it off my phone."

"Who's paying for your phone?"

"Trust the process of life, Mother."

"It's hard to be trusting when said child skips school, has grown-up sleepovers, and stays out all night. Trust is earned, Son."

"Fair point," I admit. "Let's compromise."

"I'm listening."

"That thing comes off my phone and I start paying for the bills."

"I don't want you getting a job. School is too important."

"Football will cost money," I say. She flinches. "How about I call if I'll be late."

"How about you're supposed to do that anyway?"

"What's it going to take?"

She sighs. "Finish out sophomore year with good grades

and no more of this funny business that's been happening since fall, and then we'll talk about removing it for junior year. I need to see progress." Mom hugs me. "And let me in. Talk to me. I want to be in your life."

"You are."

"Dylan."

I look up at the sunrise. Low and lazy with February's tilt. "I love Jamie." There. It's said. "But she doesn't love me and I have to accept that."

"Oh, sweetheart."

"I lost the greatest girl I've ever known because I wasn't okay with myself," I say. "And now I'm past the burnt hair, I aired out the room, it sucks I'm never going to see her again."

"Maybe we can have her over for dinner some night."

"She won't come."

"You need to put up a fight! Girls like effort. Go in there and make sure she knows that you're—"

"Jamie knows what she wants and it's not me, and I can't say I blame her," I say quickly. Mom looks all crestfallen. I put my arm around her. "Don't be sad."

"I want so badly for you to be happy, though."

"It's okay," I say. "So that's where I was all night. I needed to apologize to her."

"I guess it didn't work."

"Does it look like it worked? I'm here all alone without a time machine."

"If you could go back a couple months, what would you fix?"

"When I learned she was trans, I would say, 'Cool.' And then we would go get a pretzel."

"And what am I up to in this do-over?"

"You're into it. The omnipresent worrying is at bay."

"But you know why I worry, right? It's what moms do."

"Most moms," I say, feeling for JP.

"Maybe I'm not supposed to admit this, but in junior high when it appeared you were into girls, I breathed a huge sigh of relief. Not because being gay is bad or anything, but because you don't want your kid's life to be any harder than it has to be. People can be so heinous," she says. "When I was out in the car with Jamie's mom, Jessica, she was telling me how scared she is for her daughter. How much she loves Jamie and how every night she loses sleep worrying that bad things are always waiting around the corner. That she worries all the time about how hard Jamie's life might be. I . . . didn't want you to be involved in that. I wanted you to stay away to make things easier for you. It was wrong. Will you forgive me?"

"I guess so. It's awful, but I get it."

"So I want in on this do-over too."

"Then I guess you'd be like, how nice we get to have my son's girlfriend over for dinner. Let's make crab cakes with real crab."

"Real crab, huh?" She laughs. "I'm very happy to hear we've won the lottery in this alternate reality."

"Just sucks it's only that. This is a whole new world."

A whole new world. Since I'm delirious, all I can picture is a boat made of souls, tearing through the surf and crashing onto a beach made of stars. They explode on impact, flying into space. Some stronger than others. Some disappear completely. "I think about Dad all the time."

"Me too."

"I've never needed him more than this past year."

Mom holds me even tighter. "Oh, sweetheart."

"What do you think he'd say about me and Jamie?"

"Well . . ." She rests a finger on her chin. "I think all parents want their kids to be happy. And I think good parents learn and adapt so that happiness grows. He would do the same."

"Do you think Dad's out there?" I ask. "Not like in heaven or anywhere like that, but what made him a person, does that exist?"

"It has to. I need it to. He is still very much alive for me," Mom says.

"Is that why you never remarried?"

She swallows with a thump. "Partly."

"Why?"

"Because I can't imagine loving another person the way I loved your dad," she says. "When we met in college, I fell madly, hopelessly in love with him. All my friends thought I was nuts because he was too big and too tall and too this and too that. You know what that's like; you're just like him."

"I do."

"But I didn't care. I knew we were meant to be. Then we had our little surprise, you, right before senior year. We decided he would stay in school and I'd get my degree later. By the time we bought this house, he already had cancer. We just didn't know it yet," she says. "We had so many dreams for this place. We were going to plant a row of arborvitae right over there." She points. "Change out that ugly fence for a new one."

"Why don't we do those things, you and I?"

"Time. Money. It all slips away." Mom sits there. I don't think I ever noticed how sad she was before. I always thought the sighing and the pining was her just being a mom.

"We need to sell the house," I say.

"I'll never do such a thing."

"We can sell it, move to an apartment. It'll be fine," I say. "It'd be a lot less stress."

"You're my number one priority." She hugs me tight. "You come first."

"Don't you think Dad would want both of us to be happy? I'm not a Labrador; I don't need a yard."

She lets me go. Her gaze slides to the shitty chain-link fence.

"I think it's time we get happy," I say.

"Perhaps you're onto something."

Now I hug her. "We're going to be okay."

She stops and holds my stubbly cheeks in her hands. "I'm very proud of you."

"You are?"

"Of course I am! You're a dream kid," she says. "Most of the time."

"Ha-ha."

My hair has grown since fall and she brushes some off my forehead. "I think we should have Jamie over for dinner," she says.

"I already told you, that's out."

"Well, maybe another girl sometime. Or boy."

I look up to the sky. "I know that book you have gave you a million options to support in the most helpful Helpy

McHelp-Help way, but here's the honest truth: I'm just a guy who likes a girl. So I'm whatever that's called and that's it."

"Okay," she says. "Sounds good to me."

My face is crusty and my butt is cold. The sun is up and there's not much more to this day than an eventual trip to the hospital. I need sleep. My mom nuzzles me like a kitten or cub or something and I bust up laughing.

"What?" she cries out.

"Nothing. I love you."

"Well, good, because I love you," she says. "I'm freezing. Come inside with me and get ready for school."

I get to my knees and start to inch across the roof. "I'm going to bed."

"No way. If I have to go to work, you have to go to school."

"I promise I'll be good tomorrow, but all I want to do is sleep until my doctor's appointment," I say. "It was going to be a half day anyway."

Her mouth crunches up, but I can tell she's thinking about it.

"Play hooky with me—have a sick day. Make waffles and watch Netflix."

Now she leers at me with a wink. "Now you're the bad influence."

"Yay," I cheer.

She goes in through my window and then I do. I shut it. She closes the lock. "You need to dust, Dylan. Good lord, look at this." Mom shows me her filthy finger.

"Day off," I remind her, and collapse into bed.

Pulling up my covers, she rubs my shoulder through the blankets. "I'll wake you up when it's time to go."

The door shuts with a click and I'm out.

A heavy, deep hole opens up and I slide into it and close the lid. Warm and soft, I feel my dreams tiptoeing in after a while. Wild great things that make no sense and I'm along for the ride, until blackness hits me like a gong and I'm unconscious.

I dream of Jamie. That plane of hers is there and she's coming down the ladder. I'm waiting on the tarmac, wearing a suit.

Something stirs me.

"Dylan?"

I don't want to be awake. "Is it time to go?"

"Um, I don't know," says Jamie.

My eyes fly open. Sitting up, I see her. She's red in the cheeks, her hair is a tangled mess, and she's pulling at her hands over and over. "Is this a dream?"

"I'm afraid not." She looks to her wet boots. Then, carefully, up at me. "Hi."

THIRTY-SEVEN

Mom stays stuck to the floor in my room, eyes whipping back and forth between me and Jamie. I didn't notice her before. "I'm going to the kitchen," she says. "Does anyone need anything?"

We shake our heads no. I still can't believe Jamie is here in my house, not just in my house, but in my room and breathing and everything. It is a dream. I'm speechless.

"Okay then, um, so that's where I'll be and I'm going to leave the door open, okay?" Mom tilts her head and glares. "The door stays open."

"Fine. Open," I mumble.

Behind Jamie, Mom gives me two thumbs up before she jets away, and I laugh at her. "Am I bothering you?" Jamie asks.

"No, my mom's being a nut."

"Oh." Jamie paces the floor, leaving behind a spot of wet

and dirty carpet from where she stood. I am so happy to see that mud, but she's oblivious. Every movement is stiff with cold, and she rubs her arms inside the sleeves of her coat. Her light is dim. "I didn't mean to come up here."

"That's okay." I sit up in bed and pull the blankets in.

"I left JP's house and walked. And walked and walked and walked. Fuck-it stomped all over town. Thinking. I thought about everything. Then around midnight, I saw your crutches lying in two different places a block away from each other. I was like, those are longer than mammoth tusks; they're definitely Dylan's," she says. "I worried someone stole them or something. So I brought them here."

"Someone did steal them."

"Well, that's a shitty thing to do."

"Sometimes people are shitty." Like me.

"Hmm," she murmurs in agreement. "I was going to leave them on the front steps, but your mom saw me. She asked me if I wanted to come in."

"It's pretty cold out."

"Yeah." Jamie rubs feeling back into her ears. "So I thought okay, and then she asked me if I wanted to say hi because you were upstairs and I thought why not, so here I am. Hi."

"Are you hungry?"

"Not really." Jamie leans against my desk and takes in the shapes and sights of my room. "It looks a lot different in the sunlight."

"I guess so."

"I'll be honest with you, I'm stalling for time." Jamie hides holding a tissue to her eye and disguises it as a runny nose before putting it back in her pocket. "I don't want to go home and hear 'I told you so' from my mom."

"She doesn't mean it like that."

"The heck she doesn't. She 'doesn't approve of my choices' these days," Jamie says. "And I don't want more therapy. It took forever to get it down to two sessions a week. I'm tired of feeling like a project. I wish people would just believe me when I say I'm fine."

She sniffs, but this time it's not pretend. "Do you want a blanket?" I say, and reach for a folded one untouched at the end of my bed.

"Thanks." Jamie unfurls it, wraps herself up like a woolen burrito, and sits on the far end of the bed. "I'm just not in the mood for 'I knew you'd be one of those girls who stays out all night' right now."

"Understandable."

"Just feel . . ." Her voice slips away. Jamie buries herself completely in the blanket. "I feel so alone."

I move to touch her, but my hand hovers. Waiting for a sign. I don't know if I'm allowed to touch her in any way, but waiting for signs is a bullshit experience. Only sign I need is hers, and my hand comes down soft to rest on her shoulder.

She doesn't shake it off. She doesn't tell me to move it.

"I know that feeling," I say.

"So does JP," she says. "It's funny, when he found me I was practically bleeding from your silence. And all of a sudden it was like, who is this broken little rich boy?"

"Who cares."

"He doesn't know how to tell you how important you are to him. We were both kind of moping around over you, isn't that stupid? Especially since he disgusts me right now. What kind of ally does that? He is a very good listener, though."

"That's how he learns your soft spots."

"At least I got a show out of it."

"You did it on purpose?"

"I'm no angel," Jamie says. "Every time JP wanted me to talk to you and I said no, because I was pissed at you, which I still am, he kept upping the ante and I was like, hmm, how far will this kid go to get what he wants?"

"JP will go the distance."

"He told me about his mom."

"Whoa. That's major."

"He said you and your mom were the only people who knew."

"Well. That's accurate." I knew, but my mom did the listening and talking. Never me. But who knows, that could change. "So is that what you were thinking when you were out walking around for hours? How to bring me and JP back together?"

"Yes. No." Jamie flips her arms free from the blanket and pushes up her sleeves. "I just kept walking around, worrying about my Spanish test on Friday and all this other crap, but underneath it all, you kept bubbling up."

"In a good way?"

"Not really. I hate that I think about you all the time. I wish I didn't. I wish I could take a bath and wash everything away, instead of having it build and build. I hate that I torture myself with all these memories of us. I feel like I scared you away and I hate myself for that."

"You didn't! Please don't get that stuck in there. It was

me. Maybe I wasn't ready, maybe I was blaming my dad, maybe I was just an idiot. All of the above. Like, when you said you wanted to have sex, I was not expecting that. Made me nervous about future, um, endeavors."

"But I only said that to keep you."

"What?"

"I'm not ready either. That's what my friend Keely said to do. She said that's what boys want." Jamie wraps the thick blanket tighter. "Ugh, I feel so dumb. Like Keely knows what the hell she's talking about. She can't keep a boyfriend longer than a month."

"I wish you could've told me."

"Maybe we could . . . talk? About stuff like that? Instead of feel dumb?"

"I'd love a chance to talk about anything with you."

The new silence isn't cold. It's as warm as my hand that's still resting on her shoulder.

"When we met, did you honestly not hear me in group?"

"I was in a pity spiral, so no."

"Then why when you did learn the truth, why couldn't you just say 'Wow, I didn't know you were trans, but I don't care because I like you' instead of spit on the sidewalk and make me feel like garbage, why? Even a polite 'Thanks, but no thanks' would've been better. Why did you have to be so awful? Why are you only okay with us in the dark?" Jamie finds her camera and starts twisting the lens cap with jittery fingers. "Why do I keep coming back to this?"

The lens cap falls and she struggles to fit it onto the camera, gives up, and thumps it down in her lap with a thud. "Just feels like I've been trapped in this world where I don't know what's true anymore. When I'm with you, I only want the good and I'm too blind to see the bad. Even after everything that's happened, I'm still in this soupy shit. I hate—no, *despise*—myself for wanting the fairy tale."

"But we all want that."

"Well, make it stop," she says. "Tell me you're an all-star asshole and that if I stay here one more second you'll hurt me. Again."

"Jamie, I can't stop thinking about you either."

"No. Wrong answer." She shuts her eyes tight. "Were we ever real?"

"Yes."

"All those things you said in the tree house, were they true?"

"Every word."

"And my hand was honestly the best thing you've ever held?"

Now I close my eyes, remembering. "Always."

I've hurt a lot of people in the past, but nothing is worse than this.

Jamie hugs her knees. "Dylan, I think we . . ."

I wait, my comforter taking the form of tenterhooks, when Mom yells up the stairs, "Sweetheart! It's time to go."

"Where are you going?" Jamie asks.

"My cast comes off today. Want to come?" We have so much more to talk about.

The three of us pile into the car like it's nothing. Oh, don't mind us, we always travel in style with my mom driving the whip, my shotgun seat pushed back as far as it can go without breaking, and the girl of my literal dreams mashed in the backseat.

After a fairly awkward seventeen minutes of my mom peeking in her rearview mirror at me and Jamie, she finally pulls in to the parking lot and calls out, "We're here!"

My crutches, the ones Jamie found, are all dinged up. Scratches cut the metal where I collided with a million trash cans, cars, shopping carts, and rocks. The handles are cracked and yellowed from months of my sweaty hands gripping the foam molded to my palms. Battle-hardened.

I walk into the hospital and lean them against the wall where my height is checked for the last time. I know the drill and I stand against the stadiometer as the nurse climbs up onto a chair. "I wonder if I'll hit seven feet," I say.

"I hope not. We're running out of places to buy clothes," Mom grumbles.

The nurse slides the bar down until it taps my head. "Six feet, seven inches," she says, marking it on the paper inside a manila folder.

"I'm almost as tall as my dad." This is so great, I could pop.

The crutches come with me to the X-ray room and I leave them by the bed for hopefully the last time. When we get to the exam room, I put them down for good. I don't care what the doctor says; I won't pick them up again. I am beyond done with this broken leg. Dr. Jensen comes in, clipboard in tow, just like always. "Hop up," he commands, and I swing my leg high onto the crinkly paper bed. A nurse, not the same jerk who sized me up for pit fighting, aligns my entire right leg so it's facing out and steady. "Let's get right to it," Dr. Jensen says. "I'll turn on the saw."

Deep within my chest, my heart starts to throb. This is it. The oscillating saw looks like a motorized pizza cutter. It buzzes and Mom grips my shoulder. Jamie squeezes her hands to her stomach. "You'll feel a light to moderate tickling sensation," the nurse tells me as Dr. Jensen makes the first cut.

It goes down, starting at my foot, smooth and firm. After each pass, he goes back and does it again. Sometimes two or three times. "The bottom of this cast has a lot more wear and tear than I'd like. But the X-rays look good, so I'll let it slide."

After he's done cutting two lines on opposite sides of the cast, he takes something that looks like a car jack and a pair of pliers had a baby, and sticks its nose into the crack and pushes. The cast pops open in two pieces. I hold my breath as he lets air touch my leg. "Most plaster I've used in a long, long while, I guarantee you that," he says, prying the top off and snipping the gauze with a pair of shears. He peels it all away and tosses it to the side, and just like that, my leg is free.

And holy shit, it reeks.

Mom pinches her nose shut. "I think I'm gonna barf."

"Nice," I say, but looking at my leg, I think I'll join her. Clots of flaky beige skin mingle with my dense leg hair, and it smells worse than a dead fish inside a dead cat rotting under the porch. I lift my leg from the tomb and push the old cast out from underneath it. It's my foot. I wiggle it.

Jamie sneaks her camera from her bag. "Whoa . . . This is the most disgusting thing I've ever seen. Can I?"

"Take all the pictures you want."

She goes nuts.

"Does it hurt?" Dr. Jensen asks.

"A little." I bend my ankle for the first time in months. It feels like it wants to pop. Turning my leg from left to right, I see the scars from the pins and screws buried in the bone. The nurse comes near with a flat metal tool to scrape days and weeks of nastiness off my leg. "I'll do it," I say, and rake the dull blade up my shriveled calf.

Okay, this is gross.

Dr. Jensen pats me on the back. "Rules for now: no sports for the next three months. Football should be fine by camp—when's that, August? We'll set up one last appointment to take a look, but as long as you go slow, I don't anticipate any problems. Take it easy. Build up to running, let your leg get as strong as the rest of you. All right?"

I nod.

"But don't worry," he says. "Once a break heals, it becomes the strongest part of the bone."

"Like a scar," I say.

"Wear it proudly." He shakes my hand and leaves. "See you in two weeks for the follow-up."

The door clicks shut. Mom helps me off the table, hands me the pair of jeans she brought in her bag, and I step behind a screen. By myself, I put them on. Buttoning the button and zipping up the fly. I smooth down the denim leg I've been missing all these months. Two legs in an actual pair of pants. It's crazy how good a pair of jeans feels. I take the old pair, the one with only one leg, and ram it down into the shiny chrome trash can, crushing all the little paper cups underneath it down, down, down until my old pants, my old me, is gone. And I walk. It's a cheesy little circle, but I walk and it's amazing. Mom fusses and warns me not to go too fast, but this is heaven. No wheelchair, no crutches, just me.

Jamie snaps three pictures and stops. Her eyes peek up from behind the camera.

"Is it okay if we walk home?" I ask Mom.

"It's kind of far. I don't want you to tax your leg on the first—"

I give her a look.

Mom stands up straight. "Oh. Sure thing," she says. "But call me if it gets to be too much, okay?"

"Okay."

She pats me on the back and squeezes Jamie's shoulder. "Have a nice walk, you two. Go slow."

In the empty exam room, Jamie and I are still. She takes a breath and doesn't budge. Her nose lifts to the ceiling and she talks to the invisible sky above. "I don't know what we have. If anything. I don't know where to start."

My one new leg is tender. I shake it out as I think. Mom's voice rings in my ears. Trust is earned. "Me either, but when we go get that pretzel, I want to eat the whole entire thing in front of the universe."

A tiny grin sneaks across her lips.

I gaze down at her and it finally comes out. "I love you, Jamie."

"You don't."

"I do. And I want to show you every day."

She covers her eyes with one hand and searches for my chest with the other. It lands and I clamp it down over my heart. Her fingertips linger. Jamie peeks through her knuckles to see me smiling because I can't do anything but smile when I'm around her.

This is the girl that sees beauty in rust, that flies with or without my hand under her feet. Who meets me in a garden full of sleeping flowers. The girl who I hope will be there with me when they bloom again in the spring. The girl who changed my life. I hope she drives me crazy by taking a billion and more pictures of me and everything else in the world forever. This is the girl.

We leave.

We leave the osteo office, we leave the wing, we leave the hospital, we even leave the bus stop, and stroll into the sunlight. On the sidewalk, the steps I take are light. Nervous. I test my leg and give it more. I bend my knee and we hear my ankle pop.

People stare at us as we walk by and I'm like, yup. That's me, that's her.

That's us.

"I don't want us to be horrible anymore," she says.

It's like a little dagger that came out of nowhere. "You don't?"

"No," she says. Jamie's hand sneaks toward mine. Her fingertips brush against the back of my hand, and I weave my fingers through hers. "I want us to be good."

"Let's be good," I say.

Our shadow below shows us walking as one, stretched out and long. Jamie takes a picture. I lean my head back and take in the light. Rain again tomorrow, but I don't care about anything but her hand in mine. It's all I need.

I give it a squeeze. "Want to see how fast I can eat like ten pretzels?"

She sends me one back and laughs. "Yes, immediately."

ACKNOWLEDGMENTS

I tried to kick off thanking so many wonderful people with something witty, but it quickly devolved into why type O blood saved a significant amount of people from bubonic plague in medieval Europe and then that somehow morphed into a line about boob sweat and I was like, you know what? Forget all that. I need to salute the real MVPs because that's far more important *and* coherent.

Two people—straight up, no chaser—come first because without them, oh man . . . I don't even want to think about it. This book would be nowhere without my amazing agent, Mackenzie Brady-Watson. Tenaciously whip-smart and clever, she saw the story I first delivered and knew the bones could bear more weight. I can't thank her enough for loving Dylan and Jamie and always wanting more from both them and me. And it's almost unfair to merely say thank you to my extraordinary editor, Erin Clarke, whose thoughts and notes crackle with fire, because there's so much I need to pack into those two words. Thank you for believing in these characters and knowing just when to administer CPR. And thank you for giving this book life.

So to these two brilliant women, my eternal gratitude for all the very many big and little things. You know them all, and I thank you, thank you, thank you.

My cover. Oh my god, it's gorgeous. I was filling up my car when I first saw it and immediately started getting all weepy at the gas station. Leo Nickolls, you're the best. And when I'm done gushing about your work, I'll let you know, but I fear it will be never.

To everyone at Random House, thank you for being so very excellent. Big shout-out to the copy editors because—holy cow!—I repeat myself so much. It's a tic, repeating myself (have I mentioned I tend to repeat myself?), and they endured a whole manuscript. True professionals, I'm telling you.

I am one lucky duck because, along the way, I've gotten to know some truly great people. Major recognition and thanks to Billie Bloebaum, Kiersi Burkhart, Cara Hallowell, and Cynthia McGean. Martha Brockenbrough is a gem. Meredith Russo is a badass. To a very special person, Sara Gundell Larson: the book world is a better place for having you as its champion. Thank you for being a dear friend and good heart. With love, I thank you for absolutely everything.

And to Whitney Gardner: You knew every iteration of this book, from beginning to end and all my flailings in between. One time when I was filled with doubts about this book and everything inside it, you wrote in the margin, "If you don't finish this, I will cry and cry and cry and cry." It's tiki time. (tiki emoji)

Love is love is love. I wish all couples joy and happiness and the freedom to fight over stupid things like who gets the remote and why do you always leave your socks on the floor when the hamper is right there, why?

If you're thinking about harming yourself, please go to twloha.com.

We love you. I love you. Be well.